EMMANUEL

Copyright © 2021 Patrick Halls

All rights reserved

The characters and events portrayed in this book are fictitious. Any similarity to real persons, living or dead, is coincidental and not intended by the author.

No part of this book may be reproduced, or stored in a retrieval system, or transmitted in any form or by any means, electronic, mechanical, photocopying, recording, or otherwise, without express written permission of the publisher.

CONTENTS

Title Page
Copyright
ACKNOWLEDGEMENTS
CHAPTER 1-A CHANCE MEETING AND A LIFE DECIDED   1
CHAPTER 2-ESCAPE   16
CHAPTER 3 -BAMAKO BELLE   28
CHAPTER 4- THE CHASE IS ON   39
CHAPTER 5 - THE ACCIDENT   46
CHAPTER 6- ALIMAME CAMARA   56
CHAPTER 7 -TO WED OR NOT TO WED   67
CHAPTER 8- LOOK BACK   69
CHAPTER 9 -THE STORY TELLER   82
CHAPTER 10 – DATE NIGHT   89
CHAPTER 11-A WALK IN THE WOODS   97
CHAPTER 12- CHRIS CHYNOWETH   104
CHAPTER 13 THE ENGLISH ROSE   109
CHAPTER 14 AFTERMATH   112
CHAPTER 15-THE PROGRAMMER   119
CHAPTER 16 - THE CAT IS OUT OF THE BAG   121
CHAPTER 17-A WORK OF GRACE   124
CHAPTER 18-A WILD NIGHT   130

CHAPTER 19– CRISIS	137
CHAPTER 20 -COMMITTEE	142
CHAPTER 21- WEDDING	146
CHAPTER 22-AFTERSHOCK	150
CHAPTER 23 A COSY CHAT AT THE CHYNOWETHS	158
CHAPTER 24- AN APPLICATION FROM THE PROGRAMMER	161
CHAPTER 25 -EMMANUEL'S STORY	164
CHAPTER 26-THE MATCHMAKER	173
CHAPTER 27-SECURITY SORTED	176
CHAPTER 28-THE FOUNDLING	181
CHAPTER 29-THE PAST REAWAKENED	195
CHAPTER 30 -THE CONTACT	202
CHAPTER 31 -EMILY CENTRE STAGE	206
CHAPTER 32 SEEK OUT FATHER	217
CHAPTER 33 -DIPLOMATIC MEETING	227
CHAPTER 34 -THE FALLOUT	237
CHAPTER 35 -PATRICK DELVES	243
CHAPTER 36- ESTHER DECIDES	252
CHAPTER 37- CHURCH	256
CHAPTER 38- RECEPTION	263
CHAPTER 39 -EPILOGUE	270
AFTERWORD	275

ACKNOWLEDGEMENTS

I would like to record a massive thanks to my daughter in law Becky Halls. She is a well published novelist and helped me with the publication of the book. She writes under her maiden name 'Rebecca Paulinyi'.

I would like to give a heartfelt thanks to Kathy Barwise, who read through the whole book and carefully commented on it as well my thanks to Ian and Rose Jenkins, for their contribution too.

The profits from this book will go to a charity which gives food, clothing, faith, hope and love to the poor of Derby. This is the Hope Centre, Curzon St, Derby which is the community outreach of Derby City Church.

to Esther's boss and had plenty of places and quiet corners for smaller, how should we put it..... more private gatherings. The alcohol was certainly flowing freely. The music coming through the speakers was very loud and raucous with a real beat to it – a sort of hypnotic beat that took over your mind and transported you out of your normal course of life.

Esther was a pretty, slightly prim, twenty three year old, serious minded girl with serious minded spectacles to match. She was the pride and joy of her family, having graduated from Lagos university with a first class degree in business studies. In the process she had acquired excellent English. Her uncle Samuel, through use of his contacts, had secured her a prime job in a bank with strong African connections in the fabled City of London. This was the one of the big financial centres of business in the whole wide world and here she was right in the middle of it. She was having the time of life, her work being centred on the computerisation of the business.

She kept telling her slightly sceptical colleagues at work, 'You'll see. In twenty years from now the whole world of finance, government, entertainment, everything in fact will revolve round the computers you look down on and on the world wide web or internet.'
She always remembered what her surname Afolayan meant in her native language, 'walks like a wealthy person, walks with confidence'. She was someone special and she was going places in the world.

Then she saw him. He was on the other side of the large living room, heaving with people. Their eyes locked and he shuffled and pushed his way through the dancing, loudly chatting, gyrating, pressed together throng over to her. His English was excellent too, though like hers it had a slight but definite accent. Within a minute they realised their mutual heritage. They began chatting away in the language which was for the two of them the language of their birth. He was handsome, tall, confident, smooth talking, athletic, slim and his ebony skin was as smooth and supple as his conversation. She was a single girl and whether he was married or single, she never did find out. They were both drunk and a special sort of …. 'meeting' happened in one of the places for more private gatherings – a one to one encounter.

She never saw him again and only ever knew the first name that he gave her. She did not even learn what he did for a living. She guessed that he was rich. You needed to be if you went around with a gold Rolex watch on your wrist and a golden necklace. The next day when she had got over her first ever hangover, she felt quietly ashamed of herself for having enthusiastically taken part in the one to one 'meeting'. She had after all been brought up as a Catholic. The nuns at her convent school in Nigeria had been very clear about what girls should and should not get up to. She somehow knew also that her African nuns were stricter than the European ones.

However she was eager for him to call her. So to make certain of that, she had stuffed not merely one but two of her business cards, one in each of his trouser pockets. She had told him she was expecting him to ring. She was in fact, positively looking forward to the prospect of dating him properly – going out for meals, concerts, the theatre, walking in the park and talking. The card had not merely one but two contact numbers. One was her work phone number with its answer phone and another her mobile number. She had a mobile which in those days was the size and weight of a brick and an aerial of a size to match. And she waited, and waited, and waited for his call. After three weeks she gave up waiting, left with a sense of having been let down by him. No it was something more than that. It was a sense of bitterness and betrayal. That feeling of betrayal grew as something new, unexpected happened to her.

She found herself waiting for another 'thing'. It was a part previously of the routine of life that came with the territory of being a young adult female. Like the phone call she had been waiting for, it never came. She found herself trying to deny to herself what was going on. Surely it was just a blip, a hiccup and she had had blips before like that even when she had not had any special one to one 'meetings'. She also somehow knew deep inside herself this, that she were to acknowledge what might be happening inside her body, she would need to tell her family. Even though they too were Catholics, rightly or wrongly she was worried that they would then put her under immense pressure to do 'something'. She just could not do that 'something' to another human being. Again that was a rule that the nuns had drummed into her. It was easier not to tell her family.

When she was thirty one weeks pregnant and the baby had been kicking vigorously for several weeks inside her swelling belly, she knew she could deny it no longer. She had this friend Emily, a Brit through and through. Now Emily had a thin face, pointy nose and the most amazing long, brown, below waist, wavy hair which Esther envied since she knew she could never achieve anything similar. She was a trainee midwife. Surely if anyone would know, she would know what to do for the best. Esther's family back home still had not got a hint of what was going on. Emily took her friend to the doctors, then to the antenatal clinic at the hospital. The bored clinic doctor felt her tummy, hummed and hawed and then filled out the paperwork for a routine ultrasound scan.

It was late Friday afternoon and Esther was the last scan of the day for the radiographer, a middle aged experienced lady who had seen everything. She saw Esther waddle in and lie down on the couch. She looked at her maternity record: a late booking into the hospital but an otherwise fit young lady, hopefully a straightforward scan. Then she could go home as her own tummy was rumbling and she would not mind a mug of tea either. She squirted the jelly on Esther's belly, put the probe on top of the squelchy stuff and started the scan. Then she saw it and stopped abruptly. Esther looked at the radiographer's face chan-

ging slightly, only slightly because she was experienced.
'Is there anything wrong with my baby?' cried out Esther in alarm.
'I need to make some checks,' came the not very reassuring reply back.

Yes there was absolutely no doubt. She then checked the other relevant parts moving the scanner probe. They were normal. She breathed a sigh of relief without showing it. But all was not done yet. It was a sad rule that if one abnormality was present in a baby then it was more likely that other problems could be there as well. So she focused on the heart and the lungs then the liver and the kidneys and the face and the brain. They were normal. Then came the difficult bit, the truly tricky bit. She would have to say something to the patient before sending them back to the antenatal clinic. The patient's reactions could be so varied at this point. It was the early 1990's and the practice of not explaining to a patient fully the nature of a problem was only just beginning to disappear from medicine.

'I'm afraid that there is a difficulty with the baby and I am going to send you back to the clinic doctor now..... to have more of a complete explanation. Baby is missing his left hand and wrist and part of his left forearm but the rest of the left arm is normal..,,'
She stopped as Esther just burst into tears. Her little one was not normal and would look like a little monster. She cried silently for a few minutes while the radiographer tried to console her and gave her some tissues to wipe her eyes and stuffed up nose.

She continued on.
'He is definitely a boy and I have carefully checked the rest of baby. I am pleased to report that there are no other problems. If it is any consolation, he is kicking his legs like crazy and it would not surprise me if he were to grow up to be a footballer.'
Esther laughed through her tears, at this last remark designed to console her.

She was sent back to the doctor in the antenatal clinic who asked her some more questions and then basically said it was one of those sad things and there was nothing that could be done. She would of course see a paediatric orthopaedic surgeon after birth. He booked her in for a hospital delivery but did not anticipate problems since the baby was head down. The next thought came to him routinely – a single mother, a foreigner without family around to help, a baby with a malformation.
'Shall I arrange for you to see one of our hospital social workers?'
'No thanks,' said Esther. She did not want tea, sympathy and help filling in a maternity benefit claim form. She was starting, just starting to consider different plans for her life.

Later that night having calmed down, she reflected on the situation. Esther knew that there had been prominent sportsmen present at the party. Her country's football team were in London for an international friendly match – a warm up before the up and coming world cup. Her banker boss had invited more than just normal, boring finance people to his party. He had wanted a whole different range of African talent to come together to celebrate his good fortune with him. So there had been bankers, professors, musicians, sportspeople and even an artist. When she visualised what the baby's father looked like and his long muscular legs, she could well imagine that he was a footballer by profession. After all, surely you would need strong, well toned legs to be good at the game. She knew she could not tell her family what was happening. They would hit the roof and say that the baby's deformity was due to her 'sin'. She started to take time off from her job using various excuses.

When the time came for the baby to be born, the pains began when she was in her flat by herself. She had been out earlier for lunch and had had the special meal of that day with her friend Emily and Emily's parents. Maybe it was the particular vegetable, brussel sprouts that the English enjoyed with the turkey, that started her off. Soon however the contractions gradually got very strong and intense. It was mid evening. She was scared, alone and of course it was her very first time giving birth.

She phoned Emily, grunting out the words between the waves of pain 'Emily the contractions have started bad. You know what you told me about would happen. What shall I do?'
Emily was happily munching her way through a mince pie. No alcohol for her this Christmas since she was on stand by for Esther. She answered in a casual tone of voice.
'You remember our plan. You ring 999 for an ambulance. They take you to hospital. I meet you there to be your birth companion in the labour ward.' Her little mini car had been playing up recently and she did not want to promise to take her to hospital when she was in labour in case the vehicle broke down on the way. Also she was a bit scared that Esther might break her waters in her nice clean car and make a mess. Even worse she might give birth in her car going to hospital.
'I can't do that but I'm scared and I don't want to be alone. Emily, please come. Please come now.'

Emily wondered if she should ignore Esther's plea and call an ambulance anyway. But she had just had this training lecture on medical ethics with its emphasis on patient autonomy – the new kid on the block in terms of buzz medical phrases. So she did not feel she could override Esther. Looking back nearly thirty years later she realised she had made a crazy decision at the time. She should have called an ambulance to Esther's address. If challenged later, she could have perfectly legitimately said, 'It's a safeguarding issue. The baby needs to be born in the place where he can have the best care both before and after birth'. No midwife could have said anything against that. But again if Emily had called the ambulance, then the lives of many people would have changed radically and this story of mine would have died.... stillborn.

As another contraction came Esther put the phone down on Emily. She had told her friend what to do and now she needed to focus on herself. She somehow knew she was going to be okay. Emily sighed. Putting the wicker Moses basket with the garish colour which would hold the baby afterwards, in her car, she started driving towards Esther's flat in a posh art deco apartment block in St John's Wood. She was slightly annoyed but not worried. Esther, as a first time mum. would probably spend hours in labour, so she would have plenty of time to sort things and get her into hospital safely.

Twenty minutes after the phone call, Esther felt the urge to bear down. Ten minutes after that Emily knocked on the door of Esther's third floor flat. She was feeling just a little breathless from climbing upstairs on a stomach full of turkey and mince pies. Esther yelled, 'come in' just as she was about to give birth. Emily, a student midwife, gasped when she saw what was happening. Now she too like Esther, was scared and suddenly, unexpectedly way out of her comfort zone. Words she had just learnt in class came to her mind in horror – words like 'stuck shoulders', 'cord wrapped round neck' and 'third degree tears'. All these were things that could occasionally go wrong at the moment of birth. This situation had gone for her from manageable to very bad. She was just too young, too new to midwifery, to be having to deal with this. She tried to remember what she had been taught, 'be professional and keep the panic out of your voice'. She did know that for this sort of delivery without gloves or equipment outside a hospital setting, she had been taught it was best to do the minimum rather than fiddle too much. So she quickly fetched a clean towel from the bathroom and caught the child. Then she wrapped the tiny infant up, who was thankfully crying and a good colour.

An already half formed plan was quickly born too in Esther's brain as she pushed out her afterbirth. It was a decent exit from her situation. She was okay with only a little bleeding, merely more than a bit tired. The baby too was in fine fettle, with as lusty a pair of lungs as you could imagine. Emily relaxed, breathing a sigh of relief. She just wanted to hand Esther and the baby over to someone qualified.

So timidly she started venturing, 'We need to call the hospital to get you seen, to cut the cord and get baby checked over.'
Esther put her plan into action and said determinedly in a strong voice, 'No I'm not going to hospital. I want to stay here.'
Emily said, 'At least let me see if I can get a midwife to come here to help you.'
Esther then let Emily into the secret of her plan. Emily exclaimed in dismay, 'But I can't do that. If I am found out I will get in big trouble. They could even throw me out of the midwifery course. In fact they would certainly throw me off it.'
'Even if you refuse to help me, I am going to do it,' came the stern reply back.
Esther and Emily argued and argued but in the end, faced with Esther's determination, Emily finally caved in. The words 'patient autonomy' still resounded round her mind. She was already in much deeper than she had ever wished to be. The kitchen scissors were sterilised with boiling water from the kettle and the cord tied with thick thread and then cut. Luckily Esther had some thick thread available. She was an amateur dress maker of some note and had her own nice, elegant sewing machine of the top brand. Emily checked the afterbirth with care which thankfully, seemed to be complete. That was one thing she had definitely learnt from her short time so far on Labour Ward – check the afterbirth with care. It was then cut in pieces with the same scissors as had cut the cord and flushed away down the toilet.

'What are we going to do about the baby crying?,' said Emily as the baby's bawling increased.
'If the neighbours hear they will catch on. They might have seen you going up and downstairs from your flat with your bump. He needs feeding. We can't go out to buy formula milk not today and certainly not at this time of night.'

Esther was silent at that. She realised that, being the day of the year it was, had its down side for her plan as well as its major upside.

Emily went on, 'They won't sell baby bottles and milk at the corner shop. Even if they did, he will have woken half London town up with his noise, by the time we come back with the stuff.'

Esther thought on. This was one thing she had not planned on having to sort out.

Esther spoke in a businesslike voice, 'Give him to me Emily. I will put him on the breast like the women do back home, just after giving birth.'

Emily said in her amazement, 'What? You are going to do that?'

A woman who was going to do what she was going to do to the baby could still steel herself emotionally to breast feed the child! Esther silently ignored the comments and put him to the breast. The little one began feeding like a trooper. He quickly quieted himself and some happy, sucking noises could be heard round the small flat where Esther lived. Hopefully the neighbours were busy making merry and having a toast or two or even hopefully several drinks of something stronger than orange juice. Given what day it was, it was a very reasonable expectation that they might not have not noticed the noise.

Esther made a phone call, speaking in her native language. It was the first time she had told anyone of her nearest and dearest what was going on. Emily could see her visibly perking up and looking more relaxed as the phone call proceeded. Like many non European languages, when faced with words to describe modern or technological things, it just borrowed words from English. So when Emily heard certain words said in English, she got an inkling of what was going to happen next. That had not been part of the plan as had been revealed to her by Esther. Emily could see however that it would get her out of the way totally. She saw her finish the call, writing down an address in English on a slip of paper.

The feeding of baby was her very last intimate contact with the child while Emily was cajoled into ringing up and booking the ticket, paying with Esther's platinum credit card. It would help cover her tracks a bit if a Brit rang up instead of her. She quickly packed her possessions in a bag with Emily's help. Esther rang up the letting agent. She left an answerphone message, giving notice and saying she was moving 'up north' and that a cheque would be in the post with the rent due. Emily at this point decided it might best to put on her leather gloves. She realised that not only would they keep her warm but also stop her leaving fingerprints round which the police could find. They quietly went down the stairs into the freezing winter night.
'Are you sure you have got him well wrapped up, Esther?'
'Yes yes. Let's just hurry to your car.'

They squashed in Emily's little mini with Esther and the baby in the wicker basket in the back of the car.. .They drove together to a different London hospital to the one where Esther had been booked in to give birth at. Emily knew which side entrance would be unlocked and took them to the out patient clinic area of the hospital. Its corridors were long deserted and silent at this time of night and on this particular day. It was the perfect night and perfect time to do what they were going to carry out. Still all the time, she was frightened that they would be caught out by some wandering porter or security guard. The consequences would be far worse for her than for Esther. Esther though, did not seem to be worried at all.

The baby was well wrapped up in a blanket and Emily had even bought the child a little head cap as well as a small, cuddly, soft elephant toy grey and pink. The basket was left in a dark little corner position in a corridor just next to the entrance to cardiac out patients clinic. The place was carefully noted by Emily. A stuffed giraffe was added by Esther as her one toy to her tiny boy at the last moment. She left one last little special gift, a blue envelope with some of her cut hair and a note inside. That blue for a boy envelope and that note would come back to haunt her in less than a fortnight's time. She cried a few tears as she put that precious envelope in the basket. Emily was a keen photographer and had happened to have her camera in the glove compartment of her car. She took a couple of pictures of the baby. Their hearts told them for certain in that they would never see the baby again. Esther quickly dried her eyes that were wet with tears. She had a lot to do in the next few hours.

The two of them quickly exited the hospital the same way they came, breathing a sigh of relief as they piled into Emily's car. They had not been caught. They drove out of the hospital to a phone box five minutes away, under a tall street light shining on it. It was steadily raining in the quiet deserted street. This was a time when the iconic British red telephone boxes were still used to make calls, rather than being used as they were in later years to store communal library books or even defibrillators. Emily made the phone call since her accent was rather noticeably different to Esther's and less likely to be remarked on. She disguised her voice a bit putting on a posh upper class, British, aristocratic accent. She was rather good at that sort of thing, being an enthusiastic and talented member of an amateur dramatic society. An added advantage was that if the police were to interview her and the operator heard a recording of her normal voice, they would not be able to recognise it. Her regular south London accent sounded definitely much more down market than her la di da voice.

'Hello London North hospital here,' the bored operator replied in an equally bored voice. It had been a quiet Christmas night for her.
'There is a new born baby abandoned by the entrance to the cardiac out patients'
The operator was shocked and stunned into saying, 'Sorry what was that? Can you repeat that please.' Surely she could not have heard the words right the first time.

'Abandoned baby at the entrance to cardiac out patients. Send a porter to check it out now,' Emily practically shouted down the phone.

'What?!!'

'Shut up and just repeat what I said,' came Emily's bossy voice down the phone.

'Abandoned baby at the entrance to cardiac out patients. Send a porter.'

'Good. Do that now. This call is ended.'

She put the phone down fast with a bang in her haste so as not to allow anyone to trace the call. Emily then practically ran out of the phone box back to her car and raced off with Esther.

The switchboard operator sighed, 'Probably yet another hoax call,' she thought to herself as she rang the duty porters. Ten minutes later her peaceful night was shattered when a panicky porter rang up.

'We have found a baby in a basket, just outside entrance to cardiac out patients. Can you put me through to the paediatric ward now please. We need to get a doctor and nurse over here urgently.'

Then all hell broke loose in the hospital.

Meanwhile Emily, half aware of all the commotion her phone call must have caused, drove on through the mostly deserted roads. She took Esther to her point of departure. Emily got out of the car and she and Esther hugged and cried together on the pavement.

'You promise you will go and see a midwife or doctor to get checked out as soon as possible. You PROMISE me don't you?'

'Yes yes Emily don't fuss. I promise I will.'

Emily drove off. She was not to see Esther face to face again for many, many years.

It was now three months later. The daffodils were in full bloom in huge clumps of yellow, surrounded by grass in the parks of London town. It was a sunny but slightly cold March day.

Emily sat on the park bench, surrounded by newly cut grass and spreading trees, munching slowly on a lunchtime sandwich. Her gaze was fixed, reading and re-reading a long handwritten letter she had received that morning. The sender's address was a post box in the capital of a West African country, which she had only vaguely heard of. The letter had the most amazing postage stamp on it showing one of the really beautiful, multicoloured birds that country was blessed in possessing. She looked up and idly thought to herself, 'If you were a poor country without wonderful buildings or famous people to put on your stamps, what would you do to show your best side? Putting a beautiful bird on a postage stamp for all the world to glimpse at is not such a bad idea after all.' When she got home, she had to clamber up the stepladder into the loft of her parents' place. She dug out her old school atlas and looked up on the map of Africa where the country was. On an impulse she kept the letter. She was glad she did. It would turn out to be one of many she would keep and treasure over the years.

Four days after Esther had left her flat, a cheerful, happy family turned on the television to watch a film. The news headlines were on just before the film. Suddenly they all sat transfixed at the pictures on screen. There were three little girls sat on a sofa with their parents, aged eight, six and four, all neat in their white party dresses having just been to a lunchtime recital. Mum had had a major singing part in a Christmas production of Handel's Messiah at the Albert Hall and they had all been along to support her. They had their fuzzy hair in neat pigtails. The middle child just said, 'Poor baby.' The youngest who did not understand what was happening just looked at the screen with interest. The oldest one, who grasped far more than her sisters what was going on, looked pleadingly at her parents who were sat with them, 'Mum, Dad, can't we please?'
Mum turned and looked directly at her husband. Then with a simultaneous pleading and serious tone, Mum said, 'You know Emmanuel, we are the ideal family. He's even got your name.'

Dad slowly smiled a broad, thoughtful smile in agreement but saying nothing. He fished out his address and phone book from a little chest of drawers by his side. After searching, rustling through the leaves of the book, at last he found the number he wanted. His left hand reached over to pick up the phone on top of the chest of drawers and his right hand to dial up the number on the keypad. His wife quietly smiled. She was sure they had made the right decision.

CHAPTER 2-ESCAPE

It was a cold, dark, damp, dispiriting, Boxing day morning as Esther wandered out of the arrivals terminal of Charles de Gaulle airport, Paris. It was drizzling steadily as she headed outside towards the long rank of waiting taxis. This would be the next stage of her journey of over three thousand miles. Emily had dropped Esther off in her little mini by the pavement at Heathrow at midnight. She had popped on the first available flight to Paris, which had been booked in advance.

Esther faced a particular problem. She was going to have to have a conversation with a French person. Now the French had the reputation of being very proud of their language and not liking to speak English at all. Though her own country was totally surrounded by lands with French as the official language, it was English that the students in her country's schools concentrated on learning. This was the language of the world, the language of the old colonial power. In fact French was actually one of the official languages of her country. Not that anyone would know it, not even apparently her fellow citizens. The result was that Esther was now in France but she could hardly speak a word of French.

She had guarded with her life the slip of paper she had written in her London flat, with her cousin Mabel's address on it. There had been a few previous visits to France to see Mabel but she had been met at the airport. So Esther was now not only tired but a bit nervous. She looked to see if there was a sympathetic, female taxi driver she could approach but there was none. So she found herself having to try to communicate in English through the cab window to an elderly, male, not particularly friendly looking driver.

'Can you take me to this address?' She showed him the slip of paper. He looked at her black face, nodded and said, 'How you pay?'
'Pounds.'
'Vingt …..twenty pounds,' the English words were spoken with a heavy French accent. Esther felt the price was exorbitant but was too exhausted to care.
'You pay now.'
'No. I pay you when you get me there.'
The driver understood that amount of English and thought whether to risk it. He was not too keen on African clients. Much better for him rich Americans, from whom he would never ask for payment in advance. They would always pay on the nose whatever he demanded at the end of the journey. As well as that, they would generally add in a huge tip in dollars to boot.

'Show me money,' said with a shrug,
Esther waved a twenty pound note in his face, holding it carefully in her hand so the driver could not grab at it. He got out his specs slowly and squinted through them at the note. It did seem to be genuine English pounds sterling.
'Get in car,' he said in a not particularly nice voice. Esther wondered whether to risk it. She did not trust the guy and had heard horror stories of taxi drivers. Would he take her to the right address without hassling her? In the end she knew she had no alternative, so got in.

They seemed to drive through miles and miles of motorways before turning off. Finally to her relief, she arrived at a detached house in the suburbs, hidden behind a very high metal fence as well as several trees and bushes in front and high locked gates. Esther recognised the place, having been there twice before. This was where Mabel had moved to a year ago with her rich French boy friend Philippe. He had gone off skiing at Chamonix for a few days with some university friends, leaving her alone in the house.

Thankfully it was Mabel who answered the outside bell. She gave Esther a huge smile and welcomed her in. A dog tired Esther was soon tucked in a comfortable bed. Mabel took care of her and gave her the love and attention she craved. After a good sleep, later that day she was taken to a private and very discreet English speaking medic, who had checked her out and reassured her. The doctor had not even asked her name. Mabel paid the medical bill with crisp new French franc notes. Esther stayed quiet for a few days to recover, feeling like a huge burden had been taken from her shoulders. Philippe then came back but thankfully did not pay much attention to her.

All changed one morning. Esther was having a lie in, when she heard Philippe and Mabel shouting at each other downstairs which was unusual. Then Mabel rushed noisily upstairs, burst into her room and with a frightened voice shouted, 'Come downstairs and look at the television.'
Esther took one look at her face, raced downstairs after her and saw a picture of herself on the television screen. The news commentator was speaking in rapid French and Mabel had to translate for her. The photo of her was a not particularly good quality one of her but the picture of the baby was very clear and distinct – a new born baby without… a left hand. It was her baby and he now had a name… Emmanuel. She was shocked and questioning. Why was she being given the sort of TV coverage and exposure that an international criminal or terrorist would get? Why, why? It just did not make sense. She was scared. What was happening? How could she escape from this horrible situation?

She had not imagined she could have been found so easily. When she had quickly planned her exit from England, she had thought it would be so easy to leave without being tracked. Where did that photo of her come from? It looked very much like the picture she had had to attach to her visa application. On second look, yes it was definitely that photo. So the police and immigration authorities must now be involved. She had had vague ideas that she might travel home in a few days time and lie low in her native Nigeria for a few months. She would spin a yarn about sudden family illness to her work in the City of London, to explain her sudden departure. Since she worked for a bank with a lot of African connections, they would understand better than most employers. Esther mused for a moment. Emmanuel, that was a nice name, especially when the TV commentator informed the viewers that Emmanuel was one of the names of Jesus as well as being one of Nigerian top boys names. She knew that last fact.

The news presenter announced, 'Originally it was thought that Esther had gone to friends in the North of England but the authorities now think she has left the country. They are looking into the records of air and sea passengers leaving the country. She may well be making her way either directly to Nigeria or by way of a third country.'
'What shall I do?' Esther slowly said to Mabel.
'You cannot stay here. Philippe says you cannot stay here and it is his house.' Her tone of voice was cold and her body language was uncompromising. 'If you are caught here...,' Mabel left the comment hanging. Her manner had changed in an instant from being kind and supportive to clearly regarding her cousin as a nuisance to be moved on and out as soon as possible. Her tone of voice had sent the clearest possible signal. Esther was silently shocked at the sudden change in her cousin's manner. She was dazed, confused.

She quickly asked, 'Won't they stop me at the airport if I try to fly out of the country?'
'Not if we get you different papers. Look. I can arrange something. Give me your passport for a couple of hours.'
A short while later Mabel returned with a new Nigerian passport in a different name. It had the same photo as the old one which

did not please Esther. At least the photo was a bit different to the very old one from her visa application for the UK. That was important as it was the last one which is what the television was now showing. Presumably the authorities would be circulating that one around ports and airports.

'Oh good. I can go home to Nigeria now.'
'Oh no you cannot,' said in a very so and so tone by Mabel.
'I have just spoken to your Mum, Aunty Precious. She rang me wanting to know if you were here with me. I could not lie to her. She asked me directly if the Nigerian television was telling the truth about you and the baby. I just could not deny it. The Nigerian television is saying the same as the French TV. She hit the roof. Your Mum says that she is thoroughly ashamed of you, not just for getting pregnant but for then not facing up to things by abandoning your baby. Those sisters of hers have been saying to her that it is the judgement of God on you. You went with a man not your husband and now as a result you have a deformed baby. That has wound her up too.'

'Your parents are also getting a lot of media attention, phone calls as well, with reporters camping outside the house. The BBC has even done a report from the street outside your home in Lagos. Also some of the local newspapers back home are saying that you should not be allowed back in Nigeria. Instead you should be sent straight back to London to look after your abandoned baby. One or two of our Nigerian Senators are starting to give out the same message to reporters. Your Mum definitely does not want you back home. At present you are a hot potato.'

Esther thought to herself, 'Why what have I done that politicians are wanting to make comments about me?' Again that question 'why?'. What was the thing in this whole business that I am missing, not understanding?'
Esther continued, 'But can't I slip back home on my false papers and find somewhere else quiet to stay till things calm down?'
'The papers are a quick job, good enough to get you out of France

but not good to pass anyone except the dopiest Nigerian border guard. If you were caught, I think that the government back home would then deport you back to London.'

This was worse than she had feared – worse than her worst-est nightmare if there was such a word as worst-est in English!

Then Esther opened the passport and noticed with a start, 'The passport is in the name of Blessing Okafor. That's an Igbo name and I am not Igbo. No wonder it would only be the dopiest Nigerian border guard, who would let me through.'

'Who did you get to do the work?' she asked Mabel sharply

'Well it is a public holiday and the only person I could find not celebrating was a Polish guy, who did not know much about Nigeria. Sorry I only realised when I picked up the passport from him. By then it was too late.'

'A Polish guy? Of course he does not even know where Nigeria is. He just picked the first Nigerian name he found somewhere.'

Esther shook her head slowly in disbelief. What the dickens had Mabel being playing at?

'Sorry he was a contact of a friend of a friend. I'm not exactly used to arranging false papers for anyone.'

'Where shall I go?' Esther asked panicky.

'I've just rung Uncle Samuel in the Gambia. After all you are his favourite niece. You can go there, he says. But first let's get you out of Paris. I've got you a ticket to Bamako, the capital of Mali travelling in four hours time out of Charles De Gaulle airport. That was the first flight out to West Africa I could get you on.'

'Mali?' Esther exclaimed with shock. 'But that is not near Gambia and besides I don't speak French and ....do they speak much English there?'

'No matter. You need to go now. I cannot have you here. I don't want to get into trouble with the authorities here, as they are far more strict with us Africans than the police in England. I have a good job here. I am earning much more in Paris than back home. I certainly don't want to get deported back in disgrace to Nigeria and leave my comfy life here with Philippe.'

So Esther was bundled into a taxi fifteen minutes later and told not to say nothing to nobody about her stay with Mabel. She arrived at the airport three hours before the flight time. There she was inside this huge, modern impersonal building, all of plastic and metal soaring up in the air. She was on the mezzanine looking round, below and up above. She felt lost, clutching onto her ticket with her small suitcase in her other hand.

She took a deep breath in, remembered that she was named after Queen Esther in the Bible who had been a strong woman standing up to her enemies.
'Let me think this through,' she said to herself, 'The most difficult thing is getting through passport control. It is much more likely that, if they are looking out for me, they are looking for me without knowing that I have a ticket for this very flight to Bamako. If they do happen to have caught onto the exact flight I am on, I am totally lost anyway. They'd stop me at the embarkation gate. Let me go straight to passport control, before they might have received notification to look for me.'

She headed confidently straight to passport control. She deliberately looked as though butter would not melt in her mouth. There were two lines, each to its own passport control desk, separated by a barrier. In one line near the side of the desk, there was a group of angry, shouting, young men, with police and officials trying to pacify them. That did not seem like the line to go down. Esther wanted to keep away from the police in case they recognised her. A lot of people wanted to avoid that line, so she joined the other one and waited and waited in the long queue. Then she saw that the other queue was now filling up as the shouting lessened. Then she noticed something else. The other line was being processed faster than hers.

A small, tired looking, middle aged man with cap on and well trimmed moustache was the guy in her line checking the passports. He seemed perhaps a little to be... over meticulously doing his job. Esther could hear the mutters in French, especially from French passport holders in the queue with their documents perfectly in order. Why was this man checking so intensely? Esther tried to keep her cool.

Then she saw something that alarmed her. Three people in front of her there was an older, African woman arguing with the passport checker. Suddenly he pressed a bell and two policeman seemed to come from nowhere. They frog marched her away while she kept on shouting back in accented English, 'I am a diplomat. I claim diplomatic immunity. My passport is not fake.' Would Esther's false passport be good enough to pass this pernickety, little man at his desk?

Esther's turn came. She handed him over her fake document with as much nonchalance as she could muster. Jean-Luc, the passport officer, instantly became more alert. Esther could sense his change in manner and began wondering, worrying even more how good or rather how bad was this forgery Mabel had obtained for her. She also was conscious that Mabel had just got her an inadequate imitation of the real thing and was feeling less and less pleased with her cousin.

Jean-Luc firstly checked the photo which did match but the document somehow felt 'wrong.' As an experienced passport control officer, it just did not feel right but he could not quite put his finger on it. He was not very familiar with Nigerian passports anyway. There was no entry stamp into France and no evidence of an entry visa stamped into the passport.

He said in French slowly, 'Where was this passport issued?'
Esther shook her head, smiled politely and shook her head again. Jean-Luc sighed. This was getting more difficult as his English was not fantastic. He repeated the same question in a heavily French accented, English. Esther screwed up her face as though she did not understand him and instantly downgraded her personal excellent English.

'No understand.'

Jean-Luc sighed inwardly, 'This is getting more and more difficult if she does not speak English properly. Rustling up a speaker of Nigerian languages as an interpreter on a day and a time like this is going to be well nigh impossible.'

He also remembered that Nigeria had several main local languages as well. So they would have the additional task of finding out exactly which local language was hers. He just had to plough on in English. He was beginning to long for his 6pm break to come. He had had enough hassle from the lady, who was the so called South African diplomat. Her passport had been a clever but definite forgery and he was very familiar with South African passports. The mutters from the mostly French people in the queue behind Esther got louder and louder.

'Who gave you the passport?'
Esther realised that her passport had no entry stamp into France. She had to quickly wing it with a cover story.
'Nigeria government.'
'Yes of course it was the Nigerian government otherwise you would be telling me you were presenting me with a forgery,' Jean-Luc silently said to himself.
'Yes but where?'
'Paris Embassy.'
'Why Paris and not Nigeria?'
'Old passport lost.'
Jean-Luc realised the small print on the passport showed that the document had apparently been issued in Lagos.
'But the document was issued in Lagos, Nigeria.'
Esther screwed up her face, pretending not to understand at first. Then she slowly said, 'Not Paris Embassy but Lagos.' Esther then pretended to understand and thoughtfully said, 'Lagos sent to Paris.'

Jean-Luc considered what to do. The mutters from French people behind were louder and louder. The words spoken now included the more downmarket words not normally said in the presence of government officials. He could call his supervisor Marc but realistically to investigate this properly would mean calling the Nigerian Embassy in Paris. However this was New Years Day and the Embassy would be likely be shut.

He could see that Marc was still busy at the other queue line with a big problem – a bunch of young, aggressive, male drunks, over-eager to go through passport control. He could turn Esther off the flight and then the embassy could be contacted tomorrow. But if her document was in order, then the Embassy might start to make a complaint to the Quai D'Orsay, the French Foreign Office. That would mean him having to make a report on why he had stopped her. That could also mean a possible reprimand for him, if they were not satisfied with his explanation.

He also knew exactly what Marc would say if he was to ask him. 'Jean-Luc, let her go through. There is not enough evidence to stop her and besides she is not entering the country.'
Jean-Luc knew that if she was entering the country, he would have to be so much more strict and he would definitely have to detain her. Leaving the country and therefore no longer a problem to France was a different kettle of fish.
Marc would have carried on saying, 'She is leaving the country to go to some flea hole in Africa. The Malians won't bother. The worse they could do is put her on the return Air France flight from Bamako to Paris if they are not happy with her documents.'

Jean-Luc knew Marc's views on Africa only too well. He thought that his verdict was not totally fair. He remembered with some fondness, being in Mali doing his national service in the French Army. The Malians he had met were friendly and he had been left with a soft spot for tasty, cheap, African street food. Decision made – let her through. Jean-Luc just nodded Esther through. Esther had the good sense just not to look at him. She walked off, clutching her passport.

She had an anxious two and a half hours, waiting to be called to her embarkation gate. She was starting to be scared. She wondered if the police had tracked her to Mabel's house. Could her cousin be talking to the police and telling them all about her to save her own skin? That would not surprise Esther about her. At the embarkation gate she tried to keep calm in the queue. This time when she reached the top of the queue the pretty, immaculately turned out, Air France stewardess looked at her passport. She saw that the photo matched the face. The name in the passport was the same on the ticket so she casually nodded her through.

Esther mounted the air plane gangway with some sense of relief but still worried. Esther seemed to sit in the plane in the confined space with about half the seats occupied, for an age wondering why they were not taking off. Mentally she was waiting to see if suddenly police would arrive to take her off. However the captain announced that there was a queue of planes to use their take off runway which is why the flight was delayed. Finally at 5.20 pm the plane took off much to Esther's relief.

At 6 pm Jean-Luc gladly left his passport control desk, stretched his legs and took his coffee break in the staff room. He heard from one of his back room colleagues that the south African diplomatic passport had been confirmed as a forgery. That would be a feather in his cap as the French government were very keen on picking up fake diplomatic passports. He hoped that the South African embassy might send a nice thank you note to the foreign office. That would be seen by him and also go in his record.

As he went through the reception area, he was handed his personal daily update book of those people who he had to stop if they tried to pass by his passport desk. He flicked through the book, idly seeing pictures of criminals and terrorists, each having their own page with a photo and personal details. He would take this book back to his passport control desk as a reference.

Then he spied one page with one photo on it which stopped him in his tracks. He stared at it for a minute or so, checking and rechecking in his mind. The thought also momentarily went through his head, 'Why is this person in my book? I don't understand why.' There was a phone in the staff room. He got onto the airport switchboard.

'Could you page Marc Duval, the passport control supervisor, urgently please.'

CHAPTER 3 - BAMAKO BELLE

Esther was in a long haul jet, confined to a not particularly comfortable airline seat. Mabel her cousin had not thought or bothered to book her into business class. She had merely quickly arranged for her a standard economy class ticket to Bamako. To compensate, Esther was being served an excellent quality, airline, European style meal. After all this was with Air France, a company based in France, the home of haute cuisine. The plane was suffering from turbulence too, which made her feel a bit queasy.

Her mind was suffering from turbulence too, what with the encounter with the passport officer and the television news too. What would be the next challenge to face her? She took a decision. She would order a little bottle of French red wine with her meal. Hopefully that would help her to calm down and try to think through her situation. It was the first time she had drunk alcohol since the night of that fateful party at her boss's. The Bordeaux wine was excellent – smooth tasting, not bitter, encouraging you to drink just a bit more. After the meal washed down with red wine, she started to feel more relaxed.

The first question that came to mind was, 'Why is the television making such a big thing about my situation? After all it's not like I'm a terrorist or criminal. Maybe abandoning my baby was technically a criminal act. But the TV clearly said my boy is fine and they found him rapidly. We had contacted the hospital too. I know England well enough. If I am caught and have to go back there, I am more likely to be smothered with social workers rather than be put in the police cells.' So there was no obvious answer to that question.

However the most important question then came to mind, 'What am I going to do next?' She mused through the possible options. She decided that when she arrived in Mali, it would be too late to do much that night. Best to have a good sleep in a nice hotel. After all she did have the money. She could call Uncle Samuel in the morning and sort out a flight to Banjul the capital of the Gambia as soon as possible. The turbulence had started to settle down. The wine was having a mellowing effect too. She started to slowly drift into a pleasant power nap at this point.

While she was snoozing away, she was quite unaware of the dramatic events happening on the ground. Jean-Luc the passport controller called Marc his supervisor and told him what he had just found out. He decided to be honest and mention about his doubts at the time he had let Esther pass through.
'Are you sure it's her?'
'Absolutely.'
'Why did you not stop her at the time, with her dodgy documents and call me?'
'Because I know what you'd have said, 'Why bother? She's only going to Mali'. Also you were busy with that bunch of young drunks.'
Marc did not respond to that. The French word 'Touché' came to mind.
'Never mind that. So she is on the 5pm Air France flight to Bamako. Write a hand written report and get it into the office in ten minutes. I'll get on with looking into this.'
After a call to his boss, Marc Duval faxed through Jean-Luc's concise report to the Duty Officer at the Quai D'Orsay.

Finally the Duty Officer got the report at 7.00pm. He considered the situation. The flight was due to arrive at 11.00 pm Paris time, which was 10.00 pm Bamako time. In the past the French police would have contacted the Bamako police directly. The Malians recently had been feeling that it was too much like the old days, when the French from Paris ruled Mali and dictated their orders down the phone to Bamako. So they had recently insisted that for more routine issues it had to be foreign ministry to foreign ministry. That was one sovereign state namely France, talking to another sovereign state, namely Mali. It had been agreed that the French could really only directly contact the police in the Malian capital Bamako, if they thought there was a terrorist or really major criminal on board the plane. Esther had not committed a criminal offence in France. Even in the UK it was probably a minor offence anyway. So the duty officer did not feel he could contact the Bamako police directly.

However, given that the plane was due to be landing in Bamako in four hours, he had to do something fast. So he looked up the phone number in his special book. He then rang up what he thought was the line to the duty officer in the foreign ministry of Mali in Bamako. The phone took a time to get through. Then it rang and rang but no answer.

'So even the Malians apparently celebrate New Year,' the duty officer muttered under his breath.

He checked the number and carefully dialled it again. Again the phone rang and rang but no one answered it. Time for a cup from that exquisite ministry coffee machine in the other room – a life saver after a difficult day. After returning from his coffee break, he rang again. No answer. He reflected on the next step. Time to contact his boss, even though he too was probably celebrating and would not be over pleased.

He got through to his boss who said, 'Send them a fax but tell the Malians they should deport her back to London as she is a British problem.'

The duty officer could hear the noise of loud conversation in the background and dance music. His boss was clearly at a New Year's party and obviously in happy mood. He sounded as though he certainly had had a celebratory drink or two.

The duty officer felt bold enough to ask his boss, 'Why not send her back to us in Paris? We can then crow over the British and send her back to London with a flourish!'

'Yes it is definitely nice to get one up on the Brits. Monsieur Le President would definitely be in favour but it is more difficult to deport her from France... lawyers and all that.'

'We know she has used false papers so can't we just threaten her with a long jail sentence for using a forged passport, unless she agrees 'voluntarily' to go back to England?' The duty officer knew that tactic had been used in the past to get round legal niceties and achieve desired generally political aims.

'We could do that but it's a lot easier if she is just sent straight back to England from Mali. Just tell them to do that, be a good chap.'

So the fax was prepared to send off to the ministry of foreign affairs in Mali with the instruction, 'Kindly return Esther to London rather than send her back to Paris.' The duty officer looked at the fax before sending it. 'I suppose I had better be polite and say, 'Please kindly return ....'

He was sure that they would not find that a problem. They would merely tell her that her papers were not in order and that they would be sending her back to London. Job done. Surely the Malians were okay, doing as they had been told. After all they did not have the same problem with lawyers and legal niceties in Mali as they had in Western Europe.

Finally Esther landed in Bamako. She looked out of the plane window and saw the gangway being put next to the plane ready to disembark the passengers. Esther's heart was racing. She somehow felt sure that she would have been tracked to Paris. That must now mean too that they would have found out about Mabel, her Parisian cousin and questioned her. She did not think that Mabel would have contacted the authorities on her own bat to turn her in. The guy in Paris passport control had not been happy with her documents. She suspected that he had only let her on the plane a) because she was leaving the country b) because there was a big bunch of angry French passengers behind her swearing and cursing.

She strolled out of the plane down the gangway onto the tarmac and into the enveloping warmth of an African night. She sensed a freedom she had not felt for those last two years. How wonderful to be away from the cold and confinement and grime of London. To her pleasant surprise and relief, the Malians in the airport were not really bothered with her documents. She was quickly out into a local taxi and onto an international hotel belonging to a well known American chain. She had a lovely sleep sinking into a soft, comfortable, luxurious double bed with wonderfully clean, crisp, ironed sheets. She woke up in an incredibly better mood, relaxed, optimistic and a sense that she had made a successful escape from Paris. Surely things would go smoothly now on. She then had a soak in a large bath with gallons of suds. When it came to washing, Esther definitely was a bath tub girl rather than a shower lady.

She walked slowly down the stairs to the international style buffet breakfast in a large spacious restaurant with loads of light and open windows. She was happy, feeling comforted with the smell of nice food and the buzz round her of conversation from well fed, happy, rich people, about to start their busy days. A good night's sleep had certainly helped put things in perspective. The plan was to ring Samuel after breakfast. After finishing a leisurely meal and exquisitely tasty, fresh baked, French style croissants, she was walking through the spacious, airy, clean, tiled floor reception ready to make a call to Samuel privately in her room. The air was cool with several fans on the ceiling whirring away.

There were television sets in two corners of the reception hall on at a low volume. The French TV news channel was showing a football match which she could not understand at all. So she casually glanced over on the other which was showing the BBC in English. She reeled in visible shock. There was that poor picture of her again but this time the American newsreader was saying that she had been traced to Paris. She panicked. What to do? OK she had been traced there but she had left Paris with a false passport. Could she have been tracked to Mali? Quickly she scurried back to her room and made the phone call to Samuel.

'Uncle Samuel, it's Esther here. I'm in a mess.'
She burst out crying, 'What can I do? They've tracked me to Paris. Maybe that means that they know about Mabel and I wonder whether Mabel is now speaking to the police, giving me away either because they are threatening her big time or because she wants to save her skin. The French police are not very nice with us Africans.'
Esther let the long jumbled sentence out in her distress, not giving Samuel a chance to get a word in edgeways.

Uncle Samuel could hear the tension in her voice. He did not know immediately what to say about Mabel. Mabel was his second favourite niece and he knew her well. He also was aware that she was not so tough as Esther. If she were threatened, she would blab to save her skin and her cosy life with her French toy boy Philippe. He sensed that he would need to look into this but discretely. He did not want to cause a big family row.
'You can come to me in the Gambia and stay with me for as long as you like,' he replied in a quiet, friendly voice. Esther was grateful and started to calm a bit.
'Thank you so much but how can I get to you safely? If I go to the airport and try to get a flight to Banjul, I might well get picked up. What would they do with me? Why am I being treated like an international criminal?'

Uncle Samuel was thoughtful and reassuring. 'Esther my dear. It was that blue envelope you put in the basket with the baby, together with some of your cut hair. The note inside read, 'I will love you always my baby xxx Mummy.

PS. I shall be gone soon from this world but I will see you again in heaven'.
Those words have really caught the imagination of the world at Christmas time.'
'Why should Christmas time make a difference?' asked Esther, still not getting it.

'Because it is always a season for sentimentality and family. Country after country's media has become very interested. Look. All people are wanting to do is get you back to London to be with your baby and to help you. They somehow have the mistaken idea that that is the best thing for you both. It's been a slow news fortnight too. Pictures of a beautiful disabled baby boy do get people's attention. Also he is called Emmanuel, which is a name so touchingly sweet and Christmassy. And he is a beautiful boy. Once the next war or international row breaks out and fills the TV screens, you will be out of the news.'

So that was it, thought Esther. It was that note of hers written in a moment of sentimentality. She wished she had not put it in the basket now but it was too late.
'I still don't get why the French of all people got involved.'
'When your note was published on TV, there were some people wondering what you meant by the phrase, 'I shall be gone soon from this world but I will see you again in heaven'. There was some prominent psychiatrist or other – you know one of those talking heads on TV. He suggested that you might have big mental health problems and were contemplating suicide somewhere abroad.'
'Suicide? I'd never do that. What was the idiot thinking?' Esther almost shouted aloud in her frustration.
'I know ludicrous isn't it? But his words did have the effect of galvanising the authorities. So with all the publicity surrounding you, when the British police found out you had fled to France, they notified the French. The French government felt too that they had to be seen to do something and publicise it too.'

'I still don't totally get why the world is so interested in me and why are politicians back home sounding off? It just does not make sense.'
'What interests human beings is always unpredictable. Why is the world entranced by Chinese giant pandas when there are plenty of other beautiful creatures at risk of extinction? The politicians are easier to understand. Do you remember my brother in law Solomon, the Nigerian senator?'
'I do. He was always speaking out on any and every issue in public to the press.'
'You know why he did that, don't you?'
'No I don't, Samuel.'
'He said it kept him in the public's mind and helped him get votes at elections.'
Esther was silent at that. Now that did make sense.

Samuel continued on, 'Getting back to your original question about best way to get to me……I agree at the airport you are more likely to be picked up by the police but look, you can travel to Gambia by land. Get the informal buses to Senegal and then through to Basse in the far east inland Gambia. My right hand man Almame Camara will meet you there with a nice four wheel drive car. He will then take you to the coast where I live. Use your false documents as you are unlikely to be challenged by some dopey border guard on some far frontier.'

Then he suddenly had a thought. He remembered his niece liked to wear stylish, snazzy Western clothes with loads of patterns on – they cost a pretty penny too.
'By the way are you still wearing your clothes from England or an African style outfit?'
'My clothes from England.'
'You do need to change from your expensive London clothes or you will certainly stand out like a sore thumb in a crowd of locals in Mali and certainly here in Gambia. I also suggest you get moving. You are more likely to be picked up by the police, the longer

you are round Bamako.'

So the next step for Esther was a visit to a typical African market. A confusing, noisy mixture of crowds milling round, little stalls and shops packed together. They were selling everything from a whole amazing collection of fruit, vegetables, canned goods, electronic gadgets from cassette players to radios calculators. There were also loads of small stalls, full of clothes of every type. By many of the clothing stalls there were tailors with sewing machines, bent over busy making garments. She felt thoroughly at home – so much more informal and so much more interesting and lively than boring old English shops and even London street markets. She stopped by one stall and started looking at the possible outfits. She had already changed the US dollars she had been given in Paris for CFA – the currency of French West Africa. Even though she was going to be changing her clothes as a form of disguise, it was still going to be crucial to find an outfit that suited her. She wanted to look good again.

She did come across one design she really took to. Then the haggling started with the stallholder. Bargaining about the price was such a typical African way of relating to, of interacting with people. For Esther it was such a breath of fresh air. She was glad to do it with the Malian clothes sales woman. She could see the sales lady's brother, the tailor busy working at his manual sewing machine. He was making a nice loose fitting top. He looked the spitting image of his younger sister. In this climate you needed loose fitting clothes, else you would sweat buckets. Not like in England where what was often needed were tight clothes, hugging your body to keep the heat in. She liked his sewing and Esther did know what she was talking about. She could hardly speak any French and the clothes lady could hardly speak any English. Of course they had no African languages in common.

So the Malian lady showed her the figure she wanted her to pay on a large electronic calculator. Esther took the calculator from her and typed on it what she was prepared to pay. This too and fro process happened several times. Esther wanted to get rid of the outfit she was wearing so that it would not be so possible to recognise her. So she indicated with gestures that she would throw that in too. The Malian lady hummed and hawed but she saw that Esther was wearing a nice, smart, modern, hardly worn European outfit. She knew she could resell it after a wash and an iron to some young Bamako belle who wanted to look trendy and Western. So she agreed to reduce the price. Then came the measuring up. Finally all was agreed about the money. Esther was told to come back in two hours when the tailor would have completed the work. That was done by the sales lady pointing at her watch.

While Esther was in the market, she realised that she was squinting her eyes with the midday sun. That was something that she rarely did in British winter. She saw a wandering street vendor with hundreds of different dark sunglasses in his holders. She smiled at him and gestured on finding a stylish pair right one for her. She paid with her CFA. It would also surely act as a good disguise too. She remembered with a smile someone saying to her that to disguise yourself well, you needed a beard and dark glasses. Well, she could not do the beard but she could do the glasses!

Esther wandered leisurely back to the hotel. There she found out from the receptionist, who spoke a bit of English, about the small buses that left for various places in Mali. A natural caution made her decide she would not tell the guy exactly where she was thinking of going to. Instead she vaguely indicated that she was going to look round places like Timbuktu. That was in the opposite side of the country to where she was heading. In the room she had come across a small freebie folded map of Mali in the hotel guest pack, which she had taken with her. That would be useful showing to bus drivers where exactly she wanted to go. She checked out and paid her bill in cash, ready to go back to the clothes stall.

As she walked away from the hotel she got onto a taxi/motorcycle riding pillion that was waiting round the hotel looking for custom. They rode away leaving a huge trail of dust. She happened to turn round and saw two police cars driving into the hotel parking at high speed. She had a transient wondering thought that they might be coming for her. Surely not – she was just being paranoid. The time was a bit past twelve midday.

CHAPTER 4- THE CHASE IS ON

Earlier that same day, Colonel Oumar Sidibe of La Police National, sat in his spacious office in Bamako. He was slowly sipping his ten o'clock morning cup of percolated coffee from his fancy Italian coffee machine. He was fat, old and indolent. His main occupations during his 'work' time were reading French newspapers and playing chess with his personal assistant Yaya. He just happened to be his sister's boy. After all here in Africa you did have to help your family, giving them jobs. The trouble was that while the colonel was a wily and experienced chess player, (he had beaten a French grandmaster once) his nephew was getting better and better. He had found out that the boy was reading a chess book on the side, given to him by a visiting French policeman and aficionado of the game. He had thought he could craftily disguise this fact from his uncle but the colonel had found the book in Yaya's desk draws.

The colonel held the fax in his hands and gave it a visible whiff of disdain. It had been picked up at nine o'clock that day by the duty officer at the foreign ministry, having arrived over twelve hours earlier from France, with the details of Esther. The Foreign ministry took the laid back African viewpoint that for holidays you did not need a duty officer on. After all for anything really urgent, people would surely contact the Presidential palace. The colonel noted the end sentence 'Please kindly return Esther to London rather than send her back to Paris.'

'Typical toubabs,' he muttered to himself, using the slightly derogatory word common to West Africa for white people, 'Busy giving their orders to us Les Noirs (the black people) - wanting us to do their dirty work.'

It reminded him of a time when he was a young policeman sitting in an office in Bamako. He had heard a very loud, very angry, white person in Paris barking instructions down the phone to his black superior officer in Bamako, his boss at the time. This was when France was still the colonial power before independence. Obviously the French had missed a trick with this Esther, letting her out of the country on false papers. Now they were expecting the Malians to pick up the pieces.

The colonel knew the background to the Esther story. His two favourite newspapers were French from France - 'Liberation' where he got all the general news and 'L'Equipe' where he got his sports news. Liberation had done a full feature on Esther, unusually for a French newspaper. The colonel happened to be busy reading that very feature as he drank his coffee. Normally the French papers at the time were only really interested in England if something bad had happened or if it involved lady Di, Princess of Wales. Diana was as much a glamorous heartthrob in France as she was in the UK.

He felt sorry for Esther. Yes, she had abandoned her baby but that was in a hospital. She had promptly but anonymously told the authorities in London. The baby was safe and well and healthy. All that poor girl wanted to do was to find somewhere to hide and lick her emotional and physical sores, like any other wounded animal. Sores there were sure to be. Was what she had done so very bad? Yes, she had forged papers to get out of France but there was no indication she was involved in any other criminal activity – no drugs or terrorism or major fraud. The poor woman had done nothing to justify an international chase after her.

He sipped his large latte slowly and thought on. The French of

EMMANUEL

course still had some sway in Mali in spite of having 'graciously' or so they would think, granted Mali independence. Every year millions of French francs poured into the country in aid, not all of it well spent. If they, the French, found out that the Malian foreign office had not picked up the fax while Esther was in the air and that the opportunity been missed to arrest her as she stepped off the plane, then that would create problems. It would be best to have tried to make up for any mistakes committed. He knew he was likely to get a phone call from the police minister soon and it would good to have done something or at very least be seen to have done it.

The colonel called his nephew into his office. He knew what was needed. After all he had personally arranged the network of fax machines to send messages to the lieutenants in charge of the various police posts in the city of Bamako. Or rather he had arranged for his cousin to do the work, paid for by the government. A little kickback of course had had to go to him the clever colonel, for arranging it all.
'Yaya, can you get this faxed immediately through to all the police posts in Bamako.' He handed over the piece of paper to him. Yaya read the fax attentively.
'But Uncle, there is no photo of Esther.'
'No there is not.'
'It would be nice to send a photo of her with the fax.'
'Yes it would, Yaya.'
'I could take your newspaper with its big photo of the woman and fax that through.'
'But you cannot put my newspaper through a fax machine. The paper will rip.'
'Let me take your newspaper, uncle, and photocopy the page and then fax the photocopy through.'
The colonel reluctantly handed over his morning paper. The sacrifices he had to make in police work. He barked out, slightly grumpily, 'Bring it back sharpish, mind you, as I do want to finish reading the article.'

'Yaya is a bright boy. He will go far in the police service,' he concluded to himself after his nephew left the room.

He sipped on his coffee. Job done at least on his part. He wondered how his lieutenants would deal with the fax. Some would do very little but some like Ousmane Traore would be, to put it mildly, 'active'. Colonel Sidibe was aged sixty two and thought of the lieutenants as his 'boys'. Ousmane, that particular boy, so he considered him, made him tired by his level of activity.

The Colonel was totally right. Lieutenant Ousmane Traore was aged twenty eight, had boundless energy, was slim with an impressively muscular physique. He typically jumped out of bed each morning and did a hundred press ups in the bedroom – much to the amusement of his wife and the excited vocal delight of their eighteen month old toddler daughter, Fatoumata. He was always on the phone to his superior Colonel Sidibe with plans, thoughts and ideas. Sometimes the colonel got so tired of speaking to him that he got Yaya to take a message. He would then ring him back when he felt up to it.

His sergeant came to give the lieutenant the colonel's fax and he read it with growing enthusiasm. There was a photo too which would be a big help. If he could be the one to find this Esther girl, then that would be a real boost in his chances of promotion. His wife's family came from the Timbuktu area. If he could go back there for at least a few years, that would make her happy. He was already well recognised among his colleagues especially since he was the Captain of the police football team. Recently he had received the approbation of the Minister of Police himself, when his team beat all the other government teams in a recent knockout competition at the National stadium. It had helped of course that Yaya the colonel's nephew was on his squad. He had managed to sweet talk his uncle into ringing up the trainer of the national football squad, to plead for some extra coaching of the police team.

'Right I want you to ring up every hotel in our district and see if they have had a Blessing Olafor staying with them last night. I'm going to give my friends at the airport a call to see what more I can find out. Let's make certain we have got our squad cars ready to go in the event of action,' the lieutenant said decisively.

As an afterthought he said, 'Sergeant, can you print out a photo of Esther for everyone to take with them.'

His friends at the airport gave no help, merely telling him what he had already guessed. She had arrived last night on the Paris Bamako flight but they did not know where she had gone to. They checked for him the passenger lists of flights that morning and also upcoming ones but her name did not turn up anything. Just on the off chance he sent up a squad car to chat and show the photo of Esther to the airport taxi drivers in case any of them remembered taking a young Nigerian woman to a hotel last night. All this meant that Esther was either planning to stay in Bamako or was intending to travel by land, maybe back to Nigeria.

Then the call came through. At twelve midday, the hotel receptionist Souleymane, the one who had spoken to Esther earlier, finished his shift. He ambled through the hotel reception ready to leave for home. His eye was caught by the TV screens, both of which were showing the poor quality picture of ….her. Yes that was her undoubtedly. He switched to the French news channel as his English was not fantastic but his French was excellent. Esther had been tracked to France and now was thought to be travelling to Mali under false papers. He was fascinated and astounded – a real live international fugitive in his hotel. That was a very first for him and probably for the hotel as well. He stared at the screen and wondered what to do next. He raced back to his colleague at the desk and gave a quick explanation to him in whispers.

'What do we do now? This is so exciting,' asked Souleymane.
'You'd better call the police,' replied his colleague whispering

back.

'Do you know where she is now?'

'She checked out a few minutes ago. I think she is outside waiting for a taxi.'

'Do you think it is worth while trying to get her inside on some pretext, while I am busy ringing the police.'

His colleague thought on and said, 'Better not. She might be dangerous and have a gun or something. Just ring the police.' He had clearly read a vast number of cheap detective novels and seen too many French crime series on Malian television.

The policeman raced into Lieutenant Traore's office, all breathless.

'Boss, we've got Le Grand hotel international majestic reception on the phone. Esther has just left their hotel.'

The lieutenant literally swung from his chair into action.

'Tell him we'll be there straight away. Right team, let's go with both our squad cars.'

The 'team' arrived in a cloud of dust, just as they saw a taxi motorcycle leaving and then rushed into the reception.

'Where is she?'

'She might still be outside.'

The lieutenant gestured at two of his colleague and they raced out. They came rushing back in, 'She's gone.'

The lieutenant looked to the receptionist,'Where do you think she might have gone to?'

'Possibly to the central bus station but we don't know.'

The lieutenant looked at his team, 'I'll stay here and get more details while the rest of you take one car and go to the bus station and start searching for her. Also can you radio the squad at the airport to get over to the bus station and help you?'

Lieutenant Traore started to go through with the receptionist what he knew.

'She was wearing European style clothing and had an unusual small suitcase with snazzy grey and yellow lines on it – not a

local design at all. I see plenty of suitcases in my line of work but I have never seen one like that before.'
Esther had in fact bought it at a trendy up market shop in Carnaby St London. The lieutenant interrupted and got onto his portable radio to pass those important details on to his men. If they caught the girl with the suitcase, they could always get the receptionist to identify it later if needed.
'She also made one phone call for ten minutes while she was here from her room.'
'Have you got the number?'
'Yes sure it's a Gambia number.' The receptionist wrote it down.

The lieutenant bit his lip in intense concentration. That certainly complicated matters. If she was heading back to Nigeria using the small buses, which is what he had assumed she would do, then she would be going south or west, quite possibly through the neighbouring countries of Burkina Faso and Niger. Therefore they would concentrate their search on the buses going in those directions. However if that phone call meant that she was going to Gambia, then that implied that she would have to go through the neighbouring country of Senegal to get there. The most direct route would be initially heading north to Kayes in Mali. That is unless she had decided to be devious and go indirectly to Senegal through the other neighbouring country of the Republic of Guinea. It was all getting more and more complicated.

Also the lieutenant thought to himself, 'Why has she come to Mali in the first place? The girl does not apparently even speak French, so the fax from Paris said, and it is very unlikely that she would speak a local Malian language.'
He radioed through the new information to the squad car and headed to the bus station to join them in the search.

CHAPTER 5 - THE ACCIDENT

Meanwhile Esther was blissfully unaware of all what was going on. She arrived at the market and then wended her way slowly through the masses of people to the clothes shop to pick up her new outfit. She went to the back of the shop behind a large curtain and slipped into her new outfit, leaving her Western clothes behind. She emerged from the curtain, feeling much more African with a headscarf, top and long full length wrap round skirt. She even felt pretty again for the first time since she had realised she was pregnant. That boosted her morale no end.

She looked at her suitcase and wondered if she ought change it. She just felt she wanted to kick over traces of her old London life. On a whim, she came across a smaller hand case that was deep red. It was more what many of the locals had. So she exchanged the two and quickly transferred her clothes into it.

She found a small auto bus in an area where there were loads of small buses, waiting to go all over the country. She heard men calling out various destinations of towns in Mali, 'Timbuktu', 'Segou', 'Mopti', 'Kayes'. Some of the men had little pieces of card in their hands with the names of the destinations on. She had a clear idea of where she wanted to go and she chose the right bus. With a sense of relief she got on and manoeuvred her way with her little suitcase past the Malian ladies. With babies in their arms and bundles on their laps, they did tend to expand into the small central aisle.

She grabbed a window seat on the driver's side at the back of the bus. It was next to a small little open window at the top to get some air. If she had an inside seat, she would get less of the breeze. It looked like it would be a long, hot, sweaty journey for everyone. She hung onto her small suitcase in her lap, as if her life depended on it then wondered whether to put on her sunglasses but decided not to. She did not realise it but she had just taken two decisions, which she was to look back on with regret for the rest of her life.

As they were getting ready to drive away, she saw several policemen on foot mingling slowly with the huge crowds. They were clearly looking out for someone among all the travellers and the many vendors of drinks, snacks and clothes. Were they looking for her? Had the hotel receptionist identified her? Then she saw him. 'Him' was a young slim policeman called Moussa and he was standing directly across the road from her.

He was looking round and then he saw her. He starred, looking intently at her face. Their eyes met. He just somehow felt that it was her. She just knew that he knew. But then she was wearing African clothes, not the European ones described by the hotel receptionist. Again the suitcase on her lap was not the snazzy design as described. He quickly glanced down at the poor quality photo of Esther in his hand that he had been showing passers by. He stared intently at her for a few seconds longer hesitating, doubting his own initial judgement. He could see that the photo looked a bit different to the woman he was seeing.

Esther's bus driver put his vehicle into gear. Another bus was rushing up on the policeman's side of the road. Then Moussa made his mind up and started to move into the road ready to stop the bus and check her out. So intently had he been focused on Esther that he did not look at the road before he stepped out. The other bus hit him side on and he had no chance. Esther saw all and gasped involuntarily. Her vehicle started to drive off because her driver had not seen what had happened. The last Esther saw as she looked back through the window was the still body of the young policeman, starting to be surrounded by a crowd of gasping passers by.

She just knew this: if she had worn her sunglasses to disguise herself *and* if she had sat on an inner seat in the bus, none of this would have happened. Now not only she had ruined her own life, through what had happened at that party which seemed an age ago now, but she had now killed someone too. She very slowly, very deliberately put on her sunglasses and sat quietly, just shocked beyond belief. For the rest of Esther's life, she was haunted by nightmares of the bus hitting the young policeman.

The journey was long and bumpy. When Esther came to the first police checkpoint she was quizzical. Why was there a police checkpoint? Then she realised with a start. This was Africa not England. She remembered her surprise, the first journey she had made outside of London two years before. She had been travelling along the motorway to Leeds and not a police checkpoint in sight. But Britain was an island. African countries with their long, winding, open land frontiers had to have police checkpoints every few miles on the main roads. So checkpoints were going to be part of her life when travelling.

She was worried that they would be looking out for a young Nigerian woman, of which there would not be too many in Mali. The police approached the bus. They did not seem to want to go through passengers' papers but just looked up and down the bus then let them go. This happened several times. Each time she got scared as she had only got her fake Nigerian passport.

Lieutenant Traore received the news about Moussa with a deep sense of shock too. Nothing like this had happened before in his working life. He raced down to the bus station. His colleague was alive….just. The young policeman had a head injury and a badly broken leg. He was moaning and speaking incoherently.

The next few hours were a mass of frenetic activity on the lieutenant's part. He arranged for his sergeant to take the bus driver down to his police post for interview, as well as a whole host of witnesses to the accident.

He followed the ambulance to the hospital and fussed round the medical staff, making certain that the most senior and best people available were dealing with his injured colleague. There was a visiting professor of orthopaedics from the world famous Pitié-Salpêtrière teaching hospital in Paris. He got roped in to look at the broken leg. When finally the French professor went to theatre to deal with Moussa's broken thigh bone and crushed foot, the lieutenant went back to his police post for a few hours.

It was fairly clear that the driver was not at fault so he let him go. The lieutenant was a fair minded man. But there was one thing that three of the witnesses said about the accident. His sergeant summed it up, 'Boss, they are all saying that our colleague was looking, fixed at probably a bus across the road. It was if he had seen something or someone and was in the process of walking across the road to investigate.'

Lieutenant Traore revolved that information round mentally. He knew that at least he needed to go back to the hospital to stay with his injured colleague, until he hopefully was awake enough from the anaesthetic to speak. Maybe, just maybe, his colleague might be able to give him a clue.

When he reached the hospital and had spoken to the medical staff, he phoned the Colonel to update him at 9pm that night.
'Colonel all the witnesses say that Moussa had seen someone on the bus who he was looking at intently. I think the person was Esther. Do you think it is worthwhile putting out a nationwide alert for her?'
'Typical lieutenant Traore,' thought the colonel, 'coming up with ideas and plans for me to implement. One day he'll want my job but I will be long gone by then, either dead or enjoying

retirement.'

'Do we know where the bus that Moussa saw was going to?'

'Possibly Kayes but also possibly Timbuktu.'

'Two different directions. That does make it much more difficult,' the colonel said in a reflective mood.

A whole series of trails of thoughts ran through the colonel's mind. In the first place there was a bit of laziness inside him. He knew that to alert the other police forces in Mali would take a lot of work on his part, even with the help of Yaya. Also did he have sufficient information to justify at this time of night, alerting everyone? Was the 'crime' of Esther sufficiently serious to make a nationwide search an appropriate response? Was this a good use of scarce police resources?

There was something else too. He remembered playing 'hide and seek' as a child over fifty years ago. He would cover his eyes, turn away from the other kids and count to thirty. That would allow them time to run and hide before he went out seeking them. There was a part of him that wanted to give the same chance to Esther – to give her time to run and escape. That was something he could not even admit to himself mentally as a policeman.

He made his decision.

'Lieutenant, please get your written report as soon as possible in the morning to Yaya. I will take it from there. Please can you tell the hospital that I will be visiting Moussa in the morning to see how he is.'

'Yes sir,' said the lieutenant reluctantly. There was nothing more that the impatient young officer could do. The call ended. Then he saw the pleasant young lady Assitan, the reporter from the L'Essor newspaper. He had had dealings with her before.

'Hi Assitan.'

'Hi lieutenant. Can you tell me what is happening with Moussa Coulibaly?'

He saw his chance to get a bit of publicity for the search for Esther.

'Sit yourself down and I'll tell you everything.'
No harm upping the profile in the search for Esther even if his boss would not play ball.

Finally Moussa was back in the ward, having had his broken leg repaired. The Lieutenant waited patiently outside the ward, until the nurses said he could go in and speak to his colleague.
'Moussa how are you?'
'I'm okay, lieutenant, but my head is so sore.'
'I'm sorry to hear that. Have the nurses given you some pain-killers?'
'They have, thanks.'
'Do you happen to remember anything of the accident?'
'No I don't. The last thing I remember is travelling in the squad car to the bus station,' Moussa groaned.
'No problem. You just get some rest. The colonel will be coming to visit you in the morning.' He patted his arm kindly and walked away a bit disappointed. Moussa was a good man, who had just made a foolish mistake, walking in front of that bus. The doctors had warned the lieutenant that Moussa might never remember anything of the accident.

The next day the lieutenant turned up to the office later than was normal for him – understandable since he had left the hospital to go home at 2.30 in the morning. He wrote up his report and sent it to the colonel. The colonel had decided he had better do something, now it was morning. So he sent it on to the Gendarmerie together with Esther's picture. At 2.45 pm faxes began to be sent to every border post in Mali that had a fax machine to be on the lookout for Esther. She was to be returned to Bamako for deportation to Paris.

It was now three in the afternoon and Esther had been travelling in the small, slow, informal buses for nearly twenty four hours. She had had a break of five hours in the night when the driver stopped to have a nap. She was more than a little weary with the travelling and the bumpy roads and she ached all over. Just when they reached the Senegal border they were stalled in the queue of cars and minibuses, waiting to go through the passport control. Esther looked at one of the many small stalls on the side of the road. It happened to be selling newspapers. She saw the front page of Malian paper 'Le Essor'. To her horror at the bottom of the page, she saw the same poor photo of herself and a large headline in French 'Esther en Mali?'. Then a further sub headline, 'La police visite Le Grand hotel international majestic de Bamako'. That was the hotel she had stayed at on arrival. Esther did not need to know much French to understand those headlines.

She was now in real trouble. If she was caught, surely she would be sent back to Bamako and then deported back to France and then surely back to England. She envisioned herself arriving back at the airport in Paris. There would be bound to be loads of reporters and camera and TV and flashing lights. She would be feeling so ashamed, of being an unmarried mother who had abandoned her baby. That would then be followed by a similar scene at Heathrow airport but worse. The British media would be present in even greater numbers and they had the reputation of being worse than others. Her family back in Nigeria would see the TV pictures and feel the shame too. She preferred to die than face that and she would rather kill herself.

But she was stuck in the bus and could not go back now. If she got out and walked away from the border control, she would stand out like a sore thumb. Where would she go anyway? The border post was in the middle of nowhere. Better to hope that the border control people had not seen her photo and would accept her false papers. The policeman boarded the bus and checked everyone's documents. Everyone, except her, had either a Malian or Senegalese identity card, which were given a perfunctory glance at. When he came to her Nigerian passport he looked and looked at it. Then he gestured to Esther without a word to get out of the bus and go to the office at the side of the road.

Now Esther was really scared and her face started to show it. She entered the border post, which was a small office with a desk, chair and a phone on the desk. There was a man in the office when she walked in. He had a copy of the 'L'Essor' lying on his desk, the very paper she had just seen. Was this the end of the road for her?

The man looked at her suspiciously as though he might have seen her before. He decided instantly he did not like her. He always thought of himself as a handsome man. He also was vain enough to think that attractive young ladies should pay him due respect and flirt with him at least. Esther's face was not a smiling one, just serious. She gave not a hint of recognising what was in his opinion, his glaringly obvious beauty.

He gazed at her passport and again at her and decided on her punishment for not flirting with him. There was also the practical consideration. Tabaski, the West African name for the Muslim feast of Eid. was coming up. It was a time when every family would be slaughtering a goat to eat. It was one of the few times a year when many poor people would get the chance to eat meat. Since he had a well paid government job, he would be expected to buy a large fat and expensive animal. His father had just sent him a message saying that he had arranged to buy a goat, which was much more expensive than his son had thought it would be. That was, of course, in full expectation that he, the rich government worker, would be the one funding it. That had put him in a bad mood. He was just eager to leave for Tabaski tomorrow. His shift was about to finish for the holiday. In the background could be heard the fax machine spewing out a piece of paper.

He told her in his badly accented English, 'There is a border tax of 2000CFA to pay me now.' He would not have tried it on with a Malian or Senegalese. They have given him a long mouthful back in Wolof or Bambara, the local languages, and would have got other travellers on the bus to have done the same. He did not want the aggro but this Nigerian woman would not know any better. Esther silently got out the money and gave it him. He made no pretence to give her a receipt or even put the notes in a cash box. Instead he put the money straight in the breast pocket of his scruffy uniform and nodded to her to go. He debated in his mind whether to check out the fax that had just arrived in the office next door. In the end he decided he could not be bothered. Off he went happy to his family home, with enough money now to pay for the goat. The next on duty officer started his shift, picked up the fax twenty minutes later and looked at the picture of Esther and put it to one side. The first officer did not return to the border post for two weeks and the fax had been long ago thrown in the bin.

At the Senegalese side of the border there were no problems and the checks in Senegal were perfunctory with everyone in a Tabaski holiday mood. She started to perk up thinking she might have made it, that she had escaped successfully. Esther's heart was beginning to sing in spite of her present trials and tribulations. She was back in the hot embracing sunshine of Africa, travelling through Senegal.

She felt like a small lizard who had been in a cold place, who was now warming up, lazing in the Sun. Such a wonderful change from the pale, watery, winter sun of England. No more coping, enduring the cold wet miserable weather, no more having to wrap up with thick, very thick coats, scarves and hats and of course the vests. For some reason, Africans like her in England seemed to be especially sensitive to the cold.

She remembered with a smile a Spaniard from Malaga once saying to her, 'I feel so sorry for these poor English. They are shivering with cold. They have to come to my country for two weeks every year to warm up and relax before they go back and face the cold and rain and wind.'

She was in a small van converted into a little bus, going on a rough road, with more than a few potholes and dusty semi desert ground on either side. Everyone on the bus were Africans and there was not even the odd young, white tourist backpacker roughing it. She felt much more comfortable with that. No one looked a bit askance at her, as had happened to her from time to time in London. Mind you though, it was much less of an issue in cosmopolitan London than outside of the capital. If you went on the Underground, at least a third of the travellers seemed to come from abroad. She had had an emotionally rough ride over the last few days and her heart kept going back to the wicker basket in that London hospital. But she knew she had made the right decision for her baby and for herself. Surely a good family would take Emmanuel in.

Esther breathed a silent sigh of relief after changing buses in Senegal to get one heading to Basse in the East end of the Gambia. At Basse, she found a nice guest house and phoned her uncle in Banjul.
'Great, Esther. Stay put,' uncle Samuel's kindly voice came back over the phone. 'Stay with your cover name. I am going to send to you Alimame Camara, my fixer and a Gambian. He will take my Toyota land cruiser to pick you up from Basse and bring you to the coast to Fajara near Banjul where I live.'

CHAPTER 6- ALIMAME CAMARA

Two days later Esther was sat in the guest house reception, absorbed reading the latest issue of 'The Point', a Gambian newspaper in English. She was relieved to see there was no mention of her in the paper. When she had listened to the Gambia radio news, there was no mention of her either, which pleased her immensely too. She just wanted to lie low. She was busy reaching an article about the woes of the former Yugoslavia and the situation of the Muslims there. She had wondered at first why an African newspaper was so focused on the troubles of a far away country, with no historical connection with the Gambia. Then she had found out that the percentage of the population of Gambians who were followers of Islam was the same as in Egypt. That meant the country was overwhelmingly Muslim. No wonder they were concerned about Yugoslavia.

Her eyes looked up when she heard the sound of a car pulling up outside reception. It was a white gleaming Toyota land cruiser, the elite car of the 90's in the Gambia. It looked as it had just been washed. You were really somebody here if you drove round in one of them. In walked a tall, handsome man of about thirty with lovely ebony clear skin, an air of confidence and self assurance. He had a quick word with the reception and then strode over to her.

'Hi I'm Alimame Camara. How are you? Your uncle has sent me to pick you up.'

Esther's first impression was of how much he reminded her of

Emmanuel's father. He smiled in a way that clearly indicated he liked what he saw too. She made an instant decision that she was going to take her time with this man. She did not want to be caught out again like with Emmanuel's father.

They chatted for a minute or so. Then Almame asked her, 'How much did you pay for the hotel?'
She told him.
'That sounds like toubab prices. I should be able to negotiate a little discount,' he said with an alluring smile.
He went across to the girl at reception, chatted freely, used his charm and after five minutes came back with a grin, 'You can pay the bill now. It will be 20% less than you were quoted.'
That was the very first time of many occasions that Esther saw Alimame in his role as fixer.

The journey started. Esther already knew enough of Gambian roads and its potholes, to be glad to be travelling in a car some distance high off from the ground. Alimame, yes, he was tall, handsome, even beautiful and he had exquisite manners. He was friendly, polite to everyone and supremely confident. He knew the road like the back of his hand and had already clearly decided he would take his boss's niece under his wing. So he started to explain to Esther about Gambian life – not so very different to Nigeria but poorer.

'I am a Mandinka and we are the biggest tribe here in the Gambia. Over four in ten of us Gambians are Mandinkas so it is very worth your while learning my language.'
Esther mentally crossed her fingers, saying to herself, 'If I stay here that is.'
'Are there other tribes as well?' she asked. Then she thought to herself, 'What a silly question.'
'Oh yes but the only other language of note is Wolof which is the common language in Senegal and of Gambia. Most people know a bit of Wolof and it is the big language especially in Senegal.'
'Do the different tribes get on well together?'

'Oh yes, not perfect, but at least we have not had the conflicts and civil wars they have had in other parts of Africa.'

Esther thought about her own country, with the bloody civil war in the late sixties. The Igbos had tried to set up their own state of Biafra. Even though Biafra had failed, it had left behind a legacy of hatred. The Gambia was certainly a lot poorer than Nigeria but maybe there were other advantages to living here.

Esther noted that at every police check point, Almame was careful to get out of the car, shake hands with the policemen and greet everyone on site even the young kids selling little bags of peanuts as snacks.
'Why do you do that?'
'In three words, 'courtesy costs nothing'. The more people you know in my job the better. I do favours for the police and for people. You see that envelope on the dashboard? They don't have banks here except down the coast. So it is a cash economy and the largest note is only worth a few dollars. That means you physically have to give a whole wad of notes to pay for things. The policeman, who gave me this envelope is asking me to take it to his brother, another policeman, in the next station down the road. It is his help to pay for the family goat which has just been eaten for Tabaski or Eid. They trust me, you see. In return the police won't give me too much hassle, as I go up and down on my trips. In this country if you do people favours, they owe you one, which you can claim back discretely later.'

'What am I going to do staying here in Gambia?'
'I have some ideas but I need to sit down with your uncle and talk it through. In the meantime if people do ask you your name in the Gambia, call yourself Fatou Ceesay which is a very typical female Gambian name. Can you do that for me? The other thing is to try to learn some Mandinka. It will help you fit in. I will teach you some.'

'Cannot I be called Mary Ceesay? Where are we going to stay

tonight?'
'At a village not far off the road with some cousins of mine in a very Mandinka area of the country called the Kiangs. You cannot be called Mary as that is not a Gambian name. But you could be called Mariama, its Gambian equivalent. Lots of foreigners adopt Gambian names.'
They drove on over the potholes.

Finally after another day, they arrived late in the day in one of the richer areas by the coast called Fajara -not too far from the capital Banjul. They drove into a large villa with high walls and gates and a large single storey luxurious complex. Uncle Samuel came out of the front door to greet them. Esther was delighted, relieved to see one of her family and fellow Nigerian, someone she could trust. She spent the next hour with him, unburdening herself and recounting all her adventures to an attentive listener.

Later that day Samuel and Alimame sat to talk together alone.
'Alimame, I think Esther is likely to be going to have to be with me for years. Our wonderful President in Nigeria decided to put in his two penny worth. He took it into his head that if Esther turned up in Nigeria, he would send her back to England to 'look after her child'. Silly idea when I gather social services back in London have already placed the child with excellent foster parents. I personally think they would do far better than Esther on her own with the child. Some of our politicians here in Africa when they sound off, really take the biscuit.'

'My worry Samuel, is this. If the media find out she is here in the Gambia, the authorities here will want to get rid of a hot potato and decide to send her back to London.'
'We have to hide her. She can stay in this villa but she cannot stay locked up here for ever. She won't anyway. My worry also is if the authorities find her, they will also deport me as a foreigner back to Nigeria. My business will go down the tube too, which won't be good for you either. We both have an interest in sorting

things but I cannot abandon her. Her mother, my older sister, has pleaded with me to give her shelter.'

Alimame then went on to explain exactly his plan for disguising Esther.
'We have to make her more Gambian. I have told her she needs to introduce her to people as Mariama Ceesay. Can you ensure she does that Samuel? My longer term aim is to get her a Gambian identity card. But she does definitely need to learn the local language, like mine. If she can hardly speak a local language, then she will stand out like a sore thumb, which is what you don't want. She has the ideal opportunity on this compound. As you know, my relatives run this compound doing the cooking, cleaning and gate guarding. They are all Mandinka. I have already told them to keep mum about her being here. Let her stay inside the compound for say six weeks. not leaving but mixing with them and spending all the time learning Mandinka well.'

Alimame continued, 'This can work provided she learns Mandinka. After all the police won't expect a newly arrived Nigerian to have acquired an excellent knowledge of a local language but will think she has been here for years. Also because Wolof is more the dominant language round the coast, they would not expect a foreigner to have learnt Mandinka in a few weeks.'

'Alimame, after those six weeks I do want her in my office in Banjul. She speaks excellent English and I do a lot of business with Europe. Having a nice young lady answering the phone, speaking English well, will go down a treat. I'll need to give her a good wage though, not that I mind.'
'Best not to pay her at present because she would legally need a work permit as a foreigner. Call her a volunteer. Lots of people here start a job by being a volunteer for a few months then they start to get a salary if it is working out. Again we want to try to keep her below the radar.'

'How will she travel from here to Banjul?'
'Best she comes in the car with me. If the police stop us and want to see her papers, I'm the best one to help her – blag my way through things.'
'Okay Alimame sounds good.'
'So boss we have a plan,' Alimame said with a smile back.

Later that day Samuel and Esther sat down and Samuel explained the plan. 'I'm sure you can learn the language. After all we Africans are better than the toubabs at that sort of thing and I know that you have learnt English very well.'
'OK. But the thing that bugs me is how the police in Mali got onto me. If it was Mabel, then she has betrayed me and I could not forgive her.'
Samuel intervened, 'I had a phone call with Precious yesterday. She is adamant that she never told anyone about Mabel. The police did not interview Mabel either. I don't see how else Mabel could have been tracked.'

Esther was not totally convinced until Samuel came in later with a copy of the 'Liberation' newspaper in French which was a week old.
'Esther you might be interested in this.'
Esther looked up from what she was doing and saw he was reading a French newspaper.
'I didn't know that you could read French,' said with surprise in her voice.
'Oh yes. I can speak it too. I use it quite a bit in the office when dealing with business in Senegal especially but of course you have not been to the office yet. Let me give you the main points of the article.'

He translated them for her. It detailed the story of how Jean-Luc the passport control officer had picked up on Esther and how the Malians had been informed but had not picked up the message for twelve hours. However they denied receiving the message in time. The police had tracked her down to a hotel but then had lost her.

'They did track you they think to the bus station and it goes onto say that they lost your trail then.'

Samuel skipped over the incident about the policeman being hit by the bus and surviving. He did not think it was relevant. That apparently minor decision on his part was to leave Esther with a long lasting sense of guilt and nightmares for years.

'So you see there is no mention of Mabel. I don't think your cousin did say anything.'

It was only then that Esther could accept that Mabel was guiltless.

So Esther stayed in the compound for six weeks, spending the time listening to news and channels in English but also getting involved in the cooking, cleaning with the Mandinka ladies and picking up the language. After the six weeks quarantine was over, she went in one of her uncle's cars with Alimame to his office in Banjul to help out in the business. She picked up the ropes easily and soon became the second in command on the overseas side. Alimame of course was the chief fixer on the Gambian side, with uncle Samuel as overall boss.

After six months Esther spoke very good Mandinka even with an accent. Esther was happy – happier than she had been for a long time. Uncle Samuel treated her like the daughter, he and his deceased wife had never had. Esther started to think of him as a father figure to replace her Dad, who had died shortly after she was aged ten. Alimame was starting to wonder whether it would be the right time for the next step. Then an incident happened that made them both realise how fragile a house of cards her new life was built on – all because of her lack of documents.

She and Alimame were driving home, after a tiring day at work in Banjul. They had just gone past the infamous Mile2 prison in their Toyota land cruiser. This lay at the side of the highway linking Banjul and Serrekunda. A police check on the road then came into view.

Alimame frowned and said, 'I wonder what is up. We don't normally meet police checks on the way home.'
The policeman stopped them and started chatting to Alimame in Wolof. Esther and Alimame pretty much always spoke in Mandinka now together.
'What's up?' She asked him.
'A prisoner has escaped and the police are checking all the cars. They want to see our papers,' was his reply.
She knew she could not ask Alimame for more information in case the policeman spoke good Mandinka. She somehow knew that if the guy had been Mandinka, he would have spoken to them in Mandinka.

Alimame showed his Gambian identity card and then the policeman asked for hers in Wolof.
Esther temporised and said in Mandinka 'I ye Mandinka kango moyi?' (Do you understand Mandinka?')
She tried not to show the delight on her face when he came back with the words 'domanding dorong' (a little only).
She then launched into a long explanation in fluent Mandinka about how she had left her papers at home. The policeman was clearly lost. However since that was the biggest national language in the country and with the current President being a Mandinka, he could not be too disrespectful. He could have called over his colleague on the other side of the road who was Mandinka. His colleague however was busy having an argument with a large middle aged woman about something or other. He decided to leave it. The prisoner who had escaped was male and the description was quite unlike Alimame anyway. Besides he could easily see there was nothing or nobody else hidden in the car.

That evening Alimame and Samuel and Esther had a conflab. The problem of lack of proper papers for Esther had to be sorted urgently now. If he could get hold of an official identity card

properly issued, then that would sort out both the need for a work permit as well as hassle with the police. Esther gave a knowing smile, when Alimame revealed his plan.
'I know you can fix it, Alimame,' she said confidently.

Alimame and Esther went the next day to the alikaloo or mayor/village chief of their district. He was a Jola, a different tribe to the Mandinkas but he came from a part of the country where there were many Mandinkas. Alimame greeted him in the little Jola that he did know. Esther could see that went down very well with the alikaloo. Most Gambians did not bother with his language but that was typical of Alimame, the guy who wanted to get on with everyone. He spoke on her behalf in Mandinka, spinning the yarn while she sat silent.

'So you see that she was born in Nigeria of a Gambian father who died when she was aged ten, but with a Nigerian mother. That is why she speaks Mandinka with a bit of an accent because it is some time since she has spoken the language. But she is a Gambian citizen by birth. Unfortunately she had to leave Nigeria after a row with her family. She then came to live with her mother's brother. Because she left in a hurry, we only have her Nigerian passport which gives her Nigerian name, the one her mother gave her after her father's death.'

What happened next was most delicate piece of bribery.
The alikaloo said to Alimame, 'Leave this with me and I will see where we go with this.'
Meantime the alikaloo was thinking that technically he should not be sending the paper upwards to Banjul, with a recommendation that she be given the card, without seeing more evidence about Esther's father. He did know that Alimame was likely to give him something in return, if he did not enquire too closely. They fenced verbally for a few minutes with the alikaloo trying to find out what would be useful to him.

At last his opening came when Alimame said he was involved

with an import/export business.
'Does your firm import car parts?'
'We certainly do.'
'I wonder if you might be able to help me. My second hand Mercedes has broken down. My son who is a car mechanic says it needs some parts from Europe. Your business is in import/export. Might you be able to help?'
Alimame knew how important a running smart car was to the alikaloo. It was the symbol too of having a bit of money in the Gambia, having a Mercedes – even a second hand one exported from Europe.
'Sure, if your son could pop along to our office in Banjul with the list of the precise parts he needs.'
'Could you not go to his garage to get the list from him?'

'Unfortunately not,' interjected Esther. 'As the person in the business who deals with Europe, I need to use the computer and may have to ring up abroad and speak to them and your son at the same time. This way we can be sure we have got exactly the right parts. The list of parts for a particular car can run into thousands. But we will do our very best to help your son,' the last remark said with a friendly smile.
'Would there be a cost?' asked the alikaloo back.

Esther decided it was time for her to spin a little yarn.
'Car parts do cost us quite a big but when we put in a large order, they often throw in a few items for free. Once I knew what parts your son wants, I may very well be able to wangle those particular items at reduced cost or hopefully for free. Obviously also we would be very interested your son's business for the future. We do tend to try to give good customers a good deal.'

The alikaloo smiled. This was looking even less like bribery just someone doing him a favour at no cost to themselves. Also it sounded like his son might be able to get car parts cheap in the future. Alimame smiled too but inwardly. Esther was learning the ropes well!

'Tell you what. When my car is running again, I will get my son to personally drop your new identity card round at your house. That is the least I can do for you.'

All three shook hands on the deal with a smile.

The next day the mechanic son turned up at the Banjul office where Alimame welcomed him with a large cup of coffee, three sugars and a large breadstick and chocolate spread. He knew exactly what went down well with his fellow countrymen, who very often had a sweet tooth. After a lot of discussion between the mechanic and Esther and a long phone call to Germany, they finally ordered the parts needed. There was no mention of a price.

The next week Alimame drove the car parts, which had just arrived at the port, round to his garage. A week later the mechanic turned up at the house with the Mercedes running very smoothly and a gleaming, new Gambian identity card for Esther. He now wanted some more parts for a Toyota in disrepair. Alimame knew the form. This time he told him he would have to pay something. But because he was a friend, he would of course give him mates rates. That was the way business was done in the Gambia.

CHAPTER 7 -TO WED OR NOT TO WED

Esther was quite taking to Alimame and he invited her out for several dates. They were mostly eating out at a tourist hotel or going to a disco and sharing a coke together – no alcohol for Alimame as outwardly Muslim. She could see the way he looked in her direction. She was settled in the Gambia. She had a job in her uncle's business and was valued. She was happy to sit down with Samuel many evenings, chatting in their shared Nigerian language. Other evenings she was out with Alimame.

So Esther was not totally surprised when one morning her uncle called her into his room. They sat down together for a chat and a cup of coffee.
'So Esther are you happy here in this house with me?
'Yes very happy. I don't want to go back to Nigeria.'
'Will you be staying in the business?'
'Oh yes. I love the work and am pleased to be under the radar. I really gel with Alimame.'
'I was coming to that. Alimame has come to me, as your nearest senior relative. He has asked if he could marry you. What do you think?'
'I like him.. a lot though but I want to think it through,' Esther replied.

Later that day she went out to Serekunda market to her favourite clothes stall to buy a new outfit. She came across a white family standing out like a sore thumb among the hundreds of African faces milling round. It was a husband and wife together with three young sons. The older two looked like Dad more and the youngest like a mixture of Mum and Dad. They were clearly tanned more than the normal tourists and Dad was chatting away in fairly good Mandinka with one of the sellers. He said with a jokey voice.

'I have three wives- the grandmother, the middle wife and the bride but they are all the same person,' pointing to his wife. The Africans laughed a lot at that. He was using the Mandinka words: for first wife they use the word for grandmother. For second wife they use a word meaning 'the in between one'. As for the third wife they use the word for bride.

That joke suddenly pulled her up sharp. She knew about polygamy. After all, Alimame's brother who ran their compound, had both his wives with him. Alimame was still a bachelor yet. So if she married him she would become his first wife or grandmother, assuming he took a second or even third wife. Did she want to have him for a while to herself and then have to share him with other women, who would probably be younger than her?

She would have to think about that. She knew that things in the Gambia were slowly changing as men realised the cost of having more than one wife and decided that one was enough. You also had to bear in mind that sometimes polygamy didn't work out well as co-wives sometimes quarrelled. She wanted Alimame but she knew what she had to do.

CHAPTER 8- LOOK BACK

It was now present day and Esther was very settled in the Gambia. She had got a Gambian passport but she had rarely travelled out of the country. She reflected on her life and her mind kept turning back to the child she had given away. She could not get Emmanuel out of her mind ever since she had had that dreadful phone call – that life changing message from up country a year ago. She loved her six kids and was so proud of them. No grand kids yet. One of her daughters was training as a ICU nurse in the USA. Another son was doing law, training back in London, ready to return to the Gambia in a month and practice law in Banjul. Hopefully that would be much easier with the return of democracy to the country after the fall of the dictatorship. That should mean less need to bribe your way through life.

But there was this unsatisfied urge to reconnect with Emmanuel. He would be grown up now. Surely he would have survived in England where practically every newborn grew up to adulthood – unlike here in Africa. Was he married? Did she have grand kids she did not know about? Like many people, especially ladies in their advancing fifties, her mind was turning to the idea of having grand kids. She relished the thought of being called 'Nanny'. She had shared the thoughts that had been whirring round her mind in a letter with her special friend in England. Somehow writing down your thoughts on paper rather than just speaking them, helped her clearly define what exactly was going on in her head.

Life had been good. She had extracted a promise from Alimame that if he married her, he would not marry anyone else. Also he agreed that he would not have girlfriends either – that last being a very Gambian habit for married men. She had also had a discussion about the tough issue of circumcision of children.

'If we have kids what do you want to do with the girls about circumcision?'
'In the Gambia we normally circumcise the girls.'
'But not all girls and the government is starting to think it is not a good idea. I personally think it is a horrible idea. I want you to agree that it will not happen to our girls otherwise I will not marry you.'
Alimame thought about that.
He came back to her with, 'If I agree, it is going to be difficult to implement it. My family will try to take her off into the bush which is where they do it. Also what are you going to do with the boys? Can't they be circumcised? We have to give my family something.'

'Look, you control the family in the compound because you pay them. I do not want my girls to go alone up country to see your family in the countryside of the Kiangs, until they are aged sixteen or more. That is in case your relatives try something on. Also I don't mind you letting the boys go in the bush. In Nigeria practically every boy gets circumcised in the first few weeks of life.'

Alimame breathed a sigh of relief. It was going to be difficult to sell not circumcising the girls to his family. It would have been nigh impossible to sell not circumcising the boys to his family. Almost certainly his folks in reaction would have just tried taking the girls off to the bush to 'cut' them, the awful word used to describe the process.

Esther thought back to that decision – so glad she had taken that decision to allow the boys to be circumcised. She remembered chatting to one of her doctors when she was pregnant in 1998. He told her that he was surprised that there were not more HIV patients in the Gambia. This was at a time when AIDS was ravishing countries like Uganda and yet the Gambians had similar life style choices to the people in Uganda. She remembered ten or so years later, hearing the news that circumcising the boys reduced their risk of getting HIV. Of course in Gambia circumcising the boys was universal. So that explained it. So at least her boys would have some protection.

She and Alimame had had six kids four boys and two girls. Alimame had stayed true to his word, not to marry a second or even third wife as well as her…… or had he? Had he broken his word?

The nightmare had started for her after her husband went back to the Kiangs for a short trip, to see an elderly uncle who had fallen ill. The phone call had come to her two mornings later from his cousin, the uncle's son – the life changing message from upcountry. Alimame had gone to bed early the previous night, complaining of some chest pain. He had not got up that morning and had not responded to knocks on his bedroom door. Finally his cousin had gone into the room and found him curled up as though peacefully asleep. In fact he was cold and stiff – dead in his bed. She knew he had had heart trouble and had been to the hospital in Banjul. He had certainly piled on the pounds over his years of marriage. Recently he had been diagnosed with diabetes. Everyone in the village suspected he had had a sudden overwhelming heart attack in the night.

Esther put the phone down devastated, crying uncontrollably. Her husband of twenty five years gone just like that – buried quickly as was the Gambian wont due to the hot climate and lack of morgues. She had wept and wept and wept. Then she had slowly started to pick up life again. She was now totally in charge of her business without help of Alimame. She knew however what she was doing and had now got a group of good Gambian collaborators as a backup.

Then the shock had come just as she was picking up the pieces. It had come as totally unexpected as the call telling her of Alimame's death. One day four months later she came home from work to find, to her surprise, three visitors in her living room. They were sat drinking a fizzy orange drink given them by her cook. When she saw who the visitors were, she was even more surprised. There was the alikaloo of Alimame's village Bungbaa, Tombong Drammeh and his brother Famara Drammeh. That made her immediately think it must be some issue about land in the village, as Alimame had owned a field in Bungbaa.

What though was a young teenage Mandinka girl called Aminata Ceesay doing in the room with the other two? Esther could see straight away that the girl was quite nervous and very pregnant. She looked like a country girl, who had never been to the bright lights and sophistication of the Gambian coast, where the locals mixed with rich, white tourists and business people.

The normal greetings happened – a bit more complex and lengthy in Mandinka than in English. Esther waited to hear what the alikaloo had to say. The alikaloo finally took up the story.
'When Alimame, your late husband, visited Bungbaa two days before his demise, he visited his uncle Ebrima. Ebrima asked him to look after this young girl Aminata by marrying her. As you know Ebrima died a week after your husband's death. Alimame married her immediately. Before he died, he did manage to father the baby this girl is carrying....'
'No,' Esther cried out in amazement.

A whole series of jumbled thoughts went through Esther's head. Marrying the teenage girl was something not totally unknown among older Gambian men generally as second or third wife. Esther had known guys of sixty plus suddenly getting married to sixteen year old girls. That was totally disgusting in her opinion but it was what it was. So the story was not totally implausible but it went totally against all she knew of Alimame. She remembered how he had tenderly held an umbrella above her head for two hours. She had been heavily pregnant with her sixth child, as they stood in the queue outside the stadium to go into the Nigeria -Gambia football match. Why he even followed the toubab custom of giving his wife flowers on their wedding anniversary.

The story continued.
'I can see that you are shocked but it's true. I, as well as my brother Famara here, were present as witnesses as village elders at the traditional marriage ceremony.'
Esther knew that at the traditional ceremony neither bride nor groom would be present.
'Now for the reason for why we have come. Of course the girl has no money and Alimame had surely been going to provide for his new wife. Now alas he was dead. So it is to you we are coming for help for her and her baby.'

Esther understood what that meant. 'Help' of course was the code word to mean money from her, a rich widow to be given to the girl. The 'help' would be 'managed' by the alikaloo, with of course quite a bit going into his pocket. Of course 'help' was not going to be a one off but continual series of payments over many years. She remembered a Gambian once saying to her about this kind of situation, 'When you have a rich cow, you don't just milk her once. You keep on doing it'. Esther had heard the whole tale with a mounting sense of horror. Her automatic first reaction was to believe what she was told. It had a ring of truth and it was being told by the most senior person in the village, the alikaloo.

The girl Aminata shifted in her seat uncomfortably and looked as though she needed to lie down. Esther's good manners took over in the situation and she asked her gently, 'Are you okay?'
'I'm a bit thirsty.'
'I'll get you some water.'
Esther went out to get some water from the kitchen. She was glad to get out of the living room. She stood there in the kitchen running the tap, silently crying, thinking that her world

was shattered. Her Alimame had betrayed her. He had married someone else behind her back after so many years of keeping his promise. How could he do that? How could he betray her?

She suddenly understood how her friend Binta had felt many years ago. Binta at the time, was a very attractive nurse of thirty, with a husband in a good job in the phone company Gamtel. They had just had their first baby – a boy of six weeks old. Her husband had recently had a promotion at work and decided to celebrate his new status by bringing a second wife home unannounced – a young, exquisitely pretty, twenty three year old work colleague. Binta had rushed round to Esther's and had just cried and cried saying, 'How could he do that to me?'

Esther understood at that moment in her kitchen exactly how Binta had felt. She composed herself, wiping away her tears. She wandered back into the living room, holding the glass of water. She could see the girl was looking nervously round, clearly overawed by her surroundings. It was not her fault. She was clearly just a pawn, presumably just married off to Alimame because her family told her she had to wed a rich man twice or three times her age.

'Is this the first time you have been to the coast?' Esther asked her kindly.
'Oh yes. I have never even been to the Fonis before now,' referring to the region just next to the Kiangs and west of it and nearer the coast. You would need to go through the Fonis region to reach the coast.
'Have you had a baby scan done?'
'On yes I went to Mansakonkoo for that last week. They say I am having a nice healthy baby boy very soon.'
She was referring to the health facility in the big town to the East of the Kiangs. Aminata was pleased she had been asked about her precious baby boy. She took an instant liking to Esther.
She continued, 'If you like, I could show you a ph……'

The alikaloo quickly interrupted ....too quickly in fact, 'The scan shows two healthy boys – twins,'
The girl looked away embarrassed and blushing with her head turned to the floor. She did not say anything more. Esther was left wondering what was meant by, 'I could show you a ph......'

Then suddenly alarm bells rang in her mind. 'Very soon' implied she was much more advanced in her pregnancy than the four months that she would be if she had been with Alimame. Why did the girl not mention that she was having twins? Of course if she had been having twins, that could explain why she was so big at merely four months of pregnancy. The girl was indeed a pawn in an adults' game but a game played with deceit by the adults.

Esther said inside herself with determination, 'Two can play at that game'.
First she spoke to Aminata who now looked positively terrified, wondering what question she would be asked next and thinking how she might reply to it.
'You look hungry and you are eating for...... three.' Esther spoke the word 'three' carefully and slowly as if doubting the truth of it.
'If you go out to the other side of the compound to the big kitchen, you will find Fatou Ceesay, our cook. She will rustle up some grub for you.'

Aminata looked gratefully at her and walked out or rather waddled out. The girl definitely felt more comfortable with that. She knew from the name that the cook would be a Mandinka woman, who would speak her language. She herself only really knew Mandinka and a smattering of Wolof and English from school.

That left Esther with the two men. She noted that they breathed an almost visible and audible sigh of relief. It would be far easier for them to spin lies without the girl present, who clearly was not up to backing up their tale. She decided she would not challenge them whether Alimame had really gone through a marriage ceremony. Instead she would go for the weak link, which was the girl. To call or to suggest that they, the senior men in their village, were liars, especially about the marriage ceremony, would get her nowhere except to produce an almighty row.

'I am not quite so certain about the girl. There seems to be some confusion where she is having twins or just one baby. If she is having twins then that might well explain why she is so big.'
Esther decided to keep them on edge by qualifying with the statement,
'But not necessarily explain why she is so big. But if she is only having one child then why is she looking so big? Do you gentlemen think it was definitely my husband who got her pregnant after her marriage to him or….. was she already pregnant by someone else when Alimame went with her?'
'Oh I am quite certain it is your husband's child. She is a very good, reliable girl,' the alikaloo quickly replied.
'Um I am starting to have my doubts. She does seem unusually big and I do know about these things, having had six children of my own. Is it not unknown here in the Gambia for teenage girls to get pregnant by a man other than their husband? They then pretend very cleverly to their elders and betters that it is their husband who is the father of the baby. Is that not so gentlemen?' Esther spoke arching her eyebrows up.

The two men did not quite know what to say to this. They both knew it was true. They stayed silent. Esther now saw the opening to give the coup de grace to the two fraudsters.
'Look I want to help the girl….. assuming she is genuine of course. I presume you know about DNA paternity tests. When the baby or babies are born, bring him or them with Aminata down to the coast. My lawyer will do a DNA test on the baby to see if the baby is Alimame's.'
'How do you do the test? Won't you need a doctor? Also how

will you test for Alimame since he is dead?' were the questions quickly fired back at her.

'Alimame and I had six kids, three of my boys are still round the coast. Our three boys are the splitting image of Alimame. We will do the test on whichever of my children you choose. It is a simple mouth swab so it can be done safely even on young babies. You can bring your lawyer along too. We can then compare the DNA from both boys to see if they are half brothers.'

'So I look forward to seeing you both again with the baby for the test,' Esther said with a big smile.

They had one last try to get a few dalasi (The Gambian currency) out of her.

'Do you think you might 'help' her a bit to pay for her trip here?'

'I somehow thought you gentlemen would be sorting all that. After all I am sure you paid for her bus fare with you to come here to the coast. If the DNA test shows she has Alimame's child, be assured that I will certainly be generous,' she replied with a disarming smile.

The men slunk out of the room disconsolate.

Later that day Esther was chatting with Fatou Ceesay, her cook.
'How was Aminata?'
'She is a nice kid. I gave her a huge portion of rice and peanut sauce and she ate it all up but then she is eating for two.'
'Two?'
'She showed me a photo of her recent baby scan.'
So that is what Aminata had wanted to show her before being interrupted – a photo.
'She is so proud of her little baby boy due soon. He weighs six and a half pounds already according to the nurse doing the scan.'
'I had thought she was having twins.'
'Oh no, she only mentioned one baby.'
Esther suspicions were now fully confirmed. A four month old baby in the womb would not weigh six and a half pounds.

She expected she would hear no more from the alikaloo and Famara and Aminata. She thought they would not even try to fool her again. They were just too amateurish criminals. So she was surprised when about four weeks later, a couple of policemen a man and a woman turned up to her house and asked to see her. She sat them down and brought them out a coke each, which they accepted with gratitude. It was a very hot sultry day and police work was thirsty work.

'So what's this about?'
'We want to check out a story told us by Famara Drammeh, the brother of the alikaloo Tombong Drammeh of Bungbaa village which was, I believe, the home town of your deceased husband. He has fallen out with the alikaloo over the issue of some land which Famara said belonged to him. The alikaloo has the ultimate say and claimed it was his. The brother has come to us, saying that Tombong had hatched a plot to help a pregnant teenage girl in difficulty, saying falsely that the baby was your deceased husband Alimame's child. That was in the hope of extracting money from you, his widow.'

Esther said to herself' I thought so,' and did a mental high five inside her head. She then described the visit from the alikaloo in detail to the police.
She then said, 'Can I ask you a question which is very important to me personally?'
'Yes sure. Fire away.'
'The alikaloo told me that there had been a marriage ceremony involving the girl and my husband. Is that true?'
'That we don't know. When the alikaloo's brother came to us, he was honest and said he had lied to you about being present at such a ceremony. However he made it clear to us that he does not know for sure about whether they got married or not.'
'Have you interviewed the girl?'
'Unfortunately she was no use,' the policewoman interjected. 'She just fell apart crying and doing nothing else. She is just a kid with a week old baby. Her mother started to give me a lot of

hassle telling me that her daughter was in no fit state to be interviewed and why were we harassing a young girl. So we backed off for now.'

Esther smiled at that. She knew that some of the older Gambian women or musukeebas (grandmother) as they were called, would stand up to anyone even the police and would argue their point loudly and vehemently and not stop.
'For now?'
'Now we have talked to you, we shall visit her again and this time we will be insisting on getting the truth out of her. Are you quite sure that Alimame could not be the father?'

Esther thought through her reply with care, 'You told me that the baby was born ten days ago. You said that the baby was, according to the midwife, a full term baby. That certainly means that the child could not have been conceived about the time my husband died which was five months ago. The girl told me herself she had never been west of the Kiangs and I know for certain that my husband did not leave the coast to travel up country to see his family in Bungbaa for the last nine months of his life. He was home every night. So he could not have met the girl at another time before he visited the village for the last time.'

The policeman said, 'I like your idea of doing a DNA test on the baby and on any suspected father. After all we are now well into the 21st century. I don't suppose you have looked into how to go about it.'
'You would probably have to send the test off to Europe but it would cost maybe 200 US dollars.'
'That's a lot of money but we could always get the defence to pay if the defendant is found guilty.'

As the police left, they told her that she might have to appear in court as a witness. She was still left hanging mentally whether Alimame had married the girl or not. The deceitful plot did go to court in the end. The case was a big one making the local news-

papers as it was quite a dramatic plot.
'Alikaloo Tombong Drammeh of Bungbaa village charged with attempting extortion,' was the newspaper headline.

Esther was called to give evidence and sat outside the courtroom with other witnesses including Aminata. She was holding her little baby boy. Her own mother was there to support her. Esther went over to say 'hello' and coo at the baby. Aminata smiled shyly at seeing her and said that the boy's name was Modou Drammeh. Now in the Gambia children took the surname of the father and Drammeh was the surname not of her late husband but was the alikaloo's surname.
'Could the alikaloo be the father?' Esther wondered to herself.
Then a court official came bustling over saying, 'Witnesses are not allowed to talk to each other. You need to separate now.'
So that was the end of the conversation.

Two days later Esther's daughter Hawa went out to the little local corner shack shop to buy some fresh bread and to get a newspaper. She came rushing back and said, 'Mum, I need to show this to you'. She started reading aloud to Esther.
'Alikaloo Tombong Drammeh convicted of attempted extortion of rich businesswoman Mariama Ceesay.'
'Alikaloo Tombong Drammeh was today convicted at Kanifing High Court of attempted extortion of rich, recently widowed, businesswoman Mariamma Ceesay. He tried to pass off the unborn child of his son Ousman Drammeh by Aminata Ceesay as the baby of her deceased husband, Alimame Camara. He also falsely claimed that Alimame had married Aminata just before he suddenly died. The plot came to light because the alikaloo quarrelled with his brother Famara. Famara then went to the police to reveal the truth. The plot was confirmed by an interview with the widow Mariamma Ceesay and further confirmed by Aminata Ceesay. She revealed that she had never been married to the late Alimame Drammeh and had certainly never slept with him. Her baby was the child of Ousman Drammeh, the alikaloo's

son. This was confirmed by a DNA test done on the baby and on Ousman.'

Esther's heart leapt at this news. Alimame had been true to her. Her heart started to relax.

But after the court case was over, she was back to thinking more and more about Emmanuel. The old questions kept coming back to her mind. What was he like? Had he made a success of life? Was he married himself and did she have grand kids she had never met? Had he even survived? Had he turned out to have some abnormality not detected on the scan before birth which had killed him? So many unanswered questions and the answer lay only in England.

CHAPTER 9 - THE STORY TELLER

'Rebekah also looked up and saw Isaac. She got down from her camel and asked the servant, "Who is that man in the field coming to meet us?" "He is my master,"'
A quote from the Hebrew Book of Beginning (NIV translation)

Michael read this quote and the passage round it. He was entranced by it. It was part of his own personal story. Indeed he would not be here but for this true story. It was the story of an arranged marriage -a concept that was in so many ways alien to 21st Century mainstream Britain. Isaac lived in a sea of people. The land of what would become Israel was a bustling, busy place with surely plenty of ladies available to marry, especially for a rich man like Isaac. But there he was, aged forty and unmarried.. because his Dad (Abraham) wanted him to wed someone from his family back in the land between the rivers. The land was to be called Mesopotamia but that was merely using a later Greek word to say 'the land between the rivers'.

So his father sent his most experienced and most important servant back to 'the land between the rivers' to find a bride for Isaac. It seemed from the story that there were quite possibly several brides he could find. So the servant had clearly got a certain amount of discretion in what was to happen. The servant had prayed to the God of Abraham and chosen wisely. Rebecca was the girl he found 'very attractive in appearance' too – no plain Jane. That was not an expression Michael should use, given the lady he had fallen for four thousand years later. The rest, as they say is history.

This story was part of Michael Cohen's story. Mike's grandfather on his Dad's side, Elisha Cohen, had been one of the Kohens or Kohanim, to use the correct term or priests, in his Orthodox Jewish synagogue in Finchley, North London. Michael knew that tradition dictated and was certainly correct that Michael's ancestors would have been priests in the Second Temple or even earlier back in Jewish history in Solomon's temple. Mike's Dad Isaac, had indeed, by one of those strange coincidences, married a Rebecca Cohen who 'just' happened to be one of the prettiest girls in the synagogue. So Michael was a full Jew, descended from Isaac of the Bible and from his own Dad, Isaac.
He joked to his orthodox Jewish friends, 'If ever you get that third temple of yours in Jerusalem built, you could always give me a job as a priest there.'

But this last Isaac, unlike the Isaac in the Bible had not been subsequently quite so obedient to his Dad. He was a local GP in north London and a bit of a quirky personality. That was why he had become a GP and his own boss, rather than becoming a more regimented hospital doctor. So what happened next was not totally surprising. He started drifting away from the Orthodox Judaism of his childhood. While his wife was languishing in hospital, after the birth of baby Michael, he went for a few drinks with a 'friend' called Paddy Ryan in an Irish pub to celebrate. That was before deciding to pop round the corner to the registry office of births with this 'friend'.

He and his wife had already decided that the child would be called 'Samuel Solomon Cohen'. After a few drinks Paddy, having learnt of the previously agreed names, with more cunning than common sense had suggested naming the child 'Michael'. Of course his own surname 'Ryan' was to be the boy's middle name. So Michael Ryan Cohen had landed up with the weirdest mixture of a very Irish middle name, a totally Jewish surname and a first name that could go both ways, being common to both

Irish and Jewish cultures. It was a bit like mixing custard and fish pie in the same bowl and serving it as a side salad. His wife, when she heard what Isaac had done, did not speak to him for days. He only got back in his wife's good books by promising that all subsequent children would have 'proper names' chosen by her. Hence Michael's siblings were called Daniel and Joshua and Miriam.

He had had the little boy's operation at eight days old though, to keep Grandfather Elisha happy. At least he had had a competent Mohel or official circumciser. Later on his grandfather Isaac was desperate for little Michael to have a Bar Mitzvah ceremony as an early teenager. His mother though, had got so lax in her religion that she nearly served bacon batches at the party. That still made Michael laugh. He remembered his mother quickly rushing round to get rid of the 'criminal' rolls and opening the windows to eradicate the smell, when she realised what she had done, before Elisha got a glimpse of them.

When at the age of eighteen Michael became entranced by the person of Jesus and became a Christian, his parents' reaction had been 'whatever'. That was the typical generic late 20th century response to people with a definite faith. 'Whatever floats your boat,' was the phrase, with the clear understanding behind it that people could choose whatever they liked to believe. Grandad Elisha had been enraged that his grandson had become 'one of them Messianic Jews' and would not speak to him.

But back to the quote at the beginning of this story. Had the outcome of this arranged marriage come out well? Isaac loved Rebecca after his marriage. He was having an active relationship because twenty years later he was praying that his wife would get pregnant. What was the ultimate test of the success of a marriage? Surely it had to be if the couple stayed together, though of course that did not necessarily imply the marriage was wonderful. The internet was a maze of confusing statistics. From the quick survey he had done, arranged marriage had a low divorce rate probably lower than the rate of divorce among Western Christians.

The present 21st century ideas of marriage in the UK did not work very well. The idea was that you found a girl or a boy and started dating them. Then if you felt you were in love with them, you would take things further. If your parents did not like your choice, then that did not matter even if they could see the pitfalls or benefits of going for a particular person.

Michael could well remember his feelings of passion and love when he had married Jane. They were outside on the lawn of the rather ugly modern church building where the service had taken place. The sun thankfully had come out. He had taken up and held his bride in his arms in the air for the first time for the wedding photo. In both of them, the storms of hormones were raging on the seas of their emotions and they were hot for their honeymoon.

But when the level of passion had died down, they had discovered the solid personality in each other. He remembered the last time he had swept Jane into his arms. He was a stone heavier than his wedding photo and Jane was two and a half stone lighter. She was not physically attractive like she had definitely been on their wedding day. How could she be that with what was going on in her body? But Michael loved her with a deeper, stronger love than ever before. He would have done anything to help or save her. It was 'love as strong as death', a phrase which exactly described what was about to happen.

'Where are you taking me, my darling?' she had asked him as he walked out of the house, holding her in his arms. It took her any effort just to speak out those words,
'To the clinic, Jane. I am just going to put you carefully in the back seat of the car.'
She smiled wanly back. That was the last time he remembered her ever smiling at him. He had realised with a jolt that was

the ultimate time he would probably ever leave the house with her in the car. It would surely be the very final time he would drive her somewhere. The cushions were carefully plumped up behind and round her in the car. He then covered her with two blankets, since she now felt the cold so easily.

He drove slowly deliberately. Jane definitely would not want to experience a bumpy ride today with her bones crumbling the way they were. They had admitted her to hospital from the clinic, as he had known deep down that they would. She died on the oncology ward a few hours later, with Michael holding her left hand tenderly, adorned as it was by their wedding and engagement rings - 'Love as strong as death.'

His thoughts then took an unexpected turn and a very well known royal prince came to his mind standing in front of the TV camera with his beautiful, in fact very beautiful young fiancee. He had been asked the question whether they were in love. In his reply he had used the famous or perhaps now infamous phrase, 'whatever 'in love' means.' Michael understood why that man then in his thirties had used that ambivalent phrase. He doubtless had seen his aristocratic friends and acquaintances of similar age in his social circle to him fall in love, sometimes get married, sometimes just be together. Then they would fall out of love again and even separate. Unsurprisingly that prince's own subsequent marriage had a decade or so later shattered in a thousand pieces.

Michael so wanted to take that prince to the scene of the bedside of his dying wife with him tenderly holding her hand and say to the prince, with emphasis looking him full in the face, *'That's what 'in love' means.'*

Michael stopped his reverie and focused back on his main train of thought. Yes, marriage had worked out very well for him and Jane but the more he thought about it, he came to this conclusion: The late 20th / early 21st Century western way of dating and marriage in the Western world did not work out especially great, what with all the long engagements, loads of dating, seeing each other. Even living together as man and wife before marriage did not seem to work out particularly well. All that stuff did not work – all that time and freedom and allowing people's passions to rule them did not do the necessary. What was that horrifying statistic? 40-50% American marriages ended in divorce.

No. The modern way of marriage did not work particularly well. Could this passage give some sort of answer? Also why had the author of the Book of Beginning spent so much time in his book, describing the whole incident, giving minute details? Was he trying to send a message to the human race more than three millennia later? Did he even know that his five books series would be part of the bestseller volume of all time?

He knew from the next book the author wrote in his series of five 'The going out or Exodus', that the guy had an 'organised' marriage himself. His boss, who he was living with, suggested to him to marry his daughter – which he did. So he clearly was not against the idea of an arranged marriage. Mind you the author of the book also told the story of Leah in his first book - the unloved one whose husband only discovered he had married her the day after the wedding night. So arranged marriage had its downside when done badly. The story of Leah was too part of Mike's story, as Leah's son Levi was the ancestor forefather of the Cohens, the Levitical priests.

It was interesting that the marriage on first meeting programmes did not seem to have a good success rate. In fact they often ended with disastrous results. When he had done internet searches, it seemed to suggest that arranged marriage worked best with meetings before the wedding. Often it seemed it was more organised dating which often led to marriage rather than fully organised marriage before bride and groom ever met.

Then his turn of thought took an unexpected course. His job was telling stories – real life stories. Were there some stories in this subject of organised dating/marriage he could recount to others to earn his pennies and to entertain and inform? Then a second thought came. What a coincidence! He was going on a sort of organised date that very night.
'Dad, I was talking to you. Didn't you hear me?' the voice said a little crossly, interrupting his important train of thought.
'Oh Sorry Ellie,' came back the reply in an apologetic tone from Michael.
'Would you like a cup of tea?'
'Yes please.'
'By the way we need to get more teabags when we go to the shops later today and also have you got your clothes ready for your date night?'
Having a bossy daughter was such a pain, thought Michael.

CHAPTER 10 – DATE NIGHT

Later that evening Ellie dropped him off outside the posh curry house. She straightened his tie for him, saying in the determined voice of a young woman who knew it all, 'Just be yourself Dad and don't get too nervous. Give me a ring when you want to be picked up.'
Michael thought to himself, 'Amazing isn't it when your twenty year old daughter is giving you advice on dating.' But then it was twenty seven years since he had been on a date. As he was just about to enter the restaurant, he saw his date just getting out of a taxi.

Amanda Sollerton was a slim tallish lady of fifty with browny, greying hair and spectacles, quietly spoken with an open, friendly look on her face. She greeted Mike and in they went to the restaurant and sat down. They both looked at the menu with anticipation and made their choices.
Mike said, 'I don't know if I have got the best outfit on in a curry house – my best suit with all that sauce they use, sploshing round everywhere.'
'Don't worry. Just use a couple of big napkins well tucked in.'

They decided they would drink a bottle of white wine together. They realised that they both had a taste for the delicious Asian yoghurt drink mango lassi. It was over a glass of that that they got down to brass tacks, finding out each other.
'So Mike, what's your line of work?'
'I am a story teller. I tell stories that entertain and amuse but

also speak truth.'
'That sounds intriguing? Are you a novelist or a journalist then?'
'No. I have a film production company producing films mostly for television called 'Cohen Cinematography'..'
'How interesting. You are nothing to do with the Coen brothers, the American film makers, are you, with a name like yours?'
'Oh no. I spell my name Cohen with a 'h' in the middle for a start. But I chose the name 'Cohen Cinematography' because it sounded memorable and snazzy.'
'What kind of films do you make?'
'I like to make things outside the normal run of things – a whole range of things. I did one on foundlings in the Philippines, another on the toctoc taxis of India.'

They chatted on for a few minutes on his work and then he posed the question.
'So Amanda, how do *you* earn your daily bread?'
'I was a management consultant for many years before I decided I needed a less stressful life. I still do a bit of that freelance to keep the pennies coming into the coffers. But my main work is as head of a small Christian charity called 'Introductions for togetherness.' We tend just to call it 'Introductions' for short.'
Mike thought that was a bit of a mouthful for a name but said nothing.
'And what does the charity do?'
'We seek to pair up young, single Christians who are struggling to find a marriage partner.'
'So you are a dating agency?'
'Much more than that.'
'So you organise marriages?'
'No we don't do organised marriages. We absolutely do not do that. What we do is pair couples up, after interviewing them formally for several hours and running psychological tests. But we don't just introduce. We put them together for three days of introductions. They live in the same house together, with chaperones of course, and we get them doing a whole load of jobs as

a pair. That is so that they can see for themselves how they get on with each other, doing the nitty gritty things of life. At the end of the three days they then decide if they want to date each other. If they do decide to do so, then they exchange contact details. We let them get on with it and don't do anything more. Some couples go on to date and get married. Some don't.'
'So it is more an organised initial meeting?'
'Yes that is right.'
'How successful are you?' Michael asked with interest.
'We have a seventy percent success rate in terms of marriages from the three day introductions. That is where people have lasted the three days together and decide to date each other.'
'Wow. That is impressive.'
'Yes that is because we take a lot of care in who we match up.'
'Do some people not stick out the three days together?'
'Oh yes. We can spend ages trying to match people. Then come the first introductions day, the boy or the girl takes one look at the other person and walks out saying, 'not my type'.'
'Why do you stick to young Christians?'
'Because for a lot of them, they are only prepared to marry someone like minded to themselves. But they are often stuck in tiny churches with limited numbers of available partners.'

Their church was different but Michael knew that in many smaller churches there was preponderance of older people. If you were young, then your marriage choices came down to a handful of names and if you did not happen to take to any of them……'
'Why don't they use dating apps? A lot of young people do. I have a niece, who has just married this guy she met on the net last year. It seems to be working out for them.'
'As you say, some youngsters do and there are some Christian dating apps. Problem is that a lot of dating apps don't have good reviews and for good reason. Basically before you click on a profile, all you have is a picture and a few details supplied by the person themself. Of course also people are not necessarily hon-

est in what they say about themselves. It can be quite a risky business and you might find yourself going out with someone dodgy. At best you meet someone who you know within five minutes of meeting them face to face, is not your type.'

'What sort of personality are the candidates do you get?'
'An incredible mixture. Some are people who, if they were not limiting themselves to Christians, would find it easy to find someone on the 'secular market' as it were. Some are people, who are much tougher to find a suitable partner for. Often that is because they themselves are more 'difficult' personalities for want of a better word.'
'Tell me more.'
'Some of the candidates are people without many friends or social contacts and who think that marriage is going to solve all their personal problems. That is of course totally unrealistic. Some of the candidates are so desperate that they would marry anyone. We will only match people up who we think are going to work out as a couple long term. We are very definite about that and some people we are never going to be able to match up.'
'Are people disappointed when you cannot match them up?'
'In some cases yes. Some of the blokes are very lonely and are so wanting the companionship of marriage. That is less so with the women. Some of the older girls though are desperate to have kids, especially where the biological time clock is ticking down. So they are devastated not to be matched up.'
'What happens to those who you don't match up or who you do match up? Then it does not work out so they don't get married?'
'Some of them turn out okay. Having gone through the process, they start to get a much more realistic view of marriage. They put it in perspective that it is not the be all and end all of living a good life as a human being. Some people, when they start dating, appear too desperate to the other person. That never goes down well. Often though they learn through the process to better relate to others.'
'Do you do any counselling?'

'Yes the people who come to the interview stage, we do try to talk through about what marriage is about. We explore their views and hopes and dreams and help them see what is realistic and what is not.'

'I've got to say that I loved my dead wife deeply but her last two years of life with her cancer illness were a living hell for her and for me also. Occasionally I had thoughts which I felt very guilty about, wishing I had never got married or had got married to someone, who would not put me through so much emotional pain.'

'I can empathise with that from my own experience.'

Mike asked, by now thoroughly interested in what Amanda was saying.

'By the way how do you screen out dodgy characters from the applicants?'

'We do a full safeguarding check and we ask for full details of all criminal convictions. The really dodgy characters don't get any further and we always reveal all criminal convictions to the other party at the end of the Introduction Days. Everyone is aware of that and has to consent to that before going on the three days introductions.'

'Why is that?'

'We had this guy once who passed the normal safeguarding checks. He then got through the Introduction Days and started dating. He took the girl out for a spin in his fancy sports car and crashed it. Luckily the girl was uninjured but the car was a write off and the police decided to prosecute him for dangerous driving. It then came out that he had one previous conviction for dangerous driving that we did not know about. So after that time we decided that we would ask for details of and tell the other side about all convictions.'

'I presume that was the end of them dating.'

'Funnily enough no. They went on to get married but she insisted thereafter that she would do all the driving when they were together.'

'It is amazing how willing so many people are to forgive the faults and failings of the folk they love.'
'It is indeed.'
'You know it is funny us meeting like this, as I was thinking today about doing a story on arranged marriage. I know you don't do arranged marriage but something a bit different. But is still a bit of a coincidence.'
Michael went on to describe his line of thought that day,

The chat gradually turned to other topics as the chappatis, then chicken jalfrzei and pilau rice and naans were served. It was over the kulfi ice cream at the end that Amanda, emboldened by two full glasses of white wine, posed the question.
'So Mike, what made you decide to ask me out? Was it my obvious wit, charm and beauty?' she said with a smiling, laughing face.
'In fact it was Pastor Geoff and...' Mike said leaving the sentence hanging.
'And my obvious wit, charm and beauty,' Amanda finished off the sentence for him with a laugh.
Mike said, 'Of course' with a smile back.

Then she continued, 'Pastor Geoff came to me and said you were thinking of dating me and asked what my thoughts would be. At first I thought if a guy can't ask me out straight without going through other people well.... he is not worth going out with. Geoff Payton said that he felt you were a bit nervous after so many years of not dating and that I ought to give you a chance.'
'Umm all that is technically true but there is a bit more to that. As I mentioned earlier, my wife of twenty five years, Jane, died two years ago of breast cancer. I went to Geoff and shared some of my struggle with loneliness after her passing. It had not occurred to me about dating anyone from church. Geoff said, 'What about going out with Amanda Sollerton on a date night.' I said, 'I will think about it.' He then said, 'Leave it to me', without giving me a chance to say anything more. He then came back to

me saying that you would be willing to go for a night out with me. So decision made for me.'

'So how did you feel asking me out?' asked Amanda.
'To be honest I was a bit nervous, approaching you after the church service but you did make it relatively easy. The last time I asked anyone out was my dead wife Jane, twenty seven, twenty eight years ago. What about you?'
'The last time I went out with anyone was seven years ago. It did not last long.'

'Ever been married before?'
'Oh yes to Leo, literally the boy who lived next door to us and our parents. When I married him, I did not know he had a weakness that would end our relationship early.'
'Oh what was that?' said Michael intrigued.
'He did not know it either but…….he had a weak piece of artery inside his brain. He was big on personal fitness. One day the artery blew while he was doing his weight lifting. He had a massive brain haemorrhage and that was curtains for him. He left me with our three kids under five to bring up by myself. It took me many years to forgive God for that but I did.'
'Were you happy with Leo?'
'Up and down. We were only married a few years and we did quarrel a lot. Things though were definitely improving before he died and I think after another ten years, we would have come to a much much better place.'
'Jane and I certainly had our struggles at the beginning but obviously we had a lot longer time than you to sort things out. We had come to a place of peace when her illness struck her.'

They chatted more. Mike knew that he needed to take the lead again.
'It would be nice to go out with you again – maybe something less formal.'
'Yes that would definitely be nice,' said Amanda with enthusiasm.

Michael thought to himself, 'Why do we Brits use such a weak word like 'nice' when we really do rate something highly?'
'Look I know you have got your Jack Russell little hound. What about having a walk in Derbyshire with our dogs? I like the hike from the old Bakewell station to Edensor with a fantastic view of the Chatsworth estate. We can stop and have a cup of tea at the cafe and take a different way back to Bakewell.'
'You mean date me, date my dog?!! I don't know that particular walk but it certainly sounds good to me.'

So the arrangement was made. Mike left the restaurant, with more to think about than a pleasant evening with a nice, attractive woman. His brain was going ten to the dozen cooking up a scheme. Later that night he hit the web pages of 'Introductions for togetherness' and tut tutted in displeasure. The site had just such dated design – just so ten years ago and no version specifically for mobile phones.
'We need to do something about that,' he muttered out loud.

CHAPTER 11-A WALK IN THE WOODS

A few days later, Amanda and Michael were starting their planned walk from the old Bakewell train station along to the end of the Monsall trail. Michael had brought his playful Labrador puppy Sally and Amanda had her feisty female Jack Russell called Lita. They then got out into more open country and farmers' fields
'It looks like Alpine countryside with the hills and trees round about. So few people round. It is quiet. peaceful and beautiful. '
'Yes Mike, you cannot beat it. I always remember what Jane Austen wrote in her novel in 'Pride and Prejudice' that 'Derbyshire is the finest of counties.'
'I have a proposal to make to you which might involve Derbyshire and...drones.'
'Golly that is keen. I thought normally today guys had to wait till the third date before they proposed to the girl of their dreams. I don't see how the drones fit in with that though.'
'Oh ha ha very funny. But let me at least outline it to you.'

Mike did and Amanda listened with wide eyed growing surprise over the next five minutes.
'So you are wanting to throw in a whole load of dosh and you would film what our charity does. Any couple who went through our process and then decided to date and then got round to getting wed, you would offer them a free marriage service, which you would arrange. You would also throw in a week's free honeymoon arranged by you. And you in return,

would film it all including the Introduction Days.' It all came out in a rush from Amanda's mouth.
'Yes. So what do you think?'
'Wow, I don't know what to say. I'm a bit blown away. Yes I am very interested. It would certainly allow us to expand our operations. We are short of cash. No worse than that – we are living hand to mouth at present. I would need to consult the charity's trustees of course as well as some other people. There is one concern I have.'
'What's that?'
'Do you think that an offer of a free wedding and honeymoon might induce some people to get married just for the freebies?'
'You would have an absolute veto on whom we offered the free wedding and honeymoon to. You could interview them before marriage couldn't you? Of course all couples would have gone through your three day introduction process as well as having gone through the dating process.'
'OK but you mentioned there were other goodies you could throw our way too.'
'We would revamp your web site and pay for advertising. Also we would provide admin support and office space. I gather you are having to leave your present premises soon.'

'How do you envisage the marriage service and honeymoon?' asked Amanda.
'Well I am looking to sell the programmes to whoever will take them. I would really love to be on Christian television in the US, Canada and Far East and Africa. So I do want something spectacular. How would *you* do it, Amanda?' Michael could see that she might often have insights into his work that others including himself did not have. He had this knack of throwing difficult questions back at people and sitting back to listen to their answer.

'In what way?'
'OK, so how would you do the wedding scene?'

'Well,' said Amanda quickly drinking a sip of water from her water bottle. She wet her lips for her upcoming speech on the matter which she was composing on the spot.
'We Brits do pomp and ceremony and tradition very well. So the marriage scene needs to reflect that. People inside and outside the UK love royal weddings for example. Think of the iconic Charles and Di wedding in St Paul's Cathedral or the more recent William and Kate marriage in Westminster Abbey. Three hundred million people are estimated to have watched that last one. As for Charles and Di nearly one in six human beings in the whole world at the time are thought to have viewed that block buster. The average TV producer would, I'm sure, be prepared to die for those sort of audience figures.'

Amanda was clearly waxing lyrical.
'So okay lashings of ceremony but talk me through specifics.'
'So I think you need a beautiful old Church of England church.'
'Why ever do you need one of those?'
'Do you really want to do shots of the building we go to church in. It is hideous, truly hideous.'
Mike thought about that. For his marriage to Jane, they had had the ceremony in the Baptist church, where they worshipped. They had not cared too much about the building, which happened to be a down market edifice from the sixties. They had just been so eager to get hitched. Mike and Amanda's present church was a building that looked like an aircraft hangar outside and inside. Originally it had been built to house a garden centre. Then that business had gone bust and their church had snapped up the place for a song.
'Okay Amanda I see your point. Go on.'

She stopped a minute to catch her breath as they were going uphill through the woods. The path was ultimately leading towards the majestic view of the Chatsworth palace and the hunting tower in the woods on the other side of the main building. It was tricky, negotiating one's way uphill, along the well beaten path, past the sticking out tree roots and stones exposed by the feet of thousands of walkers eroding away the soil. Two mountain bikers out of the blue suddenly came careering past them downhill, nearly hitting them. She waited till they had passed.

'You probably need nothing so grand as Derby Cathedral but a lovely old village church would do the trick very nicely. Loads of shots outside of the old buildings. It needs old wooden pews inside and masses of beautiful flowers tastefully placed everywhere. You need a well dressed priest with a more formal traditional manner and definitely an older sounding liturgy. 'Will you take this woman to be your lawful wedded wife to have and to hold...etc.' The bride needs a stunning wedding dress, again tastefully done simple and not too fancy.'
She stopped a moment to think more.
'Why do you need so stunning a wedding dress? Surely those sort of details get lost with all the other intricacies of the wedding scene.' Mike was being teasingly provocative.

Amanda replied with an expression of astonishment. She remembered how stunning she looked in the home made wedding dress. Her late mother had lovingly cut it out and sown it together over many many hours.
She cried out, 'Mike you cannot do that. You *must* have a stunning wedding dress. Besides your programme will get a lot more female viewers than male and they will all just be longing to see close shots of Bride and dress.'
Mike smiled quietly to himself as he had been thinking along those lines anyway. She went on.

'You also need to control especially what the male guests wear – no open neck shirts and scruffiness, just lots of suits and high neck cravats. No public crafty fags or vapes while the blokes are waiting round for ages for the wedding photos to be taken. Not that so many people smoke today. The Bride and Groom need to exit to a nice church entrance and walk down along the church path slowly, with confetti thrown everywhere in oodles. Best to use eco friendly rose petals as they look more attractive than paper. Then the reception needs to be in a nice old country house hotel, large and magnificent – a Georgian or Victorian old pile with loads of mature ivy covering the frontage.'

'Oh, by the way, you could think of stopping at somewhere like the Chatsworth estate for the wedding photos. Oh another thing – use really old beautiful classic British cars – Rolls or Bentley will do nicely or perhaps a Jaguar or even Aston Martin sports car. Everything has to speak British tradition but tastefully done. The Bride needs one car to arrive at the church and a different one for Bride and Groom to go to the reception from the church in. Do I need to go on?'

'No you don't Amanda.... but you probably will anyway. I can already see my slightly old fashioned accountant raising his eyebrows and giving discreet coughs at the cost of it all,' Mike replied with a laugh.

Amanda took another slip of the water to wet her lips before launching in to the second half of her developing speech. They had now reached the point of the walk where they could see the Russian cottage down hill from them.

'For the honeymoon you need a classy hotel similar to the reception – maybe the very same hotel with lots of shots of the fantastic grounds, the trees, the happy couple in the swimming pool or even better in the hot tub, drinking champagne late at night. Subdued lighting would be great or even better, candlelight, the lovely old ivy clad buildings, fine dining etc. I'm sure that you could easily find a nice old church in Derbyshire and a great hotel in our county too.'

Mike nodded in agreement. He had been thinking a bit on the same lines but it was definitely good to have a woman's opinion. He really did want to set this in his home county, The lack of female input was something he really missed in life after the death of Jane. Ellie his daughter did help sometimes, with insight but she did not have the life experience that Amanda brought to the party. He was beginning to really take to her and was looking forward to working together if ……she could wangle it with her charity's trustees.

She interrupted his reverie.
'You have not yet explained about the drone.'
'Or rather should I say drones?'
Mike did just that.
She just laughed, 'Sound super to me. You men do like your boys' toys,' was her reply.

They had by now passed through the final wood and were on the hill overlooking Chatsworth and in the distance the hunting tower. They walked down the grassy slope and into the little village of Edensor and down to the cafe. They sat out in the courtyard in the afternoon sun and ate lemon poppyseed cake, washed down with tea. Their dogs noisily gulped down water from bowls on the ground, thirsty as they were from the long walk.

Mike started the dialogue again, 'I have had an idea about your Introduction Days. I'd like to rename them 'Flat Pack days".
'Why is that?'
'I have a desk at home with different drawers and things. We bought it as a flat pack furniture. It took us, that is Jane and I, absolutely ages putting it together…especially with the poor instructions and minute intricate diagrams that typically go with them. What about giving a really complicated flat pack for the potential couples to put together?'
'Whatever for?'
'To see how they get on together as a team doing a difficult task. My wife Jane used to say to people, only half joking, that we nearly got divorced the first time we put up wallpaper together.'
'That's a plan. By the way what are you planning to call the film programmes you make of people's journey with my charity?', asked Amanda.
"Matches made in Heaven?' Note the question mark at the end to

get the viewers thinking!'

Amanda clinked tea cups with Mike to celebrate their new venture. Unless the charity's trustees put a real spanner in the works, they knew that they would be working together closely a lot over the coming months. Amanda and Mike both secretly hoped in their heart of hearts that they would have some time for meetings other than professional ones too.

CHAPTER 12- CHRIS CHYNOWETH

Six months later Chris was sat in his living room. He was rattling round in his new five bedroomed house. Why ever had he gone for a five bedroomed house? He said to others it was because he got a huge downstairs space with it, which he absolutely loved. He did not feel confined. It gave him space to prowl in, to walk round, thinking whatever he was thinking about. But deep inside himself, he was longingly hoping that one day he would fill it with a family of his own. Inside, it was a bit of mess which he knew he had created. It needed a woman's touch with some nice pictures, ornaments, that sort of thing. Somehow though he had not got the knack to choose the right kind of stuff.

Why had he got a new house? It was really funny but it was bound up with his surname. It meant 'new house' in the original language of his family, in the dim and distant past. He wondered whether the name had been given to a great great whatever grandparent in his family's homeland because they happened to have built a new house or moved into one. In some ways his surname was a pain since people kept asking if he was English. That was a really stupid question since he spoke with as standard a Southern English accent as the people putting the question to him. He had a standard reply for them. He said he was not English but he was as British as they were. When they further asked, he said 'no' he was not Welsh, Scottish or Irish. That did leave most of them still puzzled.

He rented out a couple of his bedrooms to two students from

Derby University. They kept him from being too lonely but they had gone off for the Christmas holidays back to their parents' homes and he was on his own. He would go to his Mum's house on Christmas day to meet up with Mum and her new man, as well as his sister and her two kids and husband for Christmas lunch. Then on Boxing day he would have lunch with Dad and his new partner, who was now his wife. He had finished for the night, beavering away at his work on the diabetes audit project for the hospital he was a senior doctor at. He was just not in the mood for doing more of that, even though there was a lot more work to do on it.

He was bored. He was lonely and not quite certain the way forward in life. Friends were great but he wanted something more – a person who he could be intimate with, to share his hopes and dreams. He wanted a wife. At church there had been one or two nice girls but somehow they had got snapped up. Why was that? Because he had been over slow and cautious, as he pondered whether to date them or not. But that was his nature to be slow and cautious. While it was a large church, he had not met yet anyone else who caught his fancy.

Also he was getting a bit old to be chasing after twenty year old girls. There had been a Christian physiotherapist at work. She had been free, available and nice looking. When however he had gone out with her for a time or too, it was clear she felt he was too high powered for her. As well as that she had made it plain that, in her opinion, he was excessively serious. He did struggle to make light conversation and he could be quite a ponderous person. Jokes were not his thing. He was getting fed up of going to social dos by himself when everyone else was there with their partner.

He saw the ad on social media. He knew that he had been targeted because he was a Christian in his thirties and single. Nowadays he knew that whenever anyone went on the web, they left a trail of information behind about themselves. He looked at the enticing picture of a happy couple and said, 'Why not?'. He did not normally click on that sort of link, inviting him to a dating site but this one looked different.

He put his finger on the right place on the phone, pressed on the link and hit the web site of 'Forward together (East Midlands)'. What Chris did not know is that the previous name 'Introductions for togetherness' had been ditched in favour of something with more of a zing to it. The 'East Midlands' bit had been added to differentiate it from other organisations. Chris thought the name a bit cheesy. It sounded like a local lorry firm or train company rather than a dating site.
The web site was snazzy, modern and very well done. What Chris did not know is that it was the data science/computer firm of Ricky, the eldest son of Michael Cohen, who had sorted it all out. At least the site was honest. The application form was brutally so. It made it clear that, with the revamp of the web site, the charity was now expecting a large number of candidates for only a small number of possible places. To apply, the web form would ask you a whole heap of very personal details and it could make you take up to two hours to complete.

Chris was a man used to taking at least some significant decisions in life fast. You had to as a doctor. A few medical issues could be thought about for a few days but not too long as illnesses waited for no man. With someone who was more acutely ill, doing nothing generally was not an option. With such patients you needed to make up your mind quickly and get it right ideally. It was Saturday tomorrow and he was not on call at the hospital. Dr Witherley, the senior diabetes consultant, was looking after his sicker patients for him this weekend.

He put his mobile down decidedly and fired up his laptop. He did prefer to do more complicated forms on a computer. He grabbed a beer. The next hour and a half he wiled away, filling in the quite complicated form. He hesitated at the option of agreeing to being filmed but decided yes. He did quite take to the idea. At

least he was promised a free wedding if he was filmed. That was
a) if he was accepted by the organisation,
b) if they found someone suitable for him to meet at the Introductions Days,
c) if after the Introduction Days he and the girl decided to date together, which they would need to do without the help of the organisation,
d) if they both wanted to get married to each other after dating.

That was a lot of ands and ifs. A free filmed wedding would mean that at least they would have an excellent wedding video and photos and a superb church and reception and honeymoon venue. Chris had this funny streak in him. As a Medical Consultant in a large NHS hospital, his salary was good – no in fact very good. However he loved a bargain and one of the little pleasures of life was going to the discount supermarket in the centre of town and saving a few pennies on buying first class groceries. Yes, a free wedding would be nice if he got that far which was very unlikely.

He got to the very last stage of the 'Send' button. He hesitated a moment. He realised he needed to double check the form before sending it. That took five minutes and he found that in his haste he had filled out his middle name wrong by one letter so he changed it. He came back to the 'Send' button, hesitating again for a moment, but decided again he had nothing to lose. So he clicked it. He got an immediate email back fast, saying that his application form had been successfully received.

He was glad for that, with a sense of relief that all his work had not been in vain. He went to bed at one o'clock in the morning, feeling a peculiar sense of satisfaction in what he had just done.

A further twenty people in Derbyshire applied over the next two months including a man of fifty who decided to use false ID, two nurses and three primary school teachers, one bus driver and a contortionist, who had also just applied to be on 'Britain's

Got Talent.' He would apply for anything just to get noticed! He definitely said he wanted to be filmed. His friends would say he had a twisted mind and he would reply that he had a twisted body too!

Chris Chilvers, deputy head of Ashley Mount primary school in Derbyshire, Heather Jones, literacy lead teacher at Burnsford Common C of E school, also in Derbyshire too as well as Nicola Rose, district nurse in an area to the north of the county all applied as well. All of those people agreed to be filmed.

CHAPTER 13 THE ENGLISH ROSE

Nicola Rose was sitting in the living room of her parents' house, just feeling a bit wretched. What was a woman of her age doing, living with her parents? But she had done the maths. She knew that if she rented somewhere, it would be much smaller and cost her an arm or leg. In addition it would have much less of a garden or worse no garden at all. She was in charge of looking after the flowers in her parents' garden, having a special love of foxgloves, forget me nots, roses and dahlias. But she did feel guilty about still being with her parents. They had gone up to bed already, leaving her alone downstairs.

She too was watching the TV, before going back to her bedroom upstairs. She was feeling more than a bit trapped in life. She was aged thirty, reasonably attractive but had not got a boy friend. She was thin, slightly curvy, with an open friendly looking face, slightly pointy nose and straight brown hair, a little disorganised down to just past the level of her ears. She had had boy friends in the past but she had been a bit too picky. So pernickety had she been that she had turned down two serious offers from decent Christian men, whose minds were turned to marriage. She was also beginning to realise that the biological clock was ticking away and she was feeling a stronger and stronger urge to want to hold a baby of her own in her arms.

There was something more than pickiness in her rejection of previous offers of marriage. She had an intense introversion that made her hesitate to take decisions in her personal life. She was a sort of schizophrenic personality. In her life as a senior district nurse sister, she was decisive, well able to stand up for herself, listening to others when needed, well versed in her nursing knowledge, polite to patients, sympathetic also to the weak and suffering, putting up with and occasionally putting down idiots when needed.

In her inner thought life though she was much more indecisive. The facade of work took its toll from her. and she spent long hours by herself, wondering whether she had done this or that well in her work, going over each encounter of that day whether with a patient or a colleague. Because she was a Christian who took her faith seriously, she was only prepared to go out with others of similar ilk to her. There was no one obvious on the horizon. She had the normal hormonal urges and did have a soft spot for men who were hunks. Above all she wanted a decent bloke to share life with. She desired someone who she could talk about her work to, not necessarily someone in health care but someone who would listen. She just did so want children of her own. There had been times when she had felt really tempted to go off with some non Christian bloke and go and live with them, without getting married first.

Sadly one of her church friends had done so recently. Nicola had had a recent veiled half offer on those lines from Andy Hallpike, one of the community matrons. Andy was a very handsome man with a charming manner, who won the hearts of most people who came in contact with him. But he had no faith and was divorced with one kid – totally unsuitable for her. But if she had done what he was suggesting, she knew that she could not have lived with herself. It would go against her deeply held beliefs that living with a bloke was for marriage.

She had wondered about sharing a house with other female friends, just to get away from Mum and Dad, lovely as they were. But again, there was no one suitable to do that with. She was starting to worry that she might find herself trapped, having to look after her parents as they became older and weaker. Because she was the single girl at home and a nurse to boot, her married brother and sister would expect her to make that sacrifice. She was trapped between a rock and a hard place. This web site seemed to offer her a way out. At least it was worth a try. The worse that could come to pass is that nothing at all happened because you were not one of the chosen candidates.

The thing that she really liked was that with this programme, if you got through, you were only offered one chance. If you turned down the man, then you were out of the programme. She decided that she would pray and if she got through, she would accept whatever she was given or probably accept the person, unless of course there were problems and difficulties. All she was ultimately committing herself to is making a decision to spend three days with him and only then making the decision to date him or not. It was not like she was committing herself in advance to marry the guy. She was already sliding into uncertainty mode. But she was decisive at least in her decision to hit the 'send' button on the web site, having spent two hours filling out the long and arduous form.

CHAPTER 14
AFTERMATH

Michael breezed into the office of Cohen Cinematography Productions on the outskirts of Nottingham. He was now sharing office space with Amanda for their joint project. It was a sun filled morning and he was in an equally sunny mood. The first person he encountered was Angie, one of his young production assistants, who was up and coming on the way to become a sort of second in command to him. She was a lively young lady, aged twenty three with a gigantic ball of an Afro hair style, exactly the same one as her Jamaican Mum and Dad had. Positively huge, thin, single rings of gold dangled from each of her ears.

She too was in a happy mood and cheerily greeted him, 'Hi Boss, we have over eighty filled in application forms already since the web site was relaunched two weekends ago. It does look like the targeted social media ads have worked their magic.'
'Any of the applications look any good?'
'I'm just looking at one now. The guy's nice enough looking but not fantastic. He has a weird surname *but* he is aged thirty three, a hospital Consultant locally and he has a five bedroomed house in Belper. His income is way up there. Boss, please could I be a candidate to meet him? If you don't use him as a candidate, can I take his mobile number? He looks like a good meal ticket for a girl,' Angie said with big, jokey, smiley face.

Michael pretended to look serious for a few moments then came out with,
'No you can't. You are far too young being only twenty three. And

are you sure you can cope with four kids?' That last sentence was spoken with a grin back.
'I don't understand the four kids bits.' Angie shot back with a puzzled frown on her young brow.
'There of course is one master bedroom for Mum and Dad. There are four bedrooms one for each of the four children that you are going to have. Why else does he have such a big house? Surely he is looking for love *and* a large family.'

Angie reflected for a moment.
'No boss,' she frowned back. 'Because he is such an important man he will need one bedroom as a home office. Because I too am an up and coming woman, I will also need my own home office. So that leaves only two bedrooms left for the kids so we will only have two kids.'

'What happens if you both have downstairs offices. How many kids will you have then?' Michael had to have the last word.

Angie looked back at the screen after it pinged again twice. 'Seriously Boss, we have as of now to eighty two applications. I am whittling them down a bit but we will still have a lot.'
'Good I am going to pop into office to make some calls.'

Michael walked into his office – a bit smaller than what he probably needed but it was comfortable for him. It had one ground floor window, a large cluttered desk, papers everywhere and two armchairs as well a large yucca plant which he called for some obscure reason 'Pamela.' He sat in his easy desk chair and thought through what next. He looked at his large wall clock. He hated wearing a watch. It was time for his conversation with Geoff Payton. Amanda had asked him to call Geoff because she thought that Michael might be the best person to do it.

'Hi Geoff. How are you doing? Have you had a chance to read my proposal?'
'Yes.... Yes. It certainly is unusual and it is an interesting project. But I still am thinking about the ethics.'

That bit about ethics surprised Michael. It was not as though Geoff was being asked to actually decide who got married to who. He decided best to plough on with his prepared speech.

'What did you think about my view of the story of Isaac and Rebecca?'
'I certainly liked your take on their story and how it related to what had happened in the author of the book's life. To be honest it was certainly new to me – a take on it I had never heard before.'
'New?' That was a surprise to Michael.
'Oh yes. When you have been in the job as long I have, you have heard it all before.'
'So do you think I have convinced you enough to take part?'
'I still have a feeling it may be a step too far for me.'

'I hear what you are saying but don't you think we need to be taking some new steps changing people's attitude? It strikes me that the institution of marriage is in a sorry state in the modern world. My project is going to get people thinking more deeply about marriage. Is it all about physical attraction then you date or is about much better things? Instead I want to convey the idea that a far stronger marriage is based on shared values and interest and finally most importantly by a commitment to sticking at it. Everyone of the candidates will get extensive counselling, courtesy of you as the wise servant like Abraham's. The wedding service will be based on the old liturgy which does emphasise the lasting nature of the commitment of marriage 'Till death do us part' and all that. Also everyone will be having the flat pack test!'
Michael let the words come flowing out but afterwards he just felt what he had said sounded a bit lame.

'Michael you are flattering me comparing me to Abraham's servant. Yes, I agree that flat packs is a good test. I love assembling the fiddly things so my wife lets me get on with it but when it comes to tiling she is the tiling queen. But what you want to do is a bit risky.'

'Do you really think it is more risky than what happens now Geoff? People fall in love or whatever decide they are going to get married in church or in a register office. If they get married in church they see someone like yourself and do you ever turn them away? Have you ever performed marriages on couples who you thought were grossly unsuitable and would not work?' Michael was pushing the point with Geoff. He really wanted him on board with the project. In his heart of hearts he also wanted his approval.

Geoff considered this for some time. The phone went silent and Michael knew that it was the moment to shut up and wait for the answer. The reply came back slowly and thoughtfully.
'In my thirty five years as a pastor I certainly married people who I thought were not particular suitable. It is certainly a brave minister who will turn away single people never before wed *and* who are active church members, wanting to get married. I do remember off hand three couples in that situation. To all three of them I suggested strongly that they have a real think if they were right for each other. All three insisted that they *were* right for each other. Two of those marriages sadly ended in divorce within five years. The last couple I remember very well. She was a prim and proper school miss and he was a tattooed biker running a motorcycle repair shop. I think she was attracted by a bit of the rough stuff. They fought cat and dog with reconciliation in between and three kids together over a period of twenty years, with loads and loads of counselling and support from me. At least three times I thought they would not make it through. Then suddenly they settled down and for the last ten years have been fine. They moved out of the area to the north of Scotland about eight years ago but I have still kept in touch.'

Geoff stopped reminiscing and got back to the main subject of the conversation.
'Yes Michael you have made your point well.'
'Here is your chance to do things properly to give some couples

a much better chance of succeeding. After all you won't be deciding whether a couple actually get married but arranging who you are going to put in each other's path.'
But what exactly do I bring to the party? I don't quite totally see what I do. You have got a minister anyway as part of the team.'

'Yes Peter is there partly to give a more spiritual input but he is an unusual character. He is a qualified active GP who after that decided to train as a vicar. What he does is practice as a GP part time. Then rest of time he goes round small struggling country churches in his home county of Staffordshire as an unpaid volunteer vicar holding services etc. Because he is a doctor, he will be doing any medical checks needed on the candidates, reviewing their medical history as needed. In this process the candidate may try to hide such conditions.'

'OK yes point taken. But if you have got Pete, who I take my hat off to being a volunteer vicar, why me?'
'Pete is a great guy with a lovely wife, who is expecting their first baby but he is still a bit young. You add something different to the mix. You bring experience, a lot of experience especially in marriage counselling as a, well, maturity and depth of spiritual understanding which the other younger members of the panel just do not quite have. You also will be the only one with grown up kids. So your marriage has been tried, tested through all stages of children's development. I would like you to be the Chair of the Panel and you are there to ensure that no really stupendously bad matches are made. I am very conscious that we are juggling with people's lives here and I want someone at the helm who has that kind of concern for others.'

'You almost persuade me. Tell me about the other two members of the Panel before you try to cross my palm with silver and I turn you down because I don't need the money,' said Geoff with a grin which Michael could only sense rather than see because it was a phone call not a video call.
'We have Ellie the clinical psychologist whose role is to oversee

the psychological matching tests. She is well regarded professionally and is a Christian, married lady. No kids though. She is a very precise, ordered person who will do her job very well. She won't though be able to give you a real feel of what someone is about. She's not quite got that kind of insightful personality.'
'Then what is her value if she cannot give you a real feeling of what someone is about?'
'She will exclude the people who clearly on the basis of the psychological tests cannot be matched up with anyone else. She will also suggest all the possible combinations.'

'Who is the next one?'
'Parminder is of Punjabi heritage and a professional matchmaker of ten years experience mostly working with Asian families to marriage match some youngsters but a lot of more mature couples. She is the only of the group who has actually done the job successfully, apart from your occasional forays into matchmaking,. She is also a keen Christian and has been married for fifteen years herself with two kids.'
'It is clear what she brings to the table. What do you think her especial strength is?'
'To highlight people's more compatible interests. For example a townie who likes to party on a Saturday night is not necessarily going to go well with a country person who loves long walks in nature.'
Geoff and Michael talked on.
In the end Geoff said, 'Leave it with me and I'll give you a decision in the next week.'
'That's fine,' thought Michael, 'It will be a few weeks yet before the panel meets to look at the potential matches.'

Jenny, Geoff's wife, had been half listening into the speaker phone and half reading her book. She piped up when the phone was off.
'You know Geoff, I think you should do it.'
'We don't need the money.'

'Agreed we don't need the money. We have cash in saving accounts we don't know what to do with though mind you with the kids' minds turning to mortgages and deposits for houses, that money would soon go if we did decide to help them significantly.'

Geoff did not know quite what to say to that. Jenny had always been the more practical of the two of them.
'Why do you think I should do it then? I need another reason than wanting to possibly help the kids in the future.'
'It will get you out of my hair. Since you retired two months ago, you have been like a caged lion at home getting under my feet. You need to get out, do a project. This one is ideal for you. It's just up your street and I also very much see the point of what Michael is doing. Sadly like you, I have seen too many marriages crumble. You will make a real success of it.'
'If I don't fit in, I suppose I could always leave.'
'You could always commit for a year and then see how it goes.'
'I think eighteen months would be better.'

So decision made. Geoff got out his mobile again and texted,
'Hi Michael I'll do it and commit for eighteen months.'
A reply came straight back. 'Excellent. Your first job will be to find the most fiddly and challenging piece of flat pack furniture ready for the candidates!!'
Geoff Payton laughed and texted back, 'Will do,' with a laughing face emoji'

CHAPTER 15-THE PROGRAMMER

The young man tapped slowly on the computer keyboard. He was writing a programme in the computer language Python, a routine task for him. He just finger tapped one tap at a time. He was slower than most programmers but funnily enough that made him better at his job. He made many fewer mistakes. What non-programmers, the ordinary person in the street did not realise is this: With most computer programmes, something as simple as a single comma or semicolon absent in thousands and thousands of lines of computer code, would often mean that the whole thing would not work. He had to write code this way slowly -it was just the way it was for him.

He had sorted out the web site and now he was writing the programme for the psychological tests that the serious candidates for 'Forward together' would take. He had the test given him with the questions in front of him. So he had to create a web page for the test and a database to receive the results. His two colleagues Chris and Magdalena were constructing the program to analyse the results and produce lists for each candidate of the people nearest to them psychologically matched. He was the lead for the project so he would check their work while they would look at his work.

One of his jobs had been to look at the forms sent in by potential candidate to ensure that their data had been stored correctly in the right place on the server. He did not have to check all the forms, just enough of a sample and that included the photos. For data protection reasons he was the only one allowed to do that in the project. He had looked at the sample of the girls' photos. Some of them looked really nice and he felt wistfully envious of the blokes they would surely marry. He just knew inside himself, he could never manage to attract a woman like that.

He tried not to feel sorry for himself. When he had talked with his father about life, his Dad had sought to encourage him, 'Look son. You are doing great in life. Your Mum and I are so proud of you. I am sure that the right thing will happen for you.'
Mum just gave him a big hug without saying anything more, when he had talked of his hopes for the future. Somehow his mother, with her hug, just got through to him more than the kindly, well meant words of his father.

CHAPTER 16 - THE CAT IS OUT OF THE BAG

Nicola walked into the room where there were the interview panel waiting for her. It was the second time she had sat in that very room. She had gone through all the psychological tests and was being interviewed to see if she would be the right person for Flat Pack days with someone. As she walked in, she saw that Parminder had her back to her and was talking to Geoff. She had clearly not heard Nicola come in.

'I think Nicola would be a good match with Chris Ch...' Geoff gave Parminder a warning look and she stopped before saying the surname of the intended other. Too late... Nicola had heard the first part of the name. Her heart skipped a beat. She had always focused on the seventy percent success rate of the programme – that is if you got through to the Flat Pack days rather than the thirty percent failure rate. As she had gone through the stages, she had become more and more obsessed with the idea that this whole process was going to a hundred percent, give her a husband. She lay awake at night obsessively thinking about little else. The panel had sensed that too.

Chris .....was this the name of her possible future husband? Was her future surname beginning with a Ch? She was the sort of woman who would definitely want to take her husband's surname. Not for her the modern fashion of joining husband and wife's surnames to make some horrible, amalgamated, double barrelled hyphenated thing of a name. What did the Ch stand for? She was intrigued. Was it Chaplin or Champion or what? She longed to know but did not dare ask Parminder.

At the end of the long conversation Nicola asked directly to the panel,
'So am I going to be offered a match or not?' The eagerness in her voice and on her face was palpable.
Ellie gave her a slightly cold look back, thinking that she was far too keen. 'Have some self respect Nicola,' she said to herself. 'There is only one thing definitely that you need a husband for.' Ellie went on to reflect bitterly on her own infertility struggles, 'Sometimes they cannot even do that for you.'
Ellie was also acutely aware that her own problems made her more prickly as a person towards others, but she found it difficult to control her attitude.

Parminder, a warm hearted mother of two, shot back a look of compassion. She knew of Nicola's desperate desire for kids and she had felt the same urge for children when she had been younger. Her heart reached out to her and she longed to give her a hug.
Michael sensed what was going on and carefully said with an encouraging smile. 'What we are saying to all candidates after the second interview is this: We will be contacting them very shortly with what we see as the best way forward. Don't worry Nicola, we won't keep you in suspense for a long time. That would not be fair on you.'

An hour later Nicola received a text, 'Hi Nicola, we are offering you a match. Please see our email.'
Nicola's heart flipped over and she gulped.'This is it. I'm getting married. What will he be like?'
In her eagerness to get hitched, again she was mentally short circuiting all the steps she would need to take to arrive there, as well as the thirty percent risk she would not get there. That was

even assuming she and the guy endured the three flat pack days together.

She quickly went to her email, with details of the flat pack days which would be next week starting Wednesday. She would only find out his name when she arrived in the morning at the house in Chesterfield. She wondered about texting Rosie to break the good news to her. She quickly dismissed the idea. She knew it was far too significant an event for a text. It needed a phone call and a long chat, a very long chat.

CHAPTER 17-A
WORK OF GRACE

It was Grace Bridges who thought of the idea that would be like a pebble thrown in water causing many distant ripples. In many ways the idea was typical of her. Most people including Grace herself, would have said it showed concern for others. Some more unkindly but correctly, would have added that mixed in with that, was an element of wanting to poke her nose in other people's business.

She was chatting with Pete over breakfast. Now Pete, her husband, earned his daily bread as Minister of the Living Waters church near Belper. The slightly burnt brown toast – the way they both liked it – and the accompanying Seville marmalade and butter was being munched contently by both parties to the conversation. There were occasional interruptions to swill things down with hot strong tea.

Grace looked up from her mobile, 'Pete, I was thinking of doing something to get the younger people in the church relating more to each other. A nice set meal in the church for them on a Saturday lunchtime – a sit down affair? What do you think?'
She went on give full details of the scheme she had been cooking up in her head for the last week, waiting for the right moment to run it past him.
'It's an idea,' Pete commented, 'But the important thing in any such social event is to ensure a good mixing of people. That's what I think. You just don't want them staying stuck to their normal social groups.'

'That's a fair point. If you have a serve yourself buffet, people will grab some food and sit down with their mates. My idea is that people sit down, say in groups of six or seven comparative strangers. They are then served a nice sit down three course meal with coffee.'
'I think that six is too many for a group as there will always be some people who will be shy and not say much. I would say four people on each table – carefully chosen. You are more likely to get the shy ones talking.'
'Okay four then. I am happy to organise the whole thing, to save you the hassle. I would also like to decide who sits on what tables.'
'Who is going to pay for all this or do we get those coming to contribute?' Pete clearly had the budget in mind.
'I say make it a freebie and I promise not to get too extravagant.'
'Right then we have a plan.'

The plan for the day gradually took shape. Grace had had the normal hassles. The menu was one of the biggest troubles organising. There were now a large and growing number of vegetarians and vegans as well as gluten free folk in the church. In the end she chose for the main a pasta dish with vegetables (gluten free pasta for the gluten intolerant) and a carrot and lentil soup for starters. Puds would be something substantial – apple and blackberry crumble made with plant based margarine and a custard accompaniment available for those who wanted it. For those who were not big crumble fans, there was fruit salad, plus or minus double cream – again with plant based cream available for the vegans.

'You are going to make them fat,' said Pete to Grace.
'In my opinion it does not matter, darling. I want to get a good crowd to the meal. You know how many drop out of this kind of do and church food can sometimes be so insipid. After all this is all about building relationships and there's nothing like a good nosh to make people more relaxed and loosen tongues.'

So the meal plan was settled. The church was housed, like Michael and Amanda's church, in a soulless modern purpose built hangar of a building. Its main virtue was a large auditorium used for services which could easily be converted into a restaurant. The kitchens were at the side of the auditorium with serving hatches. It was a building designed for practicality but had zero aesthetics. Even trying to hang decorative banners round from the ceiling did not help much. Grace decided to decorate the tables with montages of green leaves and flowers and nice tablecloths.

Pete began muttering away about the budget.
Grace replied, 'Did we not get that bequest in a will to the church to be used to improve church life. It's not been all used up yet, has it?'
'No it hasn't,' Pete reluctantly agreed.
'Is this event about not improving church life?'
 No reply back. Argument won.

Grace was responsible for sorting out who sat who where. She sat in her living room one evening with a printout of who had actually accepted the invite. Pete was working on his next sermon. She was nattering away mainly to herself.
'So then Pete what do you think? Shall we put nurse Nicola with doctor Chris? Or is that too much doctor/nursey? They don't know each other hardly at all. But who shall we put them with? We have got no other medical people round and besides it might otherwise just be medical table talk – generally most unsuitable with food, all that guts and gore. Shall we put them with the Rayners, who run that small engineering business in Duffield? She has just had a baby. That sounds good.'
Her husband was too engrossed in sermon preparation to reply but just left her to it. She was far better than him at sorting out this sort of thing.

The big day dawned. It was one of those rainy Saturday summer days so frequent in England and the sky was starting to turn very dark. The interior of the church began to turn dark too, even though it was lunchtime. Grace had been hoping to avoid having the main lights on as she did not feel they contributed positively to the atmosphere. She wondered what to do. Then there came to mind the Christmas candles in holders in a store cupboard. They had last been used for the Christmas carols evening and were lovely red things in metal holders with a round circular handle rising up from the main body of the holder. Her assistants quickly put them on the tables.

The hundred or so guests wandered into the great hall and were pleased to see the candles lit. They were shown to their tables by a group of youngsters from the church youth group, all dressed in suits or nice frocks. There was a music track playing in the background. It was playing classical Chinese music which Grace felt was particularly calming.

Nicola was dressed elegantly in a posh trouser suit. Chris had decided he would wear a suit too. The Rayners were dressed more informally and their faces showed the signs of the tiredness and exhaustion that comes with a young baby in the shape of Flora Lily Rayner, aged two months old. Little Flora was being cared for at home by her doting grandparents. The four of them were also now seated at table and animated conversation started between the four of them.

Then suddenly the Rayner's mobile rang. It was Grandma.
'Hi darling,' Flora's wailing could be heard as loud as anything in the background.
'I am really sorry but I just cannot settle Flora. We have tried giving her a bottle of your breast milk, from the fridge warmed up of course but no joy. Your Dad has walked her round the room singing to her. Absolutely no use. She is actually crying worse after that.'
'Okay Mum, we'll come straight back. Give us ten minutes.'
Mrs Rayner looked round the table and said apologetically, 'Sorry

we're having to go home. Flora is playing up.'

Because she was only a learner driver, her husband had to go home with her, leaving Nicola and Chris alone at the table. They both slightly felt awkward. A couple of younger single people of the opposite sex seated alone round a candlelit table! It felt a bit like they had been put together for a date rather than a church do. They both blushed slightly especially Chris, who actually found Nicola quite attractive. It had been ages since either of them had been on a date with anyone. They began talking about work, like most medical people. Chris was a very attentive listener and Nicola was flattered that a nice but not fantastic looking guy was taking an interest in her.

Grace was wandering round the tables stopping by to talk in her role as the hostess, checking that things were going well. She was satisfied and she saw from the distance Chris and Nicola talking animatedly but ……where were the Rayners? So she wandered over and found out what had happened. She noted that Nicola was fiddling with her hair. That was, in Grace's not so humble opinion, one of the classic signs of interest in the part of a girl towards a man.

Chris and Nicola both had similar thoughts of interest towards each other. However because they were both committed to the 'Forward Together' programme, they did not share them with each other. They felt a bit embarrassed, indeed slightly ashamed that they were involved with a dating organisation. It made them both feel slightly like a failure that they could not manage to do something so basic as getting a partner, without help from others. So they would only tell that embarrassing fact to their nearest and dearest. They both fantasised for a moment what it would be like to go out with each other. Because they were due to have their flat pack days the next week, they said nothing to each other.

Grace felt that her married surname 'Bridges' gave her a little

bit of licence as a matchmaker, you know building bridges and all that. So that night over dinner, she was chatting with Pete, saying,
'I think I may have had some success with Chris Chynoweth and Nicola Rose. They seem to be getting on well. I wonder if something might develop there.'
'You mean romantically?'
'Yes.'
'Um that is a thought. I don't think I mentioned it to you but they are in the 'Forward Together' programme. I had to write a reference for each of them as their pastor.'
'I've not heard of that. What's it about?' asked Grace now very interested.

Pete gave an explanation about what he knew about the programme.
'I happen to know that Nicola is quite advanced in the programme as she told me so but I don't know whether they have a potential match for her. I have no idea about Chris. He has not confided in me.'
'I think they would be an excellent couple together. Have you wondered about suggesting to the programme about matching them up?' Grace ventured.
'I don't know if I should interfere.'
'But it would do no harm to ring up Geoff Payton to find out what is happening.'
Grace could be quite persistent at times when she had the bit between her teeth and when she sensed, she was in the right.
In the end Pete slightly reluctantly agreed, 'Okay I will make the call Monday morning.'

CHAPTER 18-A WILD NIGHT

It was turning out to be a wild, windy, rainy Saturday evening on the streets of Derby. The hen parties were filling up the clubs and bars. They too could be wild and inhibited but in a different sort of way. It was also the hen night for Maddie Chapman a hospital nurse from Chesterfield, due to get married in two weeks time. The day was also the day on which Nicola Rose went to the special lunchtime meal in church.

Maddie had moved a year ago from Derby hospital to Chesterfield to be with her fiance. Her friends from Derby as well as her new friends from Chesterfield were going to be present – a mixture of old and new. Maddie wanted to try to get both groups together for this special do. Some of them had already had a few 'pre drinks' before joining the big group at the restaurant on Friargate in Derby. There would be a good meal to soak up the alcohol but there would be a load of alcohol to soak up. In the case of some of the participants, the food would not be enough to soak up all the wine glasses and shorts that had entered and would enter the ladies' stomachs.

Alternate Chesterfield and Derby friends were sat down at the large table in the restaurant. Rosie, Nicola's sister, a nurse from Derby was sitting next to another nurse from Chesterfield. She was wearing a thin party dress more suitable to a summer night in Benidorm than a cold November night in Derbyshire. Practically all the party were nurses. The other nurse was Gill. Both Rose and Gill had had enough drinks to remove inhibitions but not enough to stop them being capable of causing mischief.

Rosie remarked to Gill, 'I might be going to another hen do in the future. Nicola my sister, has only just found out that she is hoping to meet the man of her life in four days' time. It is all a bit hush hush and I should not really be talking about it.'
'Oh why is that?' Gill asked intrigued.
'She knows nothing about who she is going to meet to except they are a bloke between twenty five to thirty five, matched by a group of experts.'
'Is the programme by any chance called 'Matches made in heaven?' run by a charity called 'Forward Together'?'
'Why yes. How did you know?' Rosie asked with a puzzled and surprised look on her face.
'Because my brother is meeting someone this coming Wednesday with the very same programme.'
'What an amazing coincidence. The very same date.'
'Do you think they are going to be meeting each other? Does that mean we might one day be related?'
'It could very well be. There is one other clue. Nicola overheard one of the panel of experts saying that Nicola was being paired up to a 'Chris Ch..' but then the person stopped there when she realised that Nicola was in the room.'
'Do you know what my brother's name is? It's Chris Chilvers. We shall be meeting again at the wedding, assuming there is going to be one!'
'Wow that is amazing that we should just meet like this. I've got a piccy of Nicola on my phone. Shall I show you?'
Rosie whipped out her mobile and showed Gill.
'She looks quite a serious girl to me. Has she got a sense of fun?' asked Gill.
'A bit of one but it's not her strongest point. Why do you ask?'
'Here's my brother Chris. He definitely has got a sense of fun. Do you know who he has got for a house companion?'
Gill showed two pictures.
'The house companion's name is Dave but she is a girl and really

quite beautiful. He does so like stroking her.'
Both girls giggled at that delicious thought.
'Do you know what Dave's favourite food is?' Gill whispered in Rose's ear.
'No!' exclaimed Rose in surprise and giggled again.
'What about playing a game on them both? Send them a picture of each other anonymously with some sort of message like 'your future intended'.'
'With or without the picture of the house companion?'
'Probably best without. I don't want to scare my sister Nic off marrying him especially since Chris seems to be a very good looking chap. '
'But how do we do it so as to make it anonymous?'
'Best way is to send an email. Only thing is that Nicola knows my email address since I have had to send her emails in the past. Tell you what! I could set up a new email account.'
'Okay then, tell you what. I have got Chris's email since I had to send him a shopping voucher on line last month for his thirtieth. Also I can send my piccy of Chris to you.'

So Rosie and Gill giggled as Rosie went through all the steps to set up a new email account for herself. Then Rosie sent two messages from the new account – one to Nicola with a picture of Chris and the words 'Your future intended a match made in heaven' and the other to Chris with a picture of Nicola with the same words. At Gill's request, she did blind carbon copy in her to both emails.

The drink flowed especially for Rosie. She and the group did a night club crawl round four different clubs. About 1.30 in the morning, Rosie was blind drunk and stumbling in the street. She was starting to feel very cold and shivering a bit. The other girls, who were well loaded with alcohol too, but not to the same extent, were getting concerned about her. So they asked for help from the doormen at a club nearby. The doorman said, 'Leave it to me,' and made a call on his walky talky radio. Rosie in the

meantime had collapsed in a
semi-conscious heap by in the doorway of a nearby shop.

In a few minutes a group of four older people, who to the youngsters looked like the Mammas and Papas, turned up in blue uniforms. Rosie vaguely remembered later a group in blue called 'street patrol' or something similar coming to help her.

There was an older chap in charge with a grey beard and a hat which was askew on his head. But it was the two ladies who started to fuss round Rosie.

She was wrapped up in a crackly foil space blanket to keep her warm and called out drunkenly, 'When are you going to put the turkey in to cook? I'm oven ready!' and then gave a cackling laugh.

They gave her some water from a bottle and she started to gradually recover.

Finally the older chap in charge said, 'Let's get her up and see if she can walk and take her to the taxi rank in Victoria St.'

One of the ladies said, 'Let's first get her high heels off her and put her in flip flops.'

The other guy, who was carrying a large rucksack on him and seemed to be a strong silent type, presented his back to one of the ladies. She took out some flip flops from the rucksack and put them on Rosie.

The two women helped her up and she rather unsteadily walked along supported by a lady in blue uniform on either side. Her friends ambled slightly drunkenly side by side. Finally the ladies in blue managed to bundle her into a taxi together, with a couple of friends who lived near her to accompany her. The three of them knocked on Rosie's door at three in the morning, to be greeted by a sleepy, rather grumpy husband Ross.

The next morning Rosie could not remember much from the previous evening. She picked up the card on her bedside with a blue logo showing people in blue uniforms on and the words

'Street Pastors'. So they must have the people who had helped her last night. She lay in bed, hung over with a headache, and idly grabbed her mobile and started checking social media. She was pleased to see some nice pictures of her from the night taken before she had imbibed too much drink. She went onto her emails. She did get an email from an email server address she did not instantly recognise. It stated she had set up a new email account with them and advised her that she had set her regular email as the recovery email. She was too woozy to take it all in. So she casually deleted it.

Then the panicky phone call came from Nic, 'Rosie, I don't know what to do.'
Nic was crying down the phone. Rosie always thought it is strange that a woman, who could so strong and decisive at work, could be, well, so weak in her personal life. Nic had had two perfectly good boy friends who would both have made excellent husbands from what she could see. Both of them had shared her weird religious beliefs. She had turned down both their offers of marriage and now she was moaning she did not have a man in her life.

'I have just had this email from an address I don't recognise, with a picture of a nice looking man and a caption, 'Chris Ch.. Your future intended – a match made in heaven?' What's happening? Has there been some sort of security breach at 'Matches made in Heaven?'? No one outside the organisation is supposed to know the pairing till the day I meet the guy at the flat pack days. I hope this won't ruin my chance of a husband.' Rosie could imagine, even if she could not see them, the tears falling down her sister's cheeks. Nic could just get overdramatic about things.

Rosie struggled through her hung over haze to know what to say. 'What's that,' she muttered, holding her head. 'I had a heavy drinking hen do last night. Look Nic, just forward me the email and I'll look at it bit later when I feel a bit brighter and give you a ring.'

Rosie pressed the call end button on her phone and went back to sleep.

At eight that evening she was feeling a lot more perky. She looked at the email from Nicola, showing the picture of Chris Chilvers. She quite took to Chris, since the photo showed him with cheeky grin. She saw the email address that Nic had received and forwarded to her. Rosie recognised it as the one she had received the earlier one from.

She had a sudden horrifying thought and rescued the earlier one from her email trash bin. She went to the web page of the new email server and tried to log into her new email account. Of course she could not do so because she did not know the password. There was the button to send a recovery email to the designated email address. She clicked it and suddenly her phone pinged. She had received on her regular email account, a recovery email to the server. She clicked on it and reset her password. She then logged into the email server with her new password and found four emails – two sent and two received. The two emails sent were pictures of Nicola and Chris. When she looked at the one of Nic, it was very obviously taken by her.

She looked at the two emails received. The first email was from Chris saying 'Not my perfect match.' together with a frowning emoji. The second was from Gill saying,
'Hi Rosie,
Nice to meet you last night. Thanks for setting up the email account. We certainly had a great laugh. Chris sent me your email to him and said 'What do you think?'. I sent him back, 'Your type?'. He replied, 'Definitely not my type. I won't be marrying her.' So it does not look like we will be meeting again ever in church. Will you be telling Nicola?
Take care Gill x'

Rosie uttered an expletive. She knew how much had been hanging on 'Forward Together' for her sister. She had just ruined her sister's life. She dared not tell her. She would just have to wait to see how events developed, with a sense of dread. Her one consoling thought was this: She doubted if ever Nic could have coped with living in a house with a female dragon lizard called Dave as a house companion, whose favourite culinary delicacy was apparently eating live locusts bought from a specialist pet store.

CHAPTER 19– CRISIS

The next day Monday, was crisis morning at Michael's office in Nottingham. Both Chris Chilvers, the teacher and Nicola Rose had contacted with the pics of each other. Security had been breached big time and Michael was holding a crisis meeting with Amanda, Angie, Geoff and lastly there was Ricky at the end of the video call.

Michael said somberly, 'Kick us off, Angie please.'
'I came into the office at 9 o'clock as normal and was just about to log on to my emails when my mobile pinged. I had been sent by Nicola Rose a picture of Chris Chilvers and the comment, 'Is this the man I'm meant to marry?'. Then the phone rang. It was a very, very upset Nicola Rose who asked what the dickens was happening and was this photo the man she was going to be meeting on the flat pack day?
I'm afraid I replied on total shock, 'How did you see the photo of the man you were to be paired up with?' She then said very agitated, 'Haven't you read your emails yet? I sent you the picture just now because you had not answered my email.'
She then practically shouted back, 'Read my email and then ring me back'. She then put the phone down on me.

So I opened my emails to find two relevant ones. The first was from Nicola as a forward of an email she received from an unknown address – a picture of Chris Chilvers and the comment 'Chris C.. Your future intended a match made in heaven?' followed by a very panicky message from Nic, asking what is happening. The second email was from Chris Chilvers equally as a forward of an email he received from an unknown address with a picture of Nicola and the comment, 'Your future intended a match made in heaven?'. It came with an email message from Chris, saying, 'This person is not my type. No point putting us together'. As we know, they were booked in together as a matched couple for the flat pack days this Wednesday.'

Michael thought that Angie's initial comment, 'How did you see the photo of the man you were to be paired up with?' had clearly given the game away. This did not seem like the time to bring that up with her though.
'What did you say when you rang Nicola back?'
'I said I had just received her email. We needed to look into what was going on and we would get back to her as soon as possible.'
'Okay. Thanks Angie. It was good to say very little at this stage. So we have two issues here,'

Michael started the ball rolling.
'Firstly, we have the security breach with the worry that we may get more breaches. Secondly, how do we deal with the fallout from the breach we have had with the flat pack days coming up? Ricky, do you think we could have had an IT information leak?'
'I don't think so, Dad. At my end we only have a team of three people plus me, who can access the data on the server from my end. All of them at my end are long standing trusted employees. The other thing about data leaks is that typically they occur from someone outside of the actual organisation who is hacking in. Typically the hacker or hackers release a whole of data at once. This data leak is only a slight amount of the data available. The other thing are the pictures. Did you think about that?'

'I don't get you Ricky.' said Michael puzzled.
'The photos that the two people were sent were not pictures from our web server. They look like they were taken from a mobile in a meeting with friends or family. The computer dates attached to the pictures are a few months ago. The only pictures we have on our web server are the passport style photos sent in the application forms with different dates of taking.'

'Of course, assuming those passport style pictures were somewhere on the internet, this would mean that someone was clever enough not only to break into our web server but also any web sites holding the pictures of the two candidates. That is a big ask to believe.'
Ricky stopped to take breath. 'But having said that, there is the concern that whoever breached security clearly knew that they were destined to be a couple at the flat pack days. That piece of information was definitely on our web server. Neither Nicola or Chris knew that they were to be paired up with each other. The only people who would have known that they were the particular pair were the committee or a potential hacker.'

'How do we know that particular bit of information about Nicola and Chris being a pairing, was on the web server?' asked Amanda.
'Because Angie uploaded the minutes with the decisions from the committee meeting and the couples pairing at 6.31 pm to the admin part of the web server on Friday evening,' Ricky interjected.

'Do you think at the flat pack days we could see them both and ask discreetly if they told anyone about having the flat pack day?' said Angie. 'They were not supposed to tell anyone till after the flat pack days but you know what people are like. Maybe they both told a mutual acquaintance or their friends or family told a mutual friend.'

Everyone fell quiet for a minute, not knowing what more to say. 'In light of what Chris has said, is there going to be a flat pack day for either Nicola and Chris?' Geoff remarked, breaking the silence.
'I agree but I don't want to contact them by phone, which is the obvious alternative first off till we have got sorted what we want to do,' said Michael.
He continued, 'Okay, we need to keep on trying to work out how

the security breach happened. We don't have an instant answer. But we now do have the other practical problem which Geoff has already hinted at. Angie, do you want to explain more please?'

'Thanks Boss. To resume, I have had two more phone calls today after Nic's panicky call. The first was from Chris, with additional comments to the email. Basically he does not fancy Nicola at all. He was even so ungentlemanly as to make a reference to a 'dog's dinner'. If she is the woman we have got him, then he is a hundred percent not interested in dating, marrying or even ever meeting her. He said in addition that he would like to see a photo of any future candidate for him before going for the flat pack days 'to ensure that does not happen again'. That is of course totally against the rules.'

'How was Nicola, when she made her second call?' asked Geoff.
'Very upset, very very upset. She asked me a series of direct questions which I tried avoiding answering directly. I think she knows that Chris was the one we had got lined up for her. She asked if the Chris whose photo she had received was a candidate and whether he had had received an email with her picture. She was interrogating me about what would happen to her marriage prospects now. I could not give her a direct answer. She then just started crying. Of all the candidates who ring me up and loads of them do, as you know, she is the one most desperate to get wed.'

They then had a long debate about possible candidates for Nicola.
'So to sum up we cannot continue with Chris Chilvers as a candidate for anyone until we have really explored what he means by wanting to see the photo in advance. He certainly cannot be paired up with Nicola. We would like to try to help her but the nearest possible partner on the psychological tests is Chris Chynoweth. He however, like Nicola, is due for a flat pack day starting Wednesday. However this Chris is already allocated to Heather Jones. We are at a bit of an impasse but I think there will be explosions from Nicola's side if we ring her to tell her flat

pack day is cancelled. I could see her getting angry and causing us problems when she is told.'

'By the way, how keen is Chris Chynoweth to get married?'
'I think in his quiet, male, British way he is very keen to marry the right person but he does not like to say too much.'
Then Geoff saw his mobile ring. He could see it was Pete Bridges. 'That's a coincidence. It's Nicola Rose's and Chris Chynoweth's minister on the phone. I'd better answer it in case Nicola has been in touch with him about what has happened and he wants to know what is going on.' He walked out to somewhere quieter.

CHAPTER 20 - COMMITTEE

Geoff pressed the button on his phone to take the call and started talking, 'Hi Pete, how are you doing?'

'I'm fine. Have you got a moment?'

'Yes sure. Fire away.'

Pete launched into a description of his wife's afternoon lunch do and how Nicola and Chris seemed to have got on like a house on fire.

'So Geoff, where are they in the candidate process?'

'Both are well on and funnily enough we were considering Nicola especially this very morning. Has Nicola been in touch with you today by chance?'

'No, why do you ask?'

Geoff went on to describe what was happening.

Pete Bridges then replied, 'Have you thought of the obvious solution – pairing Nicola and Chris Chynoweth together? My wife has very good nose for matches. There are three couples in the church she has matched up with success. What's to stop your committee considering putting those two together?'

'Could I think about it?'

'Sure. I would not mind knowing though the outcome of what you decide in case Nicola and Chris come back to me as their minister for advice a help.'

'I will give you a ring back but it may be some days before I do.'

Geoff turned his phone off. He walked back in the room where Michael and the others were still discussing the situation.

'That was an amazing coincidence.' He then went on to describe the call with Pete and the Saturday lunch meeting.

At the end Geoff said, 'Chris and Nicola's pastor is suggesting we put these two together. What do people think?
Michael responded, 'I think better to do it for the sake of both Nicola and Chris. It sounds like they might be really suited for each other. It also incidentally means that we don't need to tell them that they were originally not intended for each other. I think that information would destroy Nicola from what you are saying, Angie. It would always seem to her as if she was getting second best and that might cause problems if they were to date.'
Geoff interjected, 'But you know as they say, 'Man proposes and God disposes'. Maybe what has happened is a better outcome than we had planned originally.'
Michael asked, 'What do we then do about Chris Chilvers and Heather Jones? Is there any mileage in pairing those two up? It might just be a neat solution to our problem.'
'I am pretty hesitant to pair people up, just for our convenience, but I do think we do at least need to explore that possibility, even if only to reject it,' Geoff added.
'Geoff, can you and the Panel have an urgent long think today – maybe via video conference and give me your thoughts by the end of the day?'

This was not the easiest Panel committee meeting Geoff had ever handled, as there were some very different opinions.
Ellie the psychologist started off, 'I am not at all keen on the matching of Nicola and Chris Chynoweth and wish to point out that there were some significant differences in some scores on the psychological tests'
Geoff had his doubts about the validity of the tests but did not like to say so directly to Ellie.
'That is an important point but am I right in thinking that the difference in each of the two persons score is within the range that we are agreed as acceptable for a couple?'
Ellie reluctantly nodded, 'Yes that is technically correct but I still

have my doubts.'

Geoff decided it might be good to get Parminder's viewpoint. She would be less dogmatic, more balanced.

'Reviewing the whole situation, I personally think they might work very well as a couple. My one question is that Nicola's a vegetarian as is incidentally Chris Chilvers, which is one of the reasons we put them together while Chris Chynoweth is a meat eater as is Heather Jones.' Parminder with her Asian background, was much more conscious of food tolerances since so many Indians were vegetarians. Also with her Muslim clients, she had to think about the issue of alcohol and social drinking.

'I'll give Chris Chynoweth a ring as I think it will be less of an issue for Nicola.'

Ellie then piped up as a last shot, 'Nicola is obsessionally neat and Chris is more of a bachelor slob. How will they get on?'

Parminder nodded in agreement, 'That is a point to be considered.'

Pete pointed out that Chris was a compliant man. Geoff had a deep feeling from his extended experience that Nicola and Chris would work well and he was really bolstered by the phone call from Pete Bridges. In the end the committee agreed. Geoff was delegated to ring Chris Chilvers and Heather Jones.

It was a tricky interview with Chris Chilvers, as Geoff had the sense he was holding something back. Geoff was getting a feel of a side of Chris, that he had the potential to be a bit wild and wacky. This had apparently not come out in the psychological tests, otherwise Ellie would have highlighted it. He was trying to assess whether Chris would make good his threat and not go ahead unless he had seen the photo in advance. Now that was totally against the charity's policy going against its very ethos. Chris was now saying that he would not now want to see a photo in advance and Geoff decided to believe him.

Geoff's final chat with Heather Jones had been much easier. She was ready to get married and was looking forward to it but there was not the same desperation as he had seen in other candidates. She did not seem to have a problem with marrying a vegetarian. So in the end Geoff had recommended that they should be the chosen pair.

CHAPTER 21- WEDDING

The church was Tossington on Derwent. It was an old 15th century building in the middle of an old Derbyshire village and today was decked inside with all kinds of exquisite, sweet smelling, fragrant roses, perfectly crafted by nature. When the florist decorating the venerable old building for the day, heard that the Bride to be's name was 'Nicola Rose', she knew instantly which flower to make centre stage. Chris Chynoweth was waiting by the altar, in a purple slightly sparkling suit which looked really cool on him. Nicola came into church in a traditional wedding dress with a long train, very lacy, very intricate and obviously classy. She was very demure in manner and looked her very best. Chris glanced back and his normal serious face broke into a delighted grin, like a love sick schoolboy who has just got his first date with the most beautiful girl in his class. Michael caught every look on camera. It was his first filmed wedding for 'Matches made in Heaven?' and he was in heaven too, as it would make perfect television.

Michael mentally reviewed how the last few months had gone. Angie had rung Nicola late the Monday evening after the crisis meeting that morning and the emergency committee meeting. Nicola had been delighted and relieved that her Flat Pack Day was still happening on Wednesday. Michael had filmed the first meeting that Wednesday between Nicola and Chris Chynoweth, capturing the delight on Nicola's face and the more restrained look of pleasure on Chris'. After that, the two of them had got on like a house on fire. They had dated and decided to marry on the exact day, eight months after that first meeting. Nicola in her happiness, seemed to have forgotten about the email and the picture of Chris Chilvers sent her. When she did think about it, she just assumed that someone had just got crossed wires and was playing a practical joke. Michael was genuinely happy for them both and also delighted for his programme making too. Love and Happiness, so often was a winner on television.

After the wedding ceremony, the new husband and wife were being photographed outside with the mass of milling people and guests in the churchyard. Michael and Amanda were both slow to leave the church and he deliberately held her back with conversation until they were the only two people left inside the building. Amanda was a little bit unsure why he kept on wanting to chat with her. Michael was not worried about the filming, as Joe his best cameraman was on the job. Amanda and Michael finally moved into the central aisle out of the pew where they had been sat, ready to leave. He made some excuse to move them both nearer the altar.

Then he came out with it.

'Amanda what are you doing in two months' time on September 25th?'

Amanda's face showed her puzzlement, 'Why do you ask?'

'Would you like to marry me here in this church on 25th September? I do happen to know that the church is free,' Michael said casually.

'What ?!!!!!'

'We have been going out for months and months. I love you. I think you love me. Now is a good time to get married.'

Amanda was taken totally aback, surprised. She then smiled and broke into a big grin.

'Well I am flabbergasted. I don't know what to say.'

'You could say yes.'

'Well yes yes, I will marry you,' she cried out, grinning again with her eyes wide open. They kissed and walked out of the church hand in hand. Michael caught up with Joe, who was filming the wedding photos and touched base with him, walking on cloud nine.

All went like a dream for Chris and Nicola. Nicola was the happiest she had ever been. The reception was splendid, with a four course meal. The speeches were many and the champagne flowed.

*****

The programmer saw the film of the wedding since one of his jobs had been to write the programme to store and analyse the camera footage. He struggled to control his envy of Chris. That man had an attribute that he could never have – something that practically everyone took for granted. It was an attribute which came in handy, said he to himself, laughing ruefully at his own bad joke in poor taste.

*****

What the programmer did not see, was the struggle in Nicola's heart. From about five o'clock on the wedding day afternoon, Nicola started to feel uncertain. The old demons of indecision had reared their heads again after lying dormant for eight months. Had she made the right decision to get married? Yes she had got to know Chris well over the months but she had no idea of how it would work out living with him. She had not a clue of how it might feel being intimate with him. In fact she had no real concept of what it would be like to be intimate with any man. She was starting to wonder how she could get out of this marriage. If she told Chris now, she could surely go for an annulment as long as she told him before tonight. Her face started to cloud over. Chris noted the change when they finally left their wedding guests at nine pm to go upstairs. He wondered what was going on but did not know her well enough yet to sense what might be happening. He was feeling nervous too and did not want to ask anything.

As she started to climb the stairs to go to the wedding suite, she knew she had to take the decision whether to go through with things or not. She needed to tell him the way she felt before they met the cameras at the top of the landing but she could not tell him could she? It would devastate the guy. Surely if anyone was the right man in her life it was Chris. The cameras and flash lights and crew were there. It was 'show time' as the Americans would put it. Now it was decision time. Chris opened the door to the wedding suite and held it open politely for her, saying with a smile, 'Shall we?'

She looked at his face and saw that he was nervous too. Had he too been thinking the same as her? She dare not ask him. She just knew in that moment she had to take the risk. She could see a reassuring gentleness in his face and manner. He would be kind to her. She put on her slightly more professional smile when dealing with a difficult situation and said back, 'We shall.' She walked into the room and gasped when she saw all the lovely red roses everywhere flooding the room. On a table was a magnum bottle of champagne and two beautiful fluted glasses.

Nicola looked at the bottle and exclaimed to Chris, 'Oh my goodness. However will we get through all that?'

At least a glass or two would help relax them both, she thought.

CHAPTER 22- AFTERSHOCK

Nicola and Chris lay in bed together, just ready to go to sleep on their wedding night. After an hour of getting through over half of the champagne bottle between them, they were nicely relaxed. They had then consummated their marriage – to use a very old-fashioned word to describe that most intimate of human activities. Nicola looked at Chris, who afterwards had very rapidly fallen asleep. He was now starting to snore beside her. She thought back to what her Mum had said about marriage. 'It's a bit like climbing Everest but when after thirty five years like your Dad and me, you have got to the summit, it gives you wonderful views over the world from a place of contentment.'

Nicola felt a peace inside herself. She had taken the right decision, going into the wedding suite. She somehow knew that she and Chris had now reached Everest base camp, as it were. They were now ready to start the big, long, arduous climb up the mountain of the years, like her Mum and Dad had done. She had now just come to her first tricky rock climb – coping with a snoring, snorting husband. However could she get to sleep with that noise? Not of course that she ever snored -well she did not think that was the case. But sooner or later she would find out from Chris if she did or not. As long as he did not pull off the same trick that her brother in law Ross had done. He had recorded her sister Rosie's nocturnal sleep noises on his mobile and played them after dinner on Christmas day to the assembled family group. Rosie was so embarrassed. Nicola thought they had probably had words afterwards in private. Somehow Nicola had sensed that that was not the sort of trick that her Chris would do to her.

Nicola woke up at two in the morning. She had managed to get to sleep after all.
She wondered to herself, 'Why do I feel so hot in bed?'
Then she suddenly realised with a start that, for the first time in her life since being a young child, she was sleeping with someone else in bed with her, who was radiating heat – this large, still snoring, snorting, animal noise making being called a husband.

Next day at 9.10 in the morning, Nicola got out of bed and saw the remnant of the bottle of the now flat champagne. She went to open the large heavy floor to ceiling curtains in just her nightie. She had been told that the view from the honeymoon suite was 'very private'. She gasped out loud, with a sharp intake of breath and quickly shut the half open curtains.
She groaned, 'Chris, I cannot believe it. I have just opened the curtains and there is one of Michael's blinking camera drones about twenty yards away looking straight at me in my nightie. I am really, really, really fed up with it.'

Ten minutes later Chris made the phone call to Michael
'Hi Michael. Nicola and I are ready to leave the room. By the way there was a filming drone just outside our window. How long is the plan for that to carry on for?'
Michael mumbled an apology, something like, 'Only a little bit more today.'
Then he went on to say, 'Okay. Give us ten minutes and the crew will be outside your door.'

Nicola remarked to Chris, 'I feel like royalty about to emerge onto the balcony, ready to be filmed at Buckingham Palace.'
'Yes so do I but like you I am getting a little fed up with it.'
'But at least we have something to smile about.'
'Yes we do,' shot back Chris with a glance of a big smile.

Out they went through the door to meet the light shone towards them and the camera crew with two large cameras. Nicola shyly put her hand in Chris. Then she wished she had not, when she saw the faces of the all-male crew. She coloured up a deep red. She said to Chris later in a very prim and proper voice.
'Did you see the smirk and grin on those men's faces. I was so embarrassed. Anyone would have thought we had emerged from a naughty weekend rather than as a respectable, newly married couple.'

They walked down to breakfast in the dining room, which was a large open area, with several glass doors leading onto the garden balcony and hence down to the beautiful garden, with its sweeping lawns mown in stripes. It had been used for the wedding reception yesterday but was now set up with several round tables, where most of the forty wedding guests staying overnight were seated. As Nicola and Chris entered the restaurant, the guests began cheering and clapping. The cameras were recording it all. Rosie, Nicola's sister stood up with fluted glass in hand and cried out over loudly, 'Hey little sister, come and sit with us and tell us all about it.'
Rosie was clearly in a raucous mood, having taken full advantage of the free champagne breakfast on offer.

Nicola decided that discretion might be the better part of valour, knowing her older.
So she was very happy when Chris suggested to her in a tones loud enough to be heard by Rosie but not by everyone, 'Shall we go and sit with the parents and grandparents. It might be very appropriate today as a mark of respect towards them.'
Tina, Nicola's Mum shot Chris a grateful glance. She knew what Rosie, her older daughter, could be like after a drink or two. She was beginning to take a shine to this bloke Nicola had hitched herself up with, in this weird semi arranged marriage. She could not yet think of him as Nicola's chap in the same way as she thought of Ross, Rose's husband as her chap but she could see

that happening. Rosie sensed through her mildly merry state, some disappointment but also realised that Chris had handled it quite cleverly.

They seated themselves down on a round table with the 'oldies' group consisting of Nicola's parents, Chris' Dad and his new wife and Chris' mother with her partner as well as a couple of their grandparents. Chris' Dad had moved to Northern Ireland after his divorce and his ex-wife had moved to Berwick so they had only met Nicola and her parents for the first time yesterday.
Nicola's mum kicked off the conversation politely asking, 'So how is the honeymoon suite?'
'Very beautiful Mum, with a four poster bed and an antique bath in the middle of the room as well as an enchanting view over the gardens from the top floor and our own private balcony.'
'It sounds wonderful. Not so sure about the bath in the bedroom though. Could I have a quick peep inside the suite before we go at midday?'
'Sure Mum,' said Nicola quickly just checking with Chris by a glance that he was okay with that.

'How do you find the cameras, Chris?' asked his Dad.
'Rather intrusive Dad. We feel rather like royalty but like them, we have to smile all the time! But we will soon be getting some time off.'
'Why is that?'
'Michael wants to do some more filming today – us going for a walk round the hotel lake and also using the indoor pool. Apparently it is so as to do a promo video for the hotel and so balance the production costs. Then we have five days alone here without drones or cameras so we can just be alone. Then, though, we have to do an end of honeymoon week interview with Michael before we finally leave. In fact we have already decided we are going on a second honeymoon without cameras or anyone else except ourselves.'

'A second honeymoon! That is ambitious Son! Where would you

go to?'

'Somewhere without cameras at all, except for any mobile shots we care to take ourselves. We saw on the internet this morning, while we were listening to classical music, that there are great deals to Eilat in Israel including a trip to Jerusalem.'

'The internet? What are young people coming to these days?' exclaimed Chris's Dad with a grin.

'I thought that newly married couples weren't supposed to keep their hands off each other. This two – less than twenty four hours into their honeymoon and they cannot keep their hands off their mobiles to hit the internet – itchy fingers indeed. What's so special about Israel then?'

'If we go in November as planned we can swim in a lovely warm Red Sea – tremendous sandy beaches and fish all around you as you swim and bask in the sunshine! So different from a grey cold November in Derbyshire. Jerusalem also has got so many places of Biblical significance.'

Conversation moved onto what was going to happen after the honeymoon.

Nicola said, 'I'm going to move into Chris' house in Belper. It's a new house on a new estate.'

'Nicola or can I call you Nic? Do you know why he got a new house, why he *had* to have a new house?' asked Chris' Dad.

Nicola looked puzzled, 'Yes, please call me, Nic as many people do! I don't understand why he *had* to move into a new house – tell me!'

'Do you know what your new surname means?'

'Chynoweth – no I don't. I don't even know where it comes from. I wondered whether it might be Welsh but I had not got around to asking Chris about it. There is still lots we have got to find out about each other. After all we were only dating six months before we took the decision to get married.'

'Our family comes from Cornwall near Launceston. We have still got relatives there. Chynoweth means 'New house' in Cornish. There is a tradition in our family which goes back at least four generations: At some time during our life we have to buy a newly built house. I only bought my first one, three years ago when I married Sherrie here. Chris, my lad here, rich doctor that he is, bought his first house as a new build two years ago.'

Chris' Mum decided to pitch in then,
'Nicola, you do know, don't you, he is a slob. Yes he's a slob. He is not hot on cleaning things and leaves clothes on the floor. I would use the words 'Good luck' to any woman who takes him on. Regard him as a project, my dear.'
'Funnily enough the words, 'Good luck' were said to me a few days ago, about him. I went upstairs in his house for the first time last Wednesday and I found his bedroom an utter mess. I also chanced on his cleaning lady Laura, someone he had not deigned to inform me of. She was busy trying to vacuum around the piles of clothes and books and several years of paper copies of the British Medical Journal. She was a lovely, friendly, middle-aged lady, who told me that it was her last time working there, and wished me, 'Good luck' too.

So I went downstairs and said to Chris 'I've just met up with your cleaning lady. She's just told me that this is her last time here.' He said to me, 'Yes that's right.'
I said to him with a deliberately innocent questioning tone, 'Oh why is that?'. Do you know what he said back to me?'
'Tell us' said Chris's Mum, 'We are all agog.'
'He then said to me, 'Well I was hoping that when we got married you might take over the cleaning.'
Chris's and Nicola's Mums gasped together and laughed. Chris looked rather sheepish, having been caught out committing the ultimate social sin of the 21st century, of being a male chauvinist.
Nicola continued in also laughing tone, 'I put on my special senior district nurse face and my super district nurse voice I use to deal with difficult doctors.'
Everyone was looking at her agog to see what she would come

out with next.

'I looked him in the face and said to him, 'You are quite right. I will be happy to supervise, since you do not seem capable of that, but we will be doing the cleaning together,' that word 'together' was said with an emphasis on the word 'together'. 'He did not say anything back.'

Chris sat there with a slightly embarrassed smile on his face.

'What happened about Laura?' asked Nicola's Mum.

'Laura is working one very extra last time for us both. While Chris is out of the house, she is going tidy up everything and put it away, vacuum thoroughly, clean, then wash the bedclothes and make the bed. I have given her carte blanche to move things as needed. This means that when we get back from honeymoon, I don't have to worry about whether I'm going to be sleeping in a clean bed that first night.'

'How is Chris taking the new regime?' asked his mother with interest.

'This morning I emptied his suitcase and made him hang all his clothes up in the wardrobe. I also worked out a place, where he and I could put our dirty laundry. So far he has not protested.'

*****

The programmer saw all this dialogue on his film clips and laughed too, with the others, at Chris's faux pas. He kept his own bedroom meticulously neat in spite of the big personal challenge that he faced doing that.

*****

Sherrie, Chris' Dad's new wife, had just been having a chat with a nearby cameraman. She turned away from talking to him to face the rest of the table.

'I have just been chatting with Joe here. There was another wedding yesterday filmed by Michael at Hetherton on Dove church. By his account it was a really unusual one with a pet present.'

Joe came over and addressed the table, 'Yes I was part of the camera crew yesterday at the church at the wedding.'

Nicola had a sudden 'on the off chance' thought, 'Joe, what was the name of the groom?'
'Chris. Chris Chilvers.'
Nicola was shocked. She quickly asked, 'Could I just show you a photo? Hang on a minute while I dig round in my emails for it.'
She found the picture sent her by Rosie on that drunken Saturday night.
'Is that him?'
'Yes it is. How did you get that?'
'It's a long story, not for telling now,' replied Nicola.
She decided she would have a quiet word with Chris later and also she wanted to have a word with sister Rosie later too.

*****

The programmer finished watching the video clips. The thing that really stuck in his mind was the happiness of Nicola and Chris in that film of the breakfast. You could even use the word joy to describe what was shining on their faces. He had heard the laughter and felt the festive atmosphere in the room. He closed down the viewing application on the laptop and then shut the laptop screen with a bang. He was frustrated and he could bear it no longer. He desperately wanted a share of the gladness and he was going to take a risk. He had the number he wanted on his mobile speed dial. He went to press the screen in the right place, to start the call that might just change his life. Then he changed his mind.

*****

CHAPTER 23 A COSY CHAT AT THE CHYNOWETHS

A month later Rosie had come over to Belper to have a quiet cup of coffee with little sister. She had just finished a weekend shift as a nurse on the cardiac ward. It was Chris' day off too and he had gone off on a long cycle ride on his racing bike – his form of unwinding from work. He was heading to Carsington Water with a friend.

They were sitting in the living room which was certainly very neat and tidy. Nicola had put her imprint on the room, with some nice knick knacks and a couple of spectacular natural history photos. There were a whale's tail flipping up and another of the aerial view of a Canadian forest in autumn with all the different colours of leaves in the sunlight including some reds, her favourite.

Nicola thought it might be the right time to bring up something. She fished out her mobile. Rosie glanced and saw on her home screen a selfie picture of her and Chris together. Clearly little sister was happily enjoying marriage. Rosie wondered when she would get the announcement that a little nephew or niece was on their way. She had a feeling it might be earlier rather than later. After all Nic and Chris were both a bit older and had got a house of their own. Nicola scrolled through the screen until she got up the picture of Chris Chilvers sent her from as yet unknown to her email address.

'You remember I sent you the piccy, I was sent with the caption, 'Chris C.. your future intended.' I found out who it was, the breakfast the day after the wedding talking to that cameraman Joe. It's Chris Chilvers, the chap who was due to get his flat pack day, exactly the same day as me and my Chris, but then apparently he got it postponed a week. I think whoever sent me the email somehow got my Chris and the other Chris confused. I still don't know who sent it. It does not matter now I have got my Chris.'

Rosie breathed an inwards sigh of relief at her sister's reaction. It was blindingly obvious to Nicola at least that the programme had always intended Nicola and her Chris, Chris Chynoweth to be paired off. That chap Chris Chilvers had always intended to be paired off to what was her name Heather something.

However to Rosie, it was not so blindingly obvious and she was starting to have her doubts. She remembered exactly what Nicola had relayed to her. Angie had said to her initial reaction to Nic's phone call, 'How did you see the photo of the man you were to be paired up with?' Rosie somehow had an inkling that Nic and Chris Chilvers were the original pairing for the flat pack days. She started speculating that when that Chris had seen the photo of Nic, he had contacted the charity to say he did not want her sister. The charity then did a quick swap of the two Chris's.

Maybe that was why Chris Chilvers' flat pack day was delayed a week. It had originally been planned, surprise surprise, the same day as Nic. The change of flat pack days was to match him up with someone else. She decided instantly it might be better never to tell Nic about what she had done that drunken Saturday evening. It might really rock Nic, as well as possibly permanently ruin her relationship with her younger sister.

She went on to ask Nic, 'So are you happy, now you are finally married?

'Oh yes. I was very keen, no let me be honest, desperate – not that is a word that I would use to anyone but you, to get married. I am happy now.'
'So is Chris the perfect husband? Do you love him?'
Nicola launched into a little speech in reply,
'Chris is a nice-looking man, though one or two of my favourite actors clearly beat him. But where he so obviously comes out tops, is that he is a sweet, calm, gentle, man. You ask me the question whether I love him. That is such an important question, it seems, to people these days.'
'It always has been, Nic.'
'Parminder, you may remember me telling you about Parminder, says that she has seen so many arranged marriages start off without much previous contact between bride and groom. With well-matched couples, she thinks an intertwining love does though grow. Obviously we did date but marriage is a totally different level of relationship for us.'
Rosie interrupted with a smile, 'So sister, you have not answered my question yet. Do you love Chris?'
'Oh Yes, Rosie. We have that growing intertwining love. He has won my love by his character.'
'You do seem to have a lot in common.'
'It does help our relationship that we have so many interests in common. We do love walking together and of course we do go to the same church. We are both dedicated to our jobs and because they are in the same field of work, we unwind by talking through our days.'
'How is the food situation? Any conflicts?'
'Okay I am vegetarian and Chris isn't. He is generally okay with meals free of meat and is learning to cook some of my favourites. Getting him to tidy up after himself is still a work in progress though.'
'Don't worry my hubbie is the same and we've been married five years longer then you....'

CHAPTER 24- AN APPLICATION FROM THE PROGRAMMER

Ricky was sat at his desk, literally and metaphorically scratching his head. He was wondering what best to do about the programmer and his unusual request. The guy was one of his best workers. His current responsibility just happened to be organising work for a major UK retailer, trying to promote a new product range on their web site. He was a clever lad, having gone to Cambridge to do computer science and had got a first class degree, which was something that Ricky had not been able to achieve. All that made it more difficult to know the best way to deal with the request. Ricky did definitely not want to upset him and lose him.

It had all started off for Ricky yesterday afternoon when he had got a text from him, 'Hi can I see you tomorrow in the office about something important?'

Ricky wondered what that was about. Was that going to be a demand for more money, handing in his notice or coming with allegations of bullying from a work colleague? All those things he had already had to deal with in his short time as an employer. He had had to work hard at getting good at the human relations, or in the current jargon, the 'HR' side of life as the boss. Writing computer code was so much easier, more in his groove as it were. At least the code could not argue back at him.

Ricky texted back, 'Yes sure. Come at 9 am tomorrow. What's it about?'

'Best if I explain at 9 am,' came the not very reassuring reply back from the programmer.

Ricky took an intake of breath. Somehow he sensed there would be a difficult chat coming his way.

'I would like to apply to be a candidate for 'Forward Together' and 'Matches made in Heaven?' but I know your rules.' After the initial greetings, this was how the heart of the conversation started.

Ricky carefully replied back, 'Yeh, the rules are a bit strict but you know data protection and all that. In every project our business is involved in, no employee is allowed to be a client of the company. We cannot be storing your personal data for a project which the employee could then manipulate for their personal advantage.'

'Ricky I'm going to be honest. I am really keen to be married but when I try to date girls, they turn me down because of my well um problem. This project is my last hope. Would you be willing to make an exception…….for me?' he said in a pleading tone.

Ricky thought it over slowly and said, 'I'll give you an answer tomorrow'

Ricky decided the next move was to ring up Michael. 'Hey Dad, how are you and Amanda? How are the wedding plans going?'

They talked generally about family life and Ricky's wife's first baby in the pipeline.

'I've got a favour to ask.' Ricky went on to explain about the programmer and the particular difficulty he had.

'So Dad, if he applies, would you consider him or not?'

'What about the data protection side. He has got access to the client records. '

'I have checked the access logs to the files on the web server and the only client records he has seen was the wedding of the Chynoweth's in the past nine months. If you agreed to let him apply, I would block his access rights immediately.'

Michael, as he heard Ricky telling him about the programmer and his background, began getting excited. Could this just be the chance for his big break through with the programme – his chance to get an audience of tens or maybe hundreds of millions?

'Look Ricky I am, of course, going to have to run it past Amanda and she may say 'no' outright. He will need to go through all the preliminary checks first. We just might have a particular problem pairing him up, We would only really face that, if he passes the interview stage and if there is a suitable match. Do warn him please Ricky that his chances of getting through with a potential pairing is small. Will you do that for me please Ricky? I would hate to see a guy, like him disappointed, because he has got his hopes up too high.'

'Yes I can do that Dad. As long as your team gives him a fair shot.'

The next day Ricky called the programmer into his office.

'OK. Here is the deal. You can apply to 'Forward Together' and be a client of the web site but... I am taking you off the project and I will personally be taking the lead on it in place of you. You must absolutely not attempt to communicate with the team of developers about the web site. I will be changing all the passwords to the web server and client database which you are never, never, to try to find out by chatting with the developers. Understood?'

'Yes Ricky. Of course. Thank you thank you so much.'

The programmer practically skipped out of the office in joy. He went straight to the web site of 'Forward Together' and spent the next hour filling in the long form.

CHAPTER 25 - EMMANUEL'S STORY

Michael was troubled again. This whole project was throwing up more obstacles than he had thought it would. It was turning out to be more difficult than anything else he had done. He looked again at Emmanuel Adebayo's records. He was perfect. His psychological tests suggested that he would be an excellent match with five women. He had glowing references from his employer who happened to be Ricky his son, and from his church minister, Pastor Solomon. His safeguarding check had revealed no problems.

He was very happy to marry anyone without worries about their ethnicity. He was willing to move anywhere in the country. After all his job as a programmer, web site developer and computer coder could be done anywhere where there was a good internet connection. He had interviewed very well and all of the panel warmed to him. He was a handsome man who was slim and athletic and played football well. He had an excellent voice and was a keen member, not just of his church choir, but also of a large London gospel ensemble. He would make really good television and Michael already had visions of using recordings of his singing on the programme. Ever the film maker, he had been wondering how he might enter the Nigerian and South African television market. Emmanuel would be the ideal wedge in there.

It was just such a pity for him missing a left hand and part of his left forearm. He was born that way and the London hospital where he had been seen after his birth, could not help him.

Michael felt sorry for him but also realised that something so unusual would again make Emmanuel good television too. He was amazing, the fact he could just tap away with one hand writing computer code. Apparently according to Ricky that actually made him better at doing the code because he was more careful in what he wrote – fewer mistakes. Michael did not quite understand that but Ricky knew what he was talking about.

However all Michael's hopes looked as though they were going to come to nothing. He pondered what to do. Amanda had asked for his help sorting this situation out. In effect she had handed him the responsibility of telling Emmanuel. He could do the cowardly cop out of sending a polite letter saying sorry. But he just felt that to be the wrong thing to do. Obviously Ricky was so involved in the issue too. He felt that his son would be disappointed if he did the cowardly way. So he rang up Ricky and explained the whole situation. The reply came back swift and to the point.
'Dad, are you going to tell Emmanuel personally or not and if so how? I hope you would do better than a phone call or worse a letter.'
'How do you think he would take a face-to-face chat in the office?'
'At least he would feel you were being honest and would respect you for that. He will still be devastated.'
So Michael agreed reluctantly to a face-to-face meeting but was rather dreading the prospect. It would be rather like the occasional time he had to fire someone, or rather in modern parlance, 'let them go.'

Emmanuel turned up on a Friday morning to Michael's slightly cluttered office. He was more than a bit surprised to find out they were meeting in the office rather than the posher much bigger upstairs meeting room, normally used for all the interviews. Michael had decided it was more homely, more intimate for a meeting like this. Both the previous two interviews with the committee panel had taken place upstairs. That got Emmanuel wondering what was happening. Somehow he had a bad feeling about this meeting.

Michael walked into the office with Emmanuel and then popped out and said, 'I'm bringing in my colleague Geoff in, while we have a chat and Amanda's coming in too.'
Geoff came in and there was an awkward silence. All four sensed a difficult conversation was about to happen.
Michael looked at the others and said, 'Shall I kick off?'
Amanda and Geoff nodded, slightly relieved that they would not have to break the news.

Michael started off, 'Emmanuel thanks for coming here today. We wanted to have a chat with you face to face about where we are with your application. You are a really good candidate with three good matches among the ladies. You have got fantastic references from Ricky, my son as your employer, and also from Pastor Solomon and his wife Blessing. She has clearly got a soft spot for you.'
Michael smiled as he said that. Emmanuel thought back to the incident with the teenage girls last week.
'Unfortunately, we have a problem that I did not quite anticipate, and which I must say, I feel more than a little guilty about. As you are aware from the past, your disability, I don't know what other word to use, is an issue for some girls.'

Michael had already decided this was not the time to mention about the two girls that had outright rejected the thought of marrying anyone at all with a disability.
'We found three good matches for you – in fact excellent matches for you. All three girls were willing to marry someone with a minor disability but they all said they would like more detailed information about the….umm problem before committing themselves to Flat Pack Days. And that is our difficulty.'
'Why could you not give them more details?'
'We would need to ask your permission, Emmanuel.'

'Well I am giving it you. So go ahead and tell them all about my arm,' Emmanuel replied quickly, a little bit puzzled.
'Was that all this meeting was about?' he thought to himself with a sense of surprise.

Amanda then came in on the conversation.
'Emmanuel. It's not as simple as that. You see I had to take your case to the trustees of our 'Forward Together' charity who are the ultimate authority. They did not feel they would want us to reveal any of the details about you, in case one or the more of the girls decided to reject you on hearing about your left arm. If the girl's rejection of you were to come out in public, especially if you were then being filmed, it could cause embarrassment to the girls concerned and potentially problems in the social media for them. You know the way people can be slated on social media if others don't like what they have done.'

Amanda paused for a moment. She knew that the explanation she had just given was not very convincing because she had not been very convinced herself. She knew also as much as she tried, she could not fully hide her feelings from her face. She had argued and argued before the trustees that there was really no good reason why the girls should not be given a simple description of Emmanuel's left arm problem. The trustees though, had flatly overruled Amanda. It was of course normally against policy to give any details about the couple to each other before flat pack days so that even saying he had a 'minor disability' had been a big step forward for the trustees. The whole point of the charity was that a couple started off with a blank slate and saw how they went, not that she could say to Emmanuel that she thought that their reasons for the decision were tosh.

'Disability is a touchy subject these days. You also know the rules of 'Forward Together', that once we have a match, we put the man and woman in for the flat pack days but only one lot of flat pack days. If the couple don't hit it off, then we don't try to find someone else for either of them. The charity took the policy that it did not have the resources to keep on finding matches for people. That also might encourage pickiness.'

Amanda paused once more and continued, 'Also, it would not be good for you or the girl, to put you either of you in a very awkward situation. That is, if the girl were to take one look at you on Flat Pack Days and decide not to go any further. That would leave not just you but also the girl without a match. This puts us in a bind. We just cannot go forward with you as a candidate. I'm sorry. I know you were pinning a lot of hope on this process.'

Emmanuel looked shocked, stunned by the news. He tried to maintain his composure but was struggling.
'So is there no hope for me?'
'The only ray of light is what we are doing with candidates where we have not got spaces in for flat pack days. What we plan to do, with the permission of the boys concerned, is to give the phone numbers and name only of the boys, who are good matches to suitable girls. With the three girls who are good matches for you, two we know we plan to match up with other boys, who are very good matches for them for flat pack days. The third girl does not have really good matches except for you. We would be happy to give her your number and she may or may not ring you. We cannot promise that.'

'Why cannot you just remove all three girls from the process and give them my number?'
'Because that would not be fair on two of the girls, as that way they might not get a match. For a lot of individuals, especially some of the girls in the process, they see it as their best chance of getting married, having kids and being happy in that. Remember there are generally many more young women in church than young men.'
'Why cannot you give me the third girls' number and I could take the initiative and ring her rather than her ring me?' the eagerness in Emmanuel's voice was so very obvious.
'Because we have taken the policy decision as a team that we

would give the phone numbers to the girls not vice versa, so they could be in control of contacting the boys.'
What she did not say but implied was that it would protect the girls' privacy from over pushy boys.
'Do you think the third girl would get in touch with me?'
'I'm afraid I really cannot say.'

Emmanuel looked so despondent. There was nothing more to say. He got up and tried to hold his dignity together, went over to Michael and Amanda and Geoff. He shook hands with each of them saying, 'Thank you. Goodbye then.'
As he walked out of the room, he turned round and addressed Amanda reproachfully, 'You don't really agree with the trustees' decision, do you?'
Amanda again found it difficult to hide her true feelings and said nothing, looking down embarrassed.

Emmanuel slowly walked out of Michael's crowded little office. His head was hung down with a few tears in his eyes. He was not seeing properly and bumped hard into the first desk in the outer office and cried out with pain. He had banged his knee. Angie was sitting there, focusing on the screen, typing away. She looked up and there he was.
'Are you okay? She asked in a concerned voice, as she saw him rubbing his knee with his right arm.
He shook his head silently.
'They've just told you. Haven't they?' Angie had known in advance what the meeting he had just left was about.

He just nodded, tears silently streaming down his cheeks. Angie's heart went out to him. She stood up, went over to him and gave him a hug. She glanced round and saw the other people in the office, staring at them. They were not in on the secret of what the meeting had been about. Angie quickly whisked him off to the staff room and gave him a cup of percolated coffee from the machine. Instant coffee just would not do in this instance.

Emmanuel started to open up, slowly sobbing, 'I've tried so hard at life. I've worked my socks off and got a good job. I'm not the ugliest chap going except for this stump of mine which I hate.' He lifted it up to show her.
'It just drags me down and every now and again something happens that just reminds me so vividly of it. Last week it was those girls at church. This week it's this.'

'What happened with the girls at church?' Angie asked curiously.
'I was singing in the church choir as the lead singer as we were doing a rehearsal of our latest production. Suddenly, unusually for me, I had a frog in my throat and sung two or three bad notes. I heard some silly giggling behind me and I turned and saw two teenage girls laughing to each other and making limp wrist gestures with their left hands like this.' Emmanuel imitated the gestures with his right hand.
'What did you do?' Angie asked, her face showing her shock that something as cruel as that could still happen in the twenty first century. 'How could people treat others like that?' was what was going through her head.

'I did nothing except want to cry. My mother who was leading the choir from the front, noticed what was happening and glared sternly at them both. Then Blessing, the pastor's wife, marched over to the girls with a determined look and spoke to the two of them. She is a very strong lady and you don't want to mess with her,' he said with a slight smile.
'The girls then came over rather sheepishly and reluctantly said, 'Sorry' to me.'
'How awful,' said Angie with feeling.
Then he burst out in an angry voice, in between tears streaming down, 'I want to go to them, to the trustees of the charity and tell them exactly what I think of them, doing this to me. I saw the look on Amanda's face that she did not totally agree with their decision.'

Emmanuel suddenly felt a bit funny, blubbing in front of this girl.

He looked at her face and said, 'I feel a bit like I'm letting the side down as a bloke, crying in front of a girl.'

Angie looked him in the face and took his right hand gently, even tenderly, not that he really noticed that at the moment. He was just so wound up.

'Honestly, I don't think the worse of you – that you are less of a man. No woman would want a man who tries to be macho all the time.'

He slowly got up to go but Angie stopped him and said, 'Stay here a minute.'

She rushed out and knocked carefully on Michael's office where he, Amanda and Geoff were talking through the interview they had just had with Emmanuel.

'Hi Boss, Hi Amanda and Geoff. Emmanuel is in a bit of a tizz was and I have got him in the staff room. I wondered about taking him out to lunch and trying to talk to him more, seeking to calm him down. He's also talking of complaining to the trustees.'

Angie noted the sudden look of alarm appearing on the others' faces. What if Emmanuel was to complain to the trustees and it was all to come out in public. That would be bad press for the charity as well as for 'Matches made in Heaven?'.

'Where would you take him to – somewhere nice, top notch, I hope?' Michael replied.

'Actually, I think it might be better to take him somewhere more informal, where he would be more likely to relax and calm down more. I had a Pizza place in mind, the one in that new retail park to the north of Nottingham city. Then I'd take him to a nice place in Derbyshire to walk round so he could talk and unwind.'

Michael considered all that. Angie was much nearer in age to Emmanuel and youngsters might feel a lot more relaxed in a pizza place. It seemed to make sense.

'Okay. Do that. We'll pay of course.'

Amanda interrupted with a frown, 'I don't think the charity can pay for that sort of thing. It does rather set a precedent.'
'Cohen Cinematography will fund it this time as a one off,' Mike said determinedly.

On the Monday following the weekend, Michael looked up from his computer screen in the office and asked Angie, who was walking by, 'Oh, by the way, how did it go with Emmanuel on Friday?'
'Oh great Boss, I calmed him down a lot, told him the truth that he was a great guy and that I was sure things would work out for him eventually. I don't think there will be more problems there.'
'That's good,' Michael replied only half listening.
Michael was too busy and distracted by other things that he did not pick up on the enigmatic smile Angie had on her face. He was trying to get his head round a rather long and complicated email from the accountant about his tax bill. He mentally ticked Emmanuel off his 'issues to worry about' list and read on the accountant's turgid prose with furrowed brow.

CHAPTER 26-THE MATCHMAKER

Six months later Michael was sat in his living room with the amazing view over the valley of the river Derwent which flowed through the centre of Derbyshire. It was a cloudy day but that did not matter as he could see everything clearly. A distant house below had a little billow of smoke rising from its chimney. He was having an indulgent day off and thoroughly enjoying his eleven o'clock second cup of the morning percolated coffee – one of the wonderful, smooth, luxurious pleasures of life. Amanda, who was now his wife, was at work, leaving him alone in the house to relax.

When he had got married, Ellie had said, 'Dad you don't need me round any more. You have got Amanda round to sort out your ties and match up your socks. I am going off with my friends travelling for six months.'

By him was a box of Matchmakers orange chocolate sticks, an as yet unopened leftover from a long distant Christmas. It was a lazy day, the lull before the storm of a whole load of work next week. Angie had asked for the day off too – something or other was on for her. She had been a bit vague about why she had needed this particular day off. Recently she had got a little mysterious on him, not that she had seemed unhappy – in fact anything but that. He must ask her sometime what was up. He hoped she was not busy looking for another job. She was starting to become indispensable to him.

He looked at the Matchmakers box. He had had a 'discussion'

with Amanda that morning.

She had commented in her forthright way, that he had put on weight recently, 'I would not want to think of you as a fatty'.

'Oh Amanda you can be so cruel at times,' he thought.

He of course, denied it saying truthfully, 'My weight is the same as when we got married four months earlier.'

'Then you must have got shorter, which is why you look the way you do Michael.'

So the discussion had not exactly ended with a meeting of minds on the issue. Since he had not put on any weight, it was clearly a reasonable and responsible action on his part to take the plastic wrapping off the chocolate box and carefully place one of the delicious sticks in his mouth.

His mobile by his side pinged and he casually picked it up. It was a text from Angie.

'Hi boss,' it started off, 'I'm going to be changing my name shortly to Angie Adebayo.'

Michael was intrigued.

'What do you mean?' he texted back. The name Adebayo did not ring any instant bells with him.

'Emmanuel and I have just got engaged. Boss could we have a free wedding? Smiley face, Smiley face. You could even make a TV programme about us, Smiley face, Smiley face, Angie xx.'

Suddenly the penny dropped who she was talking about. So that was what was up with Angie. She had not given him one iota of an inkling that she was interested in Emmanuel Adebayo. That girl was certainly a cheeky young lady.

Michael grinningly thought inside himself, 'Why she had had her first date with Emmanuel at company expense – that restaurant lunch where she had taken the guy out to calm him down after I had had to break bad news to him.'

He then remembered he had asked her casually a month or so later whether she had still kept in touch with Emmanuel.

She replied, seemingly equally casually, 'Oh just the odd text or two.'

The odd text or two my foot. A full blown romance had been developing.. cheeky girl indeed. Then it hit him. His chances of being big in African television might, just might have come to life again.

Michael quickly texted back, 'Many congratulations. Very interested for you to tell me all about it tomorrow, Michael x'.

He hesitated a moment by the box of Matchmakers. Should he take another one of them or not?

Then he said to himself, 'If it had not been for my TV programme 'Matches made in Heaven?', Angie and Emmanuel would never have met.'

More confidently, he opened the box again, took one solitary Matchmaker chocolate stick out and plopped it in his mouth. Actually Angie's idea was not so bad. It probably would be very good television how they had had to reject Emmanuel because he had been born without a hand, how Angie had met him through working in his office and then fallen for him.

A few seconds later after he had finished the second chocolate stick, his mobile pinged again. He picked up the phone for a second time and read.

'Hi Michael, Nicola and I are expecting our first child. She has just had the confirmatory scan – baby due 2nd December. Thank you so much for bringing us together. Chris Chynoweth.'

Michael again quickly texted back, 'Many congratulations. I will be in touch shortly.'

It was part of the contract for couple getting wed through the programme that if they had kids, they would allow Michael to make two programmes about the birth and later on.

He clearly was going to be making a lot more programmes in the next few months than he had thought. It was their first baby too, through the programme making. Michael turned to the Matchmakers box and this time without hesitation took a third stick of chocolate. He thoroughly, thoroughly deserved this one.

CHAPTER 27- SECURITY SORTED

Chris Chilvers was making a call to Michael, to sort out the next post wedding interview with him and Heather. Angie did not take to the guy. He had been so rude and demeaning towards Nic Rose who was such a lovely girl in her opinion. Michael was much more philosophical about him. He also realised how much excellent TV the guy had been giving him, including having a new phenomenon that he had never before filmed at a wedding. Chris seemed so more much relaxed than he normally was and opened up to Michael. When people open up they sometimes let slip things better not said.

'I must tell you this. My sister Gill and I were chatting at the reception and she told me about her drunken antic one Saturday night in Derby. She met Rosie Cullen, Nicola Chynoweth's sister as part of a hen do. They got talking and realised they might one day both possibly be going to the same wedding. So they played a trick and emailed me and Nicola photos of each other. I was very glad she did because I would not have wanted to get married to Nicola. If I'd have seen her on the flat pack day, I would have walked out.'

Michael was struck dumb and did not know what to say. Mentally he quickly ran through the options.
In the end he quietly remarked, 'Have you told anyone else about this?'
'No I haven't except Heather.'
'Are you OK to keep it quiet, between you and Heather. I some-

how don't think good would come of it being out in the open. Also do you mind if I have a chat with Gill?'
'I don't mind keeping quiet about it. I have kept it under my hat so far. Here is Gill's mobile number.'

Michael was relieved. Ricky had always thought that it was not an IT problem but now it looked as if he had confirmation. It was a straight forward human security leak after all. He rang Gill and got a fuller account, backing up all Chris had said. She agreed to keep it quiet too. He then rang up Ricky to break the good news to him.

Ricky was relieved but not immensely so – not as much as his father thought he would be.
'Dad that is good news but does not totally remove all my fears. Would you totally trust a man who brings his female live lizard pet called Dave of all things to his wedding and gets his sister Gill to look after the animal during the actual ceremony? Chris Chilvers and his sister Gill are nutters, Dad. I need to be a hundred percent certain that the story you told me is totally true and that there was not someone hacking into your web site which is my web site since I run it. I get it in the neck business wise and legal wise if I have a data leak. Would you be willing to speak to Rosie to confirm the story and ideally Nicola too?'

Michael could hear the agitation in Ricky's voice which was unusual for him. He remembered that Ricky had spent hundreds/thousands of pounds paying for a specialist IT firm. They had been given the job of trying to hack into his web site, to see if there were any weaknesses allowing a data leak, after the incident with Nicola and Chris Chilvers and the photos. The firm had failed to find any back door through to the web site but Ricky was still worried in case there was an IT weakness even so.
'Okay son, I will see what I can do,' Michael said trying to pacify his son.
'When you do that Dad, can you tell me what you find out,' came the determined, slightly aggressive reply back.

Michael rolled round his mind the pros and cons of contacting Rosie. He had already got the measure of her. That lady did like her drink, from what he had seen both at the wedding reception and also at the breakfast after the wedding. Would she be able to keep a lid on things? He also definitely did not want Nicola to know the information given him by Chris Chilvers. He sensed there might be trouble if she were to discover it.

That meant he would not wish to contact Nicola to find out Rosie's phone number, in case Nicola smelt a rat. In the end Angie came up trumps. She had Rosie's number on her mobile. She had needed to contact her a few times round the time of Nicola's wedding, because Rosie had been doing a singing number at the church.
'Do you ever delete numbers from your mobile?'
'No.'
'Why is that?'
'Just in case you ever need them, Boss.'
'Creep,' Michael shot back with a big grin, 'Or are you angling for a pay rise?' followed by further big grin.
'No I'm just efficient,' said Angie with a massive smile back.
'Boss, might it not better for me to contact Rosie as she might be more open and less wondering what might be at stake?'
'No. For this one I need to speak directly so I can reassure Ricky.'

Rosie was a more than a little surprised when Michael rang. He had never rung her before. She wondered what was so important that he would contact her directly rather than through Angie. Mike explained.
'So you see Rose it is a matter of IT security which is why I am contacting you to see if Chris' story is true.'

Rosie wondered if she should just shut the conversation down by denying everything. Then she wondered whether Michael might then contact Nicola. That she did not want.
In the end she came up with, 'If you agree not to get in touch

with Nic, then I will tell you what happened.'
'Agreed.'
'Okay then. What Chris said is right. Nicola overheard Parminder speaking and mentioning the name of Chris Ch… as the one for her Flat Pack Days.'
Rosie then went on to give the whole story.

So that is where the problem had all started because Nicola had heard Parminder's indiscreet comment …..Michael was immensely relieved to hear that. At least he could totally reassure Ricky and put his mind to rest that no one had hacked into their precious web site.

Then a thought which had been niggling in the back of Rosie's mind for months occurred to her again. Now was the moment to ask Michael, while she had him on the phone. Rosie could be bold and forthright when she so chose.
Out it came from her mouth, 'Tell me though the plan all along was to introduce Nicola and Chris Chilvers to each other in the flat pack days rather than Chris Chynoweth, wasn't it.'
Michael felt like he had been hit in the stomach by the unexpected and very direct question.
He slowly replied back in a very unconvincingly tone of voice, 'Client confidentiality.'
'You have just confirmed for me what I had started to suspect recently. Don't worry. Your secret is safe with me.'
She added on, 'You are not going to tell anyone are you, especially Nic? I think it might really rock her as underneath that tough district nurse exterior, she is quite an insecure person. She might be stupid enough to start thinking she got second best with Chris Chynoweth. Chris Chilvers is a bit of a hunk after all.'
'No. As I said before, I won't tell Nicola provided of course you don't say anything to Nic.'
'Agreed.'
Michael sincerely hoped that Rosie would keep to her promise.
'Please no more boozy encounters, Rosie, like that Saturday

night in Derby,' he prayed inside.

CHAPTER 28-THE FOUNDLING

Michael was excited. Angie could see her boss's eyes alight with pleasure. He was positively jiggling with barely controlled energy. He was clearly going to thoroughly enjoy this up and coming chat with her and Emmanuel.

She knew the track his mind was working on, 'Now I have at last got my big chance to get into African television'.

Angie mused about what made Michael tick in the film business. Money was certainly a big motivation for him but in fairness to the guy, he did have a big staff and was one for paying decent wages. She was on the top end of what she could expect in her job. She also knew that he spent a lot of time in long, anxious meetings with the firm's financial manager/accountant.

So he was not just interested in making money for himself. Michael wanted to achieve success, yes to be recognised for what he undoubtedly was, as an excellent film maker. That was a very human trait. But there was another thing with Michael. Angie knew deep inside him he had ideas that he wanted to spread - good ideas – ideas of hope and faith and values based on faith – ideas that resonated deeply with her. That was what she was keen to work with him. The only trouble with her boss is that he could be too single minded, too focused at times.

'So,' Michael started, 'We make a wedding programme about you two. It's going to take some but not all of the format of 'Matches made in Heaven?' We make a preliminary programme telling your story and the start of the build up to the wedding. Then we come up with a second programme of the last preparations and the wedding itself and the honeymoon. Tell me things about yourself that I don't already know. I have got all the paperwork here but I have not really had a chance to read it yet. Ah yes I see you were adopted,' Michael said looking down.

'Yes. I was really lucky there. My adopted Mum and Dad Emmanuel and Joy Adebayo are really, really, good people. They were both born in Nigeria but have lived in London for many years. My Dad is a prominent London GP and my mother is a professional singer and music teacher. I was so blessed there. I came into in a family where there are already three daughters. So I have had three older sisters who mothered me like mad when I was a kid. There is a younger sister as well too, who is living at home like me. The three older sisters still keep a close eye on me even though they have all left home and are married with kids of their own.'

'So how did you come to be adopted?'
'I am a foundling,' Emmanuel said it so simply.
Michael had to quickly think about that one. He knew what that was. He had made a programme many years ago about foundlings in the Philippines where it was still a major social phenomenon. In modern English the term used was 'abandoned baby'. In the Philippines legal system though, they still clung to the old English word, so redolent of the 17th and 18th century Britain where foundlings were a reality of life. It had the ring of poor women, dressed in a cloak, trudging through the falling snow one winter night with their baby and leaving a basket with their little one inside at the entrance to a large forbidding hospital building.

'So tell me more, Emmanuel, as foundlings are pretty uncommon in modern Britain. You certainly have me interested.'
'I was abandoned in a hospital corridor on Christmas day night when I was just a few hours old. Someone, probably not my mother but a Brit, rang up the hospital from a pay phone to say

where I was. A hospital porter went along to check things out and there I was, all wrapped in a blanket in a red wicker basket and a cuddly elephant toy, a small giraffe with a green ribbon too and a note.'

'Have you still got the elephant and giraffe toys?'

'Oh yes. They are my two possessions from my biological Mum. That makes them so important to me. There was something else as well in the basket, something special that has helped me through the years when I have struggled with feelings of rejection because my birth mum abandoned me.'

'What was that?' asked Michael already fascinated by the tale being spun before his eyes.

'It was an envelope with some of her cut hair and a note meant for me when I was older. The note said, 'I **will** love you always my baby xxx Mummy.

PS. I shall be gone soon from this world but I will see you again in heaven'

'Wow,' even Michael started to feel the tears well up when he heard about the note. He liked the fact he was starting to feel the tears trickling down his face. That would surely mean that the eyes of many a future viewer would well up too, when they heard that part of Emmanuel's story.

Then he paused and continued on, 'What happened then?'

'I was taken to the paediatric ward of the hospital, checked over and found to be healthy, except for my missing hand and wrist. Apparently from the way my belly button cord had been tied off, it was obvious a proper midwife with equipment had not been present at my birth. So there was no special point checking local delivery wards but they did anyway with no joy. Then started a police hunt for my birth mother. The paediatric department advised the police to contact all the other local hospitals. That was to see if there had been an ultrasound scan done on a pregnant mum, where the baby had my particular abnormality. It is a pretty unusual one after all.'

'Unfortunately that year Christmas day was on the Saturday which meant they could not get started looking until the day after Boxing day on the Wednesday, when the scanning departments would be open again. They soon discovered my birth mother had had a scan with my abnormality at another hospital and would have been due round my time of birth. The police went round to her address but found that she had flown the nest. They found some blood stains in her flat so they presumed I had been born there. The stains were of the same blood group as my mother.'

'Her name was Esther Afolayan. She was a Nigerian who had come to England two years before to work in a bank. They put out a nationwide hunt for her and they even went on television. In the BBC archives I am told there is some film of me at three days old, where I was in the arms of one of the cute looking children's ward nurses. It was seeing that footage, that led to my adopted parents getting in touch with social services about me. They fostered me for a few months before legally adopting me.'

Michael's eyes lit up at the thought that there was old television footage of Emmanuel, lurking round, that he could put in his programme.

Emmanuel continued, 'The police started making enquiries at London airport and finally found out she had flown to Paris a few hours after I was born. From Paris they discovered that she had flown onto Bamako in Mali. There the trail goes cold. African countries, especially years ago, weren't too hot on keeping records.'

'Do you think she still is in Mali?'

'No I have been advised probably not. They have checked my DNA and all my DNA is Nigerian. We presume therefore that my father is Nigerian also. So she would not have any special reason to stay in Bamako. Also Nigeria is a country with an English speaking overlay to the local African languages. Mali is a country with a French speaking overlay to the local languages. As well as that Mali and Nigeria don't have any local languages in common. It is more likely she subsequently returned to Nigeria or possibly another local English speaking country.'

'My knowledge of West African geography is rusty. Which other English speaking countries are we talking of here?'

'The Gambia, Sierra Leone, Liberia, Ghana.'

Michael made a mental note of which countries he should be thinking about selling his television programmes to. He would have a chat with Angie later.

'It sounds like you have been actually looking for her?'

'I love my Mum and Dad and I will always think of them as such but I want to discover my origins. It is a driving force inside me that I have to run with. I was adopted by my parents early on. At the age of eighteen, Social Services allowed me access to my records which is where I found out all the stuff I gave you. There is one last element to the mystery of my birth. The call from the pay phone to the hospital saying where I had been left, would not have been from my birth mother. She apparently would almost certainly spoken English with a distinct accent. The phone operator at the hospital who took that call was quite certain it was a posh British accent. That could, of course, either have been someone of Nigerian heritage born in UK or much more likely a white Brit. Esther did have one friend of note, a white British lady, a student midwife called Emily Sutton. The police interviewed her but she refused to say anything. That led them to think she might have been the one who made the call.'

'Did you ever try to contact Emily Sutton?'

'Of course. However, the records from social services gave an old address and she was not known there when we tried.'

'Did you get any contact address for Esther's family in Nigeria? Surely she would have had to have given one on her visa application for the UK?'

'Yes we got one but there was no reply to the letters we sent them. In the end I forked out the cash to hire a local private detective in Nigeria, with help from the bank of Mum and Dad. He went round to the address but found a totally different family living in the house, who knew nothing. He chanced on a couple of old ladies, sunning themselves outside on a bench in the street. They did remember my mother's family and told him that they moved to an unknown location shortly after I was born. That was apparently because of the media interest in my birth. They also told the detective that my family was ashamed of my mother and of the way she had abandoned me. They had wanted to get away from all the intrusive journalists and cameras.'

'There was other thing that I had not realised before. The President of Nigeria at the time said publicly that my mother was not welcome back home since she had 'disgraced the country'. That makes me think it is even more likely that she moved to somewhere outside of Nigeria.'
'If your mother's family are still in Nigeria, as is likely, then is there no other way they could be tracked down? You must have tried internet searches.'
'Internet searches were no help. They might be looked for in other ways but I was advised that would mean bribing government officials in the capital Abuja to look at tax returns, land ownership records etc. that sort of stuff, without a definite promise of getting what I wanted.
When my Dad heard the advice from the detective, he went ballistic saying, 'No Emmanuel, no bribery. The problem with my native country is bribery and corruption. That is why I left Nigeria. Don't you dare add to the problem, son."
'So that was the end of that idea I take it.'
'Oh yes. I very much respect my Dad's opinions.'
'I notice you call your adoptive parents, 'Mum and Dad."
'Yes because that is what they are to me. When I do talk about my biological parents, which is not often, I tend to refer to them as my bio-mum and my bio-dad for short.'

'Where did you get the name Emmanuel from?'
'Apparently the cute looking nurse, holding me in her arms on the TV footage, named me Emmanuel because I was born on Christmas day. Well you know Emmanuel means 'God with us' and is one of the names of Jesus. When Social services discovered my Mum was Nigerian, they were happy to keep the name because it is an extremely common Nigerian first name. 'So culturally appropriate,' was what the social worker over the case at the time, wrote in my records. My Dad, when he adopted me, was tickled pink that I had the same name as him. So he was very happy not to change it, only give me my surname.'

'By the way how do people distinguish between you and your Dad with you both having the same name?'
'I am generally called Emmy by family and friends while my Dad is known as Dr Emmanuel outside the family. He is called Emmanuel within the family though. So when my mum calls out 'Emmanuel', I know that she is wanting Dad not me. The only person who calls me Emmanuel is my Dad or strangers, who don't know me very well.'

'You say in your profile that you have had a DNA test. Are you registered with one of those 'search for your relatives' DNA databases?'
'Yes I am registered and I have had one hit. She is a third cousin but unfortunately she is too distant a relative to have knowledge of my mother or father. She is a Nigerian living in Lagos. I know nothing about my father. All I know is that my mother was unmarried. The one bit of information that Emily Sutton did divulge to the police at that time is that my bio-mum had no regular boyfriends. So it is possible my existence came about through a casual encounter.'

'You have given me a lot of information. How do you feel about me making some TV programmes about your life with a free wedding and honeymoon thrown in?' Michael looked intently at

Emmanuel – the sixty four thousand dollar question for him.
'I am still thinking about it. Angie is keen. Clearly if we have a wedding and honeymoon paid for, we will have enough money for a house deposit. You know what the prices of houses are like. I just feel uneasy though about exposing all my personal stuff to the world.'

'Where are you planning to live?'
Angie answered this time, 'We want to live in the Nottingham/Derby area – near to my work here. Emmy can commute to London easily when needed but Ricky, your son, has been very good. He said he thinks most of Emmy's work can be done remotely by home working, so he won't need to trek down to London too often.'
'I don't know if I would like to do home working. I like to be in the office seeing, interacting with others,' Michael casually remarked.
Then he went on to ask them, 'When do you want to get married?'
Emmanuel replied this time, 'In about six months time to give us a chance to make all the arrangements. We both want to have a reception with fifty from each side. I have a goodly collection of nephews and nieces as well as aunts, uncles, my football team etc.'
'Are you sure fifty on your side is a big enough number with all that crowd?'
'No probably eighty would be about right from my side alone.'

'How keen would you be to have some of your blood relatives present at your wedding, even possibly your mother?'
'I would very much like it but surely there is no chance of that. I would be thrilled to make my birth family see they have a member they could hopefully be proud of.'

Michael put on his special face that Angie knew he used when he wanted to 'sell' something to someone, some idea or concept that was important to him. He leaned forward and made very direct eye contact with Emmanuel.

'Look Emmanuel I make TV programmes. It is the way I make my living and the living of the others I work with.' In the last remark of his, Michael was making a not very subtle reference to Angie's position in the hope of softening him up.

'But I do want to make programmes that entertain, which is a vital thing in our over busy world. Also I try to create programmes that change people's perceptions for the better. You have an inspiring story, one that will encourage many young Africans living in a continent trying to make a success of itself. I am looking to break into the African TV market and a programme or two about your story would be an excellent way in for me. But, and this is an important 'but' for you. Quite possibly someone from your blood family, or who knows your blood family, might be seeing the programme. They then might come forward and help identify your birth parents. You never know, your birth parents themselves might come forward.'

'What I would do is produce the first programme as soon as possible before your wedding so to try to get your birth family to come forward in time for the big day. What I would do then is film a traditional wedding and a couple of days at our Derbyshire honeymoon hotel and then you could go off on a longer holiday. I would pay for the wedding and a decent reception and honeymoon. I would then make a second programme showing the build up to the wedding and the wedding itself and afterwards.'

Emmanuel began thinking about this. He knew he was being given a bit of a sell and a clever sell at that. He was an intelligent guy but he had met so many different responses to his disability, not many of them very favourable to him. He had faced outright cruelty as well as being patronised and he was uncertain which of the two was the worse to bear with. He knew when he was being used by someone else. Michael, with the best of intentions, was trying to do the same. So he was cautious. He was well aware, without even looking behind him that Angie's eyes was

egging him on to say 'yes'.
'Let me think about it.'
Michael could sense he was not going to get an instant response and that he would be best to back off.
'Okay come back to me when you are ready.'

Later on Emmanuel and Angie were chewing things over privately. Angie spoke her mind as always, 'Emmy I want you to do this for me. To me, the most important thing is that it gives you the chance to complete the circle, to find out who your parents are, who our future kids' grandparents are. We are really unlikely to find out any other way. Yes, we will be able to get a free wedding which will be great help to us getting a house deposit. There is one other thing. I want to advance in my job. I am on my way to becoming Michael's second in command. If we expand into Africa, then there will be an even bigger role for me. I would like one day to set up my own production company and growing in my present job would be massively great experience for me.'

'That is all very well for you but what about me? I was rejected at birth by my mother at least and the likelihood is that I would be rejected again.'
'Why are you being so negative about it? It's our future here we are talking about,' Angie replied a little petulantly.
'At my parents' request, when I was eighteen, I went to speak to social services and they gave me the information I passed on to Michael. They also had a long chat to me about the possible outcomes if ever I were to stumble on my biological parents. My bio-mum may well be married to someone else. She may equally have had children by someone else than my bio-dad. She may never have told her family about me. Remember that Britain is reasonably tolerant with disabled people but in many other places in the world people like me are despised, rejected, regarded as cursed by God.'
'But in that case, if your Mum finds out about you, she won't contact the programme. So you won't know if you have been re-

jected again. What about your Dad?'
'My Dad may not even know that I exist. Remember that quite possibly I was the result of a casual encounter. The fact that my biological parents did not continue on with the relationship implies that one or both of them rejected the other.'

'But doesn't the love of your adoptive parents count and of your older sisters too? Doesn't it count more than the apparent failure of your biological parents?'
'It sort of does but funnily enough it is the family wall at home that always gets inside my skin.'
Angie knew what he was on about, since her parents had the same in their house. Both their houses had a wall in the living room of family photos full of significant stuff starting off with Mum and Dad's wedding. Incidentally both sets of parents since then had clearly gained a few extra pounds weight.
'What of it? You are up on there, aren't you with your sisters. Their wedding photos look great and your Mum has just made a space for our upcoming one. There are the pictures of you all when you were babies.'
'But it still gets me that my sisters had their pictures taken with Mum and Dad immediately after birth. I was obviously older in my photo and the picture was taken when I was adopted.'
'It still really gets to you being adopted. You just don't want more rejection.'
'There is another thing Angie. I wonder if my bio-mum has turned out to be a criminal or an alcoholic or just ruined her life and that I might have some genetic predisposition to be the same. I sometimes lay awake at night worrying. I feel a bit in two minds about wanting to find out about my bio-mum just in case.'
'Emmy what nonsense! You have just been having dark imaginings. I don't see any sign of you being a criminal or ruining your life. Besides from what social services said, your mother had a developing banking career.'

Emmanuel kept on being reluctant though to agree to a programme being made about his life. Angie was not certain she would ever win him over. She knew in the end she had to give way on this one.

'Emmanuel,' she called him using the long formal word for something extra specially important.

'I want to marry you wherever or however we get married. Let's forget about making a television programme. We can get wed in London in your church and pay for ourselves to have a typical Nigerian combined with Jamaican knees up for a reception followed by whatever sort of honeymoon we can afford. We will move to the East Midlands and rent somewhere and save up for a house deposit. You are much more dear to me than any silly TV programme and your happiness is the big, important thing.' She snuggled up to him as she spoke.

Angie felt a big sense of release. The pressure from inside her, wanting to advance her career, the pressure from Michael, who could be quite forceful at times in his desire to make a programme, the money pressure was all gone, all evaporated away. She also sensed that her relationship with Emmanuel had suddenly advanced leaps and bounds.

Emmanuel felt that sense of release too and somehow it made the conversation start up again. In the end though after a very long discussion it came down to money. They were both keen not to rent but to buy a house as soon as possible to start their married life in. They were both anxious to get wed fast so Michael's offer of sorting it all out nicely was irresistible. Emmanuel started to try to take a philosophical view. Probably no one would come forward either because the television programme did not get seen by the right person or possibly a deliberate decision and rejection.

Emmanuel had only one absolute precondition which Angie instantly agreed to.

'Did you hear from Joe about what Michael did with his drones on the day after the wedding of the Chynoweths?'

'Yes, taking pictures of Nicola in her nightie, just as she was opening the curtains the day after her wedding. I know he did delete them but even so.'
'I want nothing like that happening, Angie. Can you absolutely sort it with Michael? No drones round the honeymoon venue!'
'Oh yes Emmy, you can be a hundred percent certain of that.' Angie said laughing.

The next day Angie popped into Michael's office, grabbed the chair next to Pamela the yucca plant, 'He's agreed to do it – to make the television programme'.
'Oh great work Angie, persuading that future husband of yours.'
'Oh no, Emmanuel took the decision himself. He is keen to see what can be done to trace his birth parents.'
'I do think it is a long shot but I do consider it is the best opportunity he's got. I am now going to contact a big Nigerian television company to see if I can sell them the first programme, which we do still have to fully make. I would like you to contact the other four West African countries.'
A few days later Angie wandered into Michael's office.
'How's it doing with the other countries?' he asked.
'The main TV stations in Ghana Liberia and Sierra Leone all claimed they were interested but they all without exception wanted a price reduction. However even when I went down to the minimum selling price you had set me, they made it plain though they wanted to see what the reaction was from the Nigerian audience. Specifically they wanted to know viewing figures, before they came to a final decision. Gambia television said straight out to me that they did not think that sort of programme with a big traditional churchy wedding would appeal to their audience. I suppose that is logical given they are a heavily Muslim majority nation.'
'That is going to make finding Emmanuel's parents with my programmes even more of a long shot.' Mike said reflectively.
'Agreed.'
'I did manage to sell the programme to Nigerian television and

also I have got something else in the bag television wise. Let me tell you about it, Angie.'

CHAPTER 29-THE PAST REAWAKENED

She flopped down exhausted, sinking into the very comfortable soft armchair. The light of the sun was starting to fade. She had just spent two hours of the warm summer evening, working on her vegetable and flower patch in the plot of land with the amazing name of the Jawbones allotments. She had weeded round her broccoli and replaced the fine netting, put over them to protect them from the cabbage white butterflies. These beautiful creatures loved to lay their eggs on the broccoli leaves. They would turn to larvae who would then munch away at the tasty green food source available.

She was thirsty, but a bit too tired to raise herself up again and get a drink. Besides she was still entranced by the view from her living room, even after five years living in the house. She lived on the south side of a very large steep valley. Her house and garden were located far up the hill on the edge of the town, which crept upwards towards the top of the valley where it met countryside and cows. There was a very broad river at the bottom of the valley, full mainly of small boats. If she turned her head to her left, she could see the Naval College, the one which Prince Philip and Prince Charles had attended. If she looked the other way to her right, there could be seen the small castle and the exit out of the river into the sea of Start Bay and the English channel.

Finally, thirst got the better of her and she slowly, achingly, got out of her armchair. She went to the kitchen fridge and poured herself a drink of cool refreshing cider – the emblematic drink of the West country. She started to pull bits of leaves, twigs and weeds out of her long wavy brown hair, now streaked with many a grey strand. With her length of hair, it was practically impossible to keep it free from the soil and plants when bending down to weed. She sat down again in the armchair and turned towards the large TV screen. Her property developer husband Ralph, was away that evening at a council planning meeting in Totnes, something to do with two bungalows he was wanting to build in Bigbury on Sea.

She idly pressed the remote control of the television, just looking for something light to watch and unwind with. There it was, this chat show. A thinnish, intense, middle aged man called Michael was being interviewed about some programme or other he was making. He had straight black hair with some shades of grey, a very thick pair of spectacles and a neatly trimmed moustache and beard. He was apparently making this film about a disabled adult. She was only half listening and then she heard the word 'Emmanuel'. At that she sat up and took notice. She listened on and yes it was definitely 'her' Emmanuel. Then she heard her very own name, Emily, being mentioned. That really set her mind in a whirl. She needed to know what this programme was all about. She glanced at the television and saw there was an option to view the whole thing from the beginning. So she started to watch the whole of the programme.

Michael Cohen was being interviewed by Mark Berry, one of the big Friday night talk show hosts.
'So Michael, what are you up to these days?'
'We have a new reality television programme coming out next week and this one is about an amazing young man called Emmanuel.'
'Tell us more.'
'Emmanuel is a foundling, now aged twenty seven who is a remarkable young man who has overcome obstacles from his disability.....

'He is now engaged to my production assistant on the show.'
'Sounds intriguing. Foundling....that word has echoes of old London and babies wrapped up in swaddling clothes left out in the snow on a cold night by some hospital.'
'Well it certainly was cold the night he was born, with below freezing temperatures..... Emmanuel was left on Christmas day in the corridor of the North London hospital in a wicker basket wrapped in a shawl with some toys. His Nigerian mother Esther Afolayan....'
'We know that Esther had a good British friend, Emily.....'
'One reason we are making the programme before Angie and Emmanuel get married is this: They would love to find Emmanuel's birth parents and then invite them to the wedding. One or both of them would be very welcome,'
'If Esther or Emily are watching this programme, they could contact me at Cohen Cinematography...... That would be wonderful....'
'And Mike, just remind me when your programme is on?'
'It is being shown on BBC1 at 10pm this Sunday evening...'

Her mind was working furiously. What to do? She had just had a letter from.... abroad. Normally she would reply to it in two or three days. Was this time to close the circle and bring lives to completion?
It was now dark and the moon was shining on the river Dart below in the valley and she could see the lights of the centre of the town of Dartmouth below her.
At that moment, Ralph came breezing back through the front door from the planning meeting. She gave him a kiss and asked, 'How did it go, my love?'
'We got full planning permission,' he said with triumph.
'Sit down a minute as I have got some news.'
Emily sat him down and told him about the chat show.
'What do you think I should do, darling? Esther is one of my oldest and best friends.'
'Is she wanting to be discovered now? Surely she wants to move

on. It was so many years ago.'
'No. I forgot to tell you and we have not really had much chance to chat this week, but a letter arrived from her the day before yesterday. She is now really wanting to find Emmanuel and probably try to get in contact with him.'
'So this programme may have come as serendipity – at just the right moment. Umm......I think you should send an email to Esther saying what you have seen tonight and telling her you will watch the documentary on Sunday night. That way she has some warning before Sunday night. She can start to think about what she would like to do, if anything at all. You can send her another email after Sunday night when you have watched the programme.'

'As I said, she has been thinking a lot about Emmanuel and she even mentioned to me in this last letter about hiring a private detective to find Emmanuel. But this way would save all that.'
'It could also mean that your role in it all is exposed too. Apart from Esther, I am the only other person who knows what you did those many years ago.'
'Could that be risky to me if my role in it all comes out in public? After all I am sure I probably did something illegal – not that that has worried me much over the years. Surely the police would not be interested in something that happened years ago.'
'I don't know. Yes, it did all happen twenty seven years ago but ..... What you could do is speak to that brother in law of mine.'
Emily pulled a face at that.
'I know he is not your favourite brother in law but he is family, when all is said and done.'

Hugh Pratt was married to Charlotte, Ralph's younger sister. He was the latest member of his family to join the firm of solicitors of Pratt, Pratt, Whitney and Pratt in Exeter. As Emily always joked, he was the latest 'pratt' in the firm. He was posh, rather hoity toity and not particularly friendly but he was a solicitor specializing in children's and young people's law. So if anyone

should know, he would be aware of how Emily stood legally.
'Okay, I will speak to him on Monday morning after the programme.'

Sunday evening came and Emily listened carefully to the television, making copious notes. She then sent off a detailed email to Esther. She was rather hoping that Hugh might say to her that she was at risk of being charged with a criminal offence if she came forward. That would give her the perfect excuse not to get further involved. She could then leave it up to Esther to contact Michael Cohen directly.

Emily rang the law firm's office first thing Monday morning.
'Unfortunately, Mr. Pratt Junior is in crown court all today but he will probably ring into the office at lunchtime to check in. You may be assured that I will pass the message on, as soon as possible,' came the friendly reply back.
At 1.45 that afternoon Emily got the call on her mobile. She was nervous and had been anxiously awaiting it all morning.
'Good afternoon Emily. Forgive me but I have had such a busy morning in court. The social workers were such a bore. How can I help you?' his voice dripped lawyerly disdain, condescension and a touch of boredom.
'I have got a bit of a legal conundrum. If I tell you the details, would you agree to keep it to yourself?'
'Of course. Lawyer client confidentiality,' His voice drawled out the words in a posh accent.

Emily did not totally believe him. She could imagine him and Charlotte discussing and dissecting her over supper, as they ate off their Royal Worcester porcelain plates and drank their crystal goblets of Chateauneuf de Pape, some posh French plonk. They were definitely that sort of couple. She decided to risk it and plunged into describing her role in detail of Emmanuel's birth and abandonment.

He listened carefully to Emily's lengthy account saying, 'Really' in his posh voice from time to time.

Emily was quite sure inside herself that he was thinking, 'I'm now related to a criminal. What a come down!'.

She wondered if she and Ralph would be seeing much less of Hugh and Charlotte in the future.

He finally posed the question, 'And what makes you think your particular criminal offence is important to engage the attention of the police at a time when they are overwhelmed with work, fighting terrorism and drug trafficking?'

It was the tone of contempt in his voice that drove Emily to want to scream and shout back at him. She bit her tongue and mustering all her self control, replied, '*That* is surely up to you to tell me.'

At the end though, to give the guy his due, Hugh did give a firm legal opinion.

'As I see it Emily, yes, you did commit a criminal offence, aiding and abetting the crime of abandoning a baby, but it is clear that you were an unwilling accomplice enticed on by the mother of the baby. In fairness to the pair of you, you made every effort to ensure that the baby was found rapidly. You cared for the baby well before abandoning him. It all happened twenty seven years ago and I very much doubt the police would be particularly interested, especially with their present work load difficulties. The only problem I could foresee is if ever you wanted to take up midwifery again. The incident might be regarded as a safeguarding issue but I gather you have definitely retired from that line of work. So, in summary, don't worry.'

He gave a reassuring smile down the phone which Emily could not see, but his tone of voice could be heard, calming her fears. Emily thanked him and thought in the end that Hugh was not so bad an old stick after all. At least he had not sat on the fence. But it did mean she did not have a good legal reason not to get involved.

Then her phone pinged. It was a long email from Esther, full of detailed instructions to her. Hugh's phrase, 'an unwilling accomplice enticed on by the mother of the baby' came to mind again, as once more, Esther was insisting on getting her involved. Once more she was assuming correctly that Emily would do it. Emily wondered why Esther could not just go directly but she saw her point. She hummed and hawed. It was difficult to refuse one of her oldest and closest friends. But even if there were no legal problems for her, would it have a negative impact on her estate agent business? How would it all look in the public eye if it came out she had helped a woman abandon her deformed baby?

In the end she decided she had to risk it. Ralph, funnily enough, when she asked him, took the viewpoint that the publicity might actually help the business.

CHAPTER 30 - THE CONTACT

On Tuesday morning at nine o'clock while her river front office in the centre of Dartmouth was quiet, Emily went into the back kitchen. She fished out her mobile with its blingy sparkly back cover and looked up on line the phone number of Cohen Cinematography. She dialled the landline, having made certain her mobile number was put as private. At least that way she could not be traced. She got through to the receptionist and said she had information about the whereabouts of Emmanuel's mum. She added in that she also knew the first name of his Dad.

This was the fifth call since the Sunday evening programme from people claiming to have significant information about Esther and Emmanuel. All the previous four ones had turned out to be hoaxes. But, the reception had strict instructions to put all such calls through to Angie. She had her own way of sorting out the real ones from the fakes.

She had her own little test to separate the truthful from the liars. But first she asked a general question to Emily, 'How can I believe your story?'
'I am going to give you a few details that you did not say in your TV programme which were also not revealed at the time of Emmanuel's birth. Firstly, the baby had a dimple just above the stump of the left arm, unless of course it has since been surgically removed.'
Angie had seen that dimple so many times before on Emmanuel's arm that she was taken aback.

'Secondly, he did not have a teddy with him, as your Sunday night programme seemed to imply but two toys – a small cuddly soft elephant, grey and pink and a stuffed giraffe.'

Thirdly, the wicker basket was painted red – an unusual colour for a wicker basket and that detail was not revealed, either at the time of Emmanuel's birth or in your Sunday programme.

Angie sat up at all that. She did not need to give the little test she had devised.

'You have my full attention. Who exactly are you?' she asked with a questioning tone.

'I was Emily Sutton, but at this stage I am not going to give you my current name. I heard your blurb on Emmanuel on the programme. But tell me about what he is really like.'

Angie thought dreamily for a moment and slowly shot back.

'He is very tall.... very handsome.... pretty tall at six foot five inches. A real gentleman... extremely kind, very gentle, softly spoken. He is a real catch. The girls who turned him down in the past are fools, utter idiots. His family adore him rightly so. But he is ... incomplete. He wants to close the circle. He wants to find out about his biological family. I want him to be complete. I... love him so much.'

'You introduced yourself on the phone to me as, 'Angela Smith'. Are you Angie his fiancee?'

'I am.'

'You sound a little less posh than you do on the television,' Emily said laughingly.

'Well I suppose I am not quite so posh in real life.'

'How did the two of you meet?'

They got talking and talking and Emily warmed to Angie.

'Angie, I cannot give you all the information you want but I can give you some. Firstly, Esther is alive and well, living in West Africa and is a successful businesswoman.'

Angie's heart leapt at that. Emmanuel had started to wonder if his bio-mum, as he called her, might be dead. At least he would know that there was a possibly of contacting her. Also, his fears came to Angie's memory that she would turn out to have wrecked her life or even been a criminal. Being a successful businesswoman did not sound as though she had ruined her life.

'Don't try to trace her as her name has changed. She has six other kids by her husband but has just recently been widowed after twenty five years of marriage.'
Angie assumed the name change was because Esther was married. She only found out later how wrong she was. Emmanuel would be thrilled to know that he had half brothers and sisters. Family always had been a big thing to him.
'Secondly, Esther's mind in recent years has been turning to her other son, that is, Emmanuel. I think she may be ready to be in touch with him directly. I do though, need to discuss things with her and I cannot promise a hundred percent that she will finally say 'yes'. So he should not get his hopes up. You say he has had to struggle with rejection. He may face that again from his biological mother, which I should imagine, is very difficult to deal with.'
'I try to put myself in his boots but it's not easy since my Mum and Dad have been round together for all of my life.'
'Same for me. Mum and Dad were together, until they both died.'
'Are you by any chance in contact with his father?'
'No, neither is Esther.'
'Do you know anything about him?'
'His name was Goodluck and he was Nigerian and I don't know if he is dead or alive. He only met her once at a party, but of course once was enough as it were. She never saw him again, He never told her what he did but she thinks he was part of a diplomatic mission to London at the time she met him. Actually, she did see him again but not in the flesh.'
'What do you mean?' Angie asked quizzically.
'She was about eight months gone in her pregnancy and we were watching the television news together one day. The Nigerian foreign minister was making an important speech at the UN in New York about South Africa and he was surrounded by a

group of his officials. Esther got up from her chair and excitedly pointed out one man in the group on the screen, 'That's him. I am quite sure that is him.' I looked closely and could see that he was very tall and handsome. Now I have seen Emmanuel on television, I can see where he gets his good looks from. Did I hear you mention that Emmanuel is very good at football?'
'Yes, he plays centre forward in an amateur team.'
'Well when Esther saw the TV, one of her theories about Goodluck's profession bit the dust.'
'Why's that?'
'Esther had been convinced that Goodluck, because he had strong muscular legs, must be a professional footballer until she saw the clip of him at the UN.'
'Do you happen to know which television news channel you were watching at the time?'
'I'm sorry I cannot remember. It could have been one of the BBC or ITV channels or even Sky news or CNN.'

Angie was a bit disappointed by this. If she knew what channel had broadcast the news, she could try to contact them. Getting in touch with all the television companies and trying to access their archives would take a lot longer. It was not like Nigerian foreign ministers appeared every day on British Television. If they could access the archived footage, they could surely get a photo of Goodluck. That might be a start to identifying and contacting him.

Angie was soaking this in ready to relay it all to Emmanuel and to Michael. They would be both equally excited but in different ways. In the end Emily said she would try and ring back in a week's time, with maybe some more news from Esther.

CHAPTER 31 - EMILY CENTRE STAGE

It was Angie who had talked her into this.

'Look Emily, you have a real story to tell and it brings a new dimension to the events round Emmanuel's birth. I think people will feel a lot more sympathetic to Esther, when hearing your account. I don't think it will harm you and your husband's business.'

'Are you sure Angie?' Emily had asked nervously.

'As sure as I can be of anything,' replied Angie reassuringly.

Emily and Angie had had a long call the previous evening trying to arrange something special for the next day. This was hopefully going to be a surprise for Emmanuel.

Emily had ended the call saying, 'Angie, you promise not to say anything to Emmanuel in case I cannot pull it off.'

Angie said 'Of course. You can rely on me.'

Emily was quite nervous as she sat with Michael as the host together with Emmanuel and Angie. Her nerves had not been helped by the last call she had had with Esther.

'So, you know what to do, Emily?'

'Yes I am not to give your new name in the interview or even hint at which country you are now in.'

'And what else?'

'I am not to say what your business is.'

'And there is one other thing. I think I'm finally ready to speak to Emmanuel, but I would want you round in case it got awkward. So I need you to do one important thing for me before I say yes.

I want you to suss him out. How would he be, if he gets to speak to me? Will he get angry with me for abandoning him or over-emotional? I need your help, your insight. I definitely don't want that Michael Cohen in on the meeting.'

'If I have got Emmanuel, Angie and Michael all together in the same house, how do I get rid of Michael?'

'I leave that to you to sort.'

Somehow Emily was not comforted by that. She was worried that Esther would be resentful if she got things wrong.

In addition to the pressure from Esther, it was the first time that Emily had ever been on film or television except for amateur home videos, as made by family and friends. Though she tried hard to cover it up, she had jelly wobbles in her tummy. Her living room was spacious open plan. It had a magnificent view out onto the river Dart through floor to ceiling glazed window that stretched along the length of the room. The morning sun gleamed on the river. It had been quite a kerfuffle, getting all the film equipment into the house. The narrow old streets of Dartmouth were difficult for the large transit van to manoeuvre round, with its ornamentally calligraphed sign of 'Cohen Cinematography' on the side. Of course there was very little parking round the town. So they had had to drop everything off at Emily's house and then go and park the van in the park and ride car park at the top of town.

The only other two people in the room with Emily were the cameraman Joe and the sound man or rather sound woman, a rather intense young Polish lady called Irene. Michael had had the camera running all the time from the start of the meeting. He could see that Emily was on edge. So he began talking about her beautiful house and the view of river and how long she had been in it – some fairly neutral subjects to start with which he would probably not use in the video. It was one of his standard techniques he used with nervous interviewees. He could see Emily visibly relaxing with the warm-up questions.

Then started the more formal part of the interview which was done with her, Angie and Emmanuel together and Michael as the question master. He wanted to see how Emmanuel coped with the answers.
'So, tell me Emily, how you met up with Esther?'
'We met up regularly in a writers' club that had fortnightly gatherings. Esther was working for a firm in the city of London that traded a lot with Nigeria and I was a student midwife. We are of similar age and were both keen on writing poems and short stories as a form of relaxation from work. She liked writing as a way of improving her written English, not that it needed much improvement, but she always was a perfectionist. We became friends and went out for a drink regularly, with one or two others from the group.'

'Tell us when you found out Emmanuel's father.'
'I remember the day she told me about your father. We were meeting the Tuesday after Easter. She told me excitedly that she had met this wonderful man called Goodluck, your father, at a party on Easter Saturday and she had given him her phone number. She waited and waited and waited for a phone call from him which sadly never, never came.

Then I noted that she seemed to be getting a bit fatter and she was wearing loose fitting clothes and I began to wonder. Then I was sure she was pregnant but I did not any have the opportunity to ask her privately. Then one day after a writers' group meeting she broke down in tears and told me what had happened. By that time she was well over thirty weeks. I took her to the clinic and she had a scan showing the problem with your left arm. She kept on saying to me that she was the wrong mother for you, Emmanuel, and that she wanted you to be adopted by a good family. I tried to reason with her and say that yes, it was not ideal being a single mum but it was still possible.'

'Can you tell me about his birth?'

'Then came the call Christmas day evening from her flat. When I arrived there, you were literally about to be born,' said Emily looking at Emmanuel. He was intensely interested. Angie had recounted him all the details that Emily had given her, but it was something quite different hearing it first-hand.

'So, since I had already had some practical midwifery training, I delivered you. You were the first baby I had ever helped into the world on my own and the most special one ever,' Emily smiled at that.

'I wanted to call an ambulance to get you and Esther seen in hospital to be checked out but she absolutely refused. She was fine with very little bleeding. You were obviously in equally fine fettle with a good set of lungs, in fact too good a set of lungs.' Emily and Emmanuel laughed at that.

'We were really worried that the neighbours would hear you bawling and get suspicious. Esther was adamant she did not want everyone to know what had happened. She just wanted anonymity – to quietly go back to Nigeria without a fuss. So her plan was to leave you in a safe place, hoping you would be adopted by a good family and then for her to fly away. I booked a flight to Paris for her as she wanted to go to her cousin there for a rest. From there she planned to fly back to Nigeria. I then helped her empty her flat.' Emily paused.

'We then drove to the hospital where I worked. I knew a side entrance that was open at night without being monitored much. I had already picked up the wicker basket dyed red from my house to put you in after you were born. I had expected to be using it in the hospital. We laid you down in the basket ever so gently, well wrapped up with the toys at each side. Esther put the envelope in, the one you know about already. She shed a tear or two then we walked away fast, back through the door. We got into the car and then ...' Emily changed voice and put on an aristocratic voice for the next sentence.

'I drove five minutes and stopped at a phone box, did my aristo voice and rang the hospital switchboard. They wanted to keep me on the phone but I would not let them, just repeating the message twice. I then put the phone down and off we went. I dropped her off at Heathrow, not expecting ever to see her or hear from her again. There was the publicity about your birth that you know about and I was interviewed by the police but told them very little. Then three months later I got a letter from her and it was not from Nigeria. Since that we have corresponded regularly, then about three years ago something changed...'

'What changed?' asked Emmanuel eagerly.
'I saw her for the first time for well over twenty years.'
'Do you mean you saw her face to face?'
'No, I got all modern and technological, as it were, and we started doing video calls.'
'When was the last time you saw her?'
'We spoke last night.'
Emmanuel took this in.
'Does this mean that you could ring her now and put me through to her? What stops you doing that now?'

Emily could see the eagerness on his face and the sadness and the longing. She looked at Angie who was in on the secret.
Angie stepped in and gently put her hand on Emmanuel's right forearm and said, 'Darling let's leave that be for the moment and focus on finding out more about your birth.'
Emmanuel sensed it was time to keep quiet.

Michael saw an opportunity and plunged in, stopping the camera. 'So Emily, you could just ring up and see Esther now?'
Emily said, 'Yes, that is technically correct, but Esther has made it thoroughly plain to me she will only go further in her own good time.'
Michael replied, 'When she is ready, can you tell me?'
The eagerness too in his voice was palpable. He had never filmed the first meeting between an adult adopted child and birth mother and he was so obviously dying to do so. Emily had

already been prewarned by Angie that Michael could be quite pushy. That was the other reason why she was nervous. She decided it was best to say nothing at all to that last question of his. The meeting carried on and the filming continued.

Finally, about twelve midday, the filming was finished and Michael and his team packed up and left. The large transit van started to slowly make its way downhill. Emmanuel got up to leave too but Angie stopped him. Emily said with a beam, 'Would you like to stay for lunch?'
Emmanuel said, looking at Angie, 'That would be lovely.'
Emily got the food ready – tomatoes, lettuce, cucumbers and beetroot all from her allotment, with home made bread followed by strawberries, again from the allotment, with Devon clotted cream. They sat down to eat at the table at the back of the living room. Angie and Emmanuel both noted silently that Emily had deliberately taken a lot of care, preparing the lunch with homemade and home-grown food. She could have so easily spent five minutes and grabbed some stuff from the supermarket shelves instead.

'The butter on the bread and the clotted cream come from a local farm shop,' Emily said smilingly.
Clearly the lunch was important to Emily and both Angie and Emmanuel sensed a strong desire on Emily's part to help them.
Emily looked at them straight in the face and said, 'Emmanuel please, tell me how life has really been for you, both good and bad. It's important for me and for Esther to know and also for you.'
Angie understood the slightly cryptic comment and looked at Emmanuel, 'Please Emmy.' That was her pet name for Emmanuel.

So Emmanuel launched in. He told of the wonders of being bought up in the Adebayo family and the love and support he had had from his adopted family, not just Mum and Dad but his three older sisters.

'My sisters are lovely people and they are forever inviting me for meals and they ring me up all the time. They are as bad as Mum. As soon as I told them I was going out with Angie, they wanted to meet her, to give her the once over.....'

'I have done well in my job and I love doing computer coding. I hope one day I might set up my own company. I love singing and I am good enough to be helping doing a big Christmas performance in the Albert Hall. I love football too and am centre forward for a large amateur team.'

'I could not be goalkeeper though,' he said jokingly.

'Why not goalkeeper?' asked Emily puzzled.

She was not a sporty lady then she suddenly realised why not and blushed a deep beetroot red, 'Oh I'm sorry. Stupid me.'

Emmanuel laughed and said 'Don't worry.'

Emily talked on, 'You have talked about the good things in life – which I like but tell me about the down side of your life.'

'There was all the bullying at school about my disability, tinged with more than a touch of frank racism. That drove me as a teenager to think that life was not worth living. But it was my Christian faith that kept me going. If I was good enough for God to interest himself in me, then I was good enough for anyone to get to know. However, the bullying has even continued into adult life but less so. Even a few months ago it happened in church.'

'In church?' Emily interjected, surprised.

'I was the lead singer at the church's Pentecost production. I was singing a new song solo in the choir rehearsal and unusually for me I hit two or three bad notes. I heard some giggling behind me and two of the teenage girls in the choir were making gestures with their left hands pretending they were limp. I was shocked, nearly tearful and I almost felt like hitting them. Blessing, the Pastor's wife, came to the rescue and went over and roundly told them off.'

'Tell me how you and Angie got together.'

Emmanuel told the whole story. Emily showed the shock on his face, when she heard about his rejection from the programme because of the charity trustees. That was new information to her, which Angie had not shared with her. She brightened up when she heard the story of how he and Angie had fallen for each other.

'Amazing isn't it that an event that looked pretty awful for you turned out to be one of the best things that could ever happen to you. How do you feel about it, Emmanuel?'

'I felt pretty awful at first and I still feel a bit sore of the way I was rejected, but I can certainly see how all things work together for good.'

After an hour or so chatting Emily said, 'I just need to make an important phone call. I'll be back soon.'

Emmanuel still did not suspect what might be happening. She came back in less five minutes and announced calmly, 'I have just spoken to Esther and she is very happy to take a video call from us now, if you would like to.'

Suddenly, Emmanuel felt like he had been hit in the pit of his stomach with flutterings galore. So this was it – the chance to see his biological mum for the first time ever, but it was not face to face. It would be a more awkward video call. He was not a big fan of video calls, especially for more difficult conversations, but he knew he just had to take this one on.

Emily brought out her laptop, because it had got a bigger screen than a mobile and started making the clicks necessary. She was waiting to be let in by Esther. Finally Esther let her in.

Emily waved at her, 'Hi Esther, I've got Emmanuel and Angie here. Shall I hand you over to them?'

'Yes please.'

Emily handed over the laptop to Emmanuel and Angie who were sitting on the sofa next to her.

Emmanuel and Esther looked at each other via the screen and did not know what to say. They looked and looked at each other, searching for the physical resemblances.

Then Angie dived in, 'Hi Esther, I'm Angie, Emmy's fiancee. How are you?'

Emily decided it would be an appropriate moment to tactfully disappear into the kitchen, to do the washing up from lunch. She would listen in though from a distance, according to Esther's instructions and if the conversation got too fraught, intervene.

'Hi Angie, Hi Emmanuel, I am doing okay,'

'What's the weather like where you are at?'

'Here on the Gambian coast, it is nice and warm but not so hot as inland. Is it raining in England at present? When I lived in London it always seemed to be bucketing down.'

So that is where Esther had landed up in – the Gambia on the coast of West Africa. The weather theme seemed to be a good one to start off a very awkward conversation.

Emmanuel decided he needed to say something.

'No it is not raining at present. It's quite sunny and the temperature has gone up to 20C today.'

The conversation stopped and no one knew quite what to say next. Angie decided to plunge in to help.

'So Esther, why don't you tell us a bit about yourself and we'll tell us about us if you like.'

'Well I changed my name to Mariamma Ceesay, years ago – much more Gambian sounding. I run an export/import business in Banjul the capital of the Gambia. I'm a widow, aged fifty-three. My husband died two years ago. We have six kids – the oldest is twenty four and my youngest is twelve, so I am pretty busy.' She went on to describe her family life.

'Wow six kids seems a lot,' Angie spoke. 'Emmy and I are only planning two when we get married.'

'A lot cheaper,' Esther laughed.

She went on, 'So, tell me about yourselves. I have heard loads from Emily about you but I would like to hear first-hand.'

So on they talked most descriptive stuff without dealing with much emotional content. Both Emmanuel and Esther were skating over the difficult issues. Both wondered when the other would take the plunge. In the end it was Emmanuel who took the plunge. He looked intently even slightly fiercely, getting closer to the laptop screen.

'I must ask you. I am wanting to know. Why did you abandon me? Why did you not let me be adopted normally, giving me up openly?'

Esther had known that some such question might be coming at some time. She felt a love for this long distant son of her.

She spoke with tenderness and gentleness to him, 'Emmanuel, I was single. living in a strange country, with no partner. I knew that I could not make it alone in the UK, with a baby. I was also aware that if I returned to Nigeria with a baby and a baby with an abnormality at that, I would not be accepted by my family. I did not want all the prying and questioning in a London hospital of doctors, nurses, social workers and the possibility that the information might leak out. When I was in labour, I knew that, with Emily's help, I could safely leave you in a secure place which is what I did.'

Emmanuel did not know what to say to that. He still felt sore inside but did not know quite how to express what was going on in his heart. The talk turned to the wedding of Angie and Emmanuel. They had agreed beforehand that Emmanuel would ask Esther to the wedding. In the end it came straight out from his mouth, directed towards Esther. He did not know how else to say it at the moment.

'Angie and I would very much like you to come to our wedding.'

Esther looked confused at that. It was unexpected, so direct and so early in their renewed relationship. She had already known from Emily, that one big reason for Emmanuel looking her out, was to have her at his wedding.

'Could I think about that? I feel most honoured, but what will your adopted parents think about it? I must think. It is possibly a step too far at present.'

Emmanuel was crestfallen. His face showed it all. He felt rejected again.

The video call ended shortly after with a time arranged for another video call in a week's time. Emmanuel was left with a mixture of emotions and thoughts.

However, just before they left Emily's, Emmanuel whispered something to Angie. He then spoke up,

'Emily, thank you so much for inviting us and for everything, not least for the lovely lunch. My future wife and I wondered if you and your husband would be able to come to our wedding as our honoured guests?'

Emily's face beamed her delighted approval. This would be a very special wedding for her.

Angie said, 'We'll send you a 'Save the date'.'

Angie thought it so typical of Emmanuel that he would want to do the kind and gentlemanly thing, even when he had so much on his plate.

Angie and Emmanuel were talking it over later in the car driving back to the East Midlands on the long trek up the motorway.

Angie summed it up, 'I feel that you, and presumably Esther as well, are rather like ponds now, with a lot of sediment of things at the bottom from the past, which have been stirred up by the video call. The pond is now dirty and you both need to allow time for the sediment to settle again and then be able to see clearly where you go.'

Emmanuel thought it a rather apt metaphor to describe his present state of mind.

CHAPTER 32 SEEK OUT FATHER

Things had moved on and Esther was now in regular contact with Emmanuel and Angie, but she also had started to deal with Michael. She had finally agreed to help find Emmanuel's father.
'So do you remember which channel showed the news item of the Nigerian foreign minister, in New York, at the UN surrounded by a group of officials?' Michael asked her.
He knew the rough date late November, early December of the year of Emmanuel's birth.
'I don't remember the name of the news channel, but I do remember it was the one with the newsreader, that guy from Trinidad called Trevor and a funny Scottish sounding name 'Mc' something or other.'
Michael said a mental hallelujah and said, 'Trevor McDonald from ITV news'
'Sounds right Michael,' said Esther.
Michael thought, 'There cannot be many television items about the Nigerian foreign minister in New York at the UN surrounded by a group of officials within the date range.'

Michael of course had his contacts. It was fairly easy to manage to track down in the ITV archives, the video of the news item showing the Nigerian foreign minister in New York at the UN, surrounded by a group of officials which consisted of four people. There was one woman, leaving three men as possible Goodlucks. Two of the men appeared far too old to be the ones and also a bit ugly. That left a young, very good looking, very tall man who funnily enough bore a very strong resemblance to the adult Emmanuel.

Michael showed Esther the video, 'What do you think?'
'The two older guys I would never have gone for, even when drunk - too old and ugly,' she said with a smile.
'I know that I was drunk at the time and it *was* twenty eight years ago, but I think that is probably him,' pointing to the young man.
Michael also remembered Emily saying that at the time, Esther had been quite definite that she had seen Emmanuel's father in the video.
'Okay, let's go with it.'

Michael wondered the best way of trying to find out who it might be. He did not really have the contacts in Nigeria to know who best to ask. He got started off by ringing the Nigerian High Commission in London. He spoke to a pleasant young man, who was an Assistant Cultural Attache, without giving him the exact reason why.
'It's just that I am doing a film about a disabled British Nigerian and we believe that the picture is of a relative of his,' was all he said.
'Can you give me more details?'
'We are still in the early stages of doing the film but we think he is some sort of relative. We though, are not certain of all the details which is why I could do with your help trying to identify him.'
'Okay, you can email me the picture and I will look at it.' So Michael sent off a cropped picture from the video of Goodluck alone.
Then nothing happened. Finally, after waiting a week for his reply, Michael phoned the nice young man.
'Hi. How are you getting on with the picture?'
The young man's voice suddenly became very cagey, 'I don't think I can help you any more.'

'Why is that?'
'I just don't think I can help you.'
'Do you know anyone else who could help?'
'No. I don't know anything.'

Then the phone went dead. Michael had just been hung up on. Somebody had something to hide. He knew that in today's connected world, anyone could just google him. They would quickly discover that he had not merely a reputation as a film maker but as an investigative journalist. That phone call has just confirmed for him, something that he had been starting to suspect. Given that the video of Goodluck showed a junior diplomat, umpteen years ago, he could very likely be someone in the present day, high up in the current business or political or diplomatic world of Nigeria.

He pondered his next move. Then he remembered who might, if anyone, be able to help. The name of Patrick Peyton floated to Michael's consciousness. He was a South African journalist who he had worked with in the past on a film item, to do with changes in the water supply to Cape town. He was now based in London and specialised in reporting on African affairs as a freelance. He had published loads of articles for the likes of 'The Economist' and 'The Financial Times' and similar high brow, quality, political and economic newspapers and magazines. He was respected, knowledgeable and helpful. Time for a business lunch which could be tax deductible. Michael's only slight niggle was that if Goodluck did turn out to be someone important, then Patrick might want to follow things up to get a story. He might not also tell Michael he was chasing it up. Michael would only find out, when Patrick had published an article with information which might not necessarily be to his taste. But that was a risk that had to be taken.

Michael's guest turned up five minutes late, stroking his trademark bushy moustache. Patrick knew that Michael was chatting him up for a purpose. He did not mind too much. Hopefully there might be a story in it for him too. The two of them sat down in the posh, discrete, spacious, West End hotel bar, with its plush leather armchairs and pictures of Victorian hunting scenes on the wall with its wooden panels. Together they ordered lunch from the agreeable, extensive bar menu. There were very few people there and soothing gentle background music was playing – ideal for a quiet private meeting.

The wine came before the food – a full glass of house red wine that Michael ordered for Patrick and a fizzy water for him.
Patrick kicked off the conversation, 'You are not exactly being subtle, Mike, giving me a very large glass of my favourite red while you have meager fare of sparkling water. I presume this little jolly is tax deductible.'
'Oh yes it is.'
'You could have something stronger you know. It won't do you any harm.'
Mike ignored that comment deliberately. He wanted to keep a clear head, as he started the difficult game of getting information out of Patrick without revealing too much.

'I want you to help identify someone for me.' He showed Patrick a still photo on his phone of Goodluck. Unlike the photo shown the Nigerian High Commission official it included the other people in the picture from the video.
'Who is this?'
'I don't know who it is, which is why I am asking for your help, from your extensive knowledge of African affairs.'
'Can you give me more of a clue to help?'
'Yes certainly. The photo was taken about nearly thirty years ago and is of a junior Nigerian diplomat present at the UN, together with the Nigerian Foreign Minister of the time, who had just been giving an important speech about South Africa which of course was one of the hot topics of the time.'
'Do we know if the guy was permanently based at the UN or merely visiting New York?'

'Not certain about that.'
'Do we know a name of any kind?'
'We don't for certain, but possibly his first name might be Goodluck. That could though be totally off beam.'
Michael had not discounted the possibility that the drunk Diplomat had not been so drunk as to want to cover his tracks with Esther.
'A typical common Nigerian first name,' commented Patrick.
He thought on for a minute, 'I presume you are wondering whether the young man in the photo has now become a big enough fish in the sea to have been picked up by a specialist journalist of the likes of me.'
'That is correct.'
Patrick knew that Michael liked to delve into unusual topics. They had worked on a story on the impact of tourism on the Masai in Kenya five years before, as well as the story on the Cape town. water supply.
'Will there be a story in there for me?'
'There might be but I can make no promises.'

Patrick thought for a minute, muttering to himself through his prominent moustache, 'Goodluck, Goodluck...excuse me Mike while I just do like the youngsters do, and play with my phone endlessly for hours, ignoring the world and people round me.'
Michael laughed and said 'Go ahead!'
Patrick had an intent look on his face as he flicked with his finger through phone screen after phone screen and typed away.
After five minutes, he suddenly said with a slight shout, 'Got it.'
He handed Michael his phone. On the screen was pretty much an identical photo to the video.
'Who is this?'
'This is a gentleman who is now Ambassador Goodluck Adeyemi and the photo was taken twenty-five years ago at a diplomatic reception in Abuja, Nigeria's capital. An images search is such a useful function these days.'
'Okay. So where is he an Ambassador?'

'Here in the UK in London. He took up his post about a month ago.'

'I thought that Commonwealth countries did not have Embassies here in the UK but High Commissions'

'That is correct but the Nigerian chappie is called Ambassador on their official web site.'

Suddenly Mike realised why the young man at the High Commission had been so cagey. Goodluck was his boss! He had a great urge to ask Patrick for his low down on the guy, but he sensed instinctively that the more interest he took in Ambassador Goodluck, the more Patrick would become suspicious. He also realised that if Patrick started investigating him, that is Michael, he might come across his latest project and put two and two together. After all, his first television programme had gone out and Emmanuel, the young adult, bore an uncanny resemblance to young Goodluck Adeyemi. He put on his poker face.

'Okay, thanks for that, but that was not exactly the information I wanted.'

That was at least partly true since approaching a senior diplomat about Emmanuel might prove more complex.

'So what is happening in your world?'

This last comment was said by Michael, in the slightly forlorn hope of diverting attention from his request, as Patrick imbibed his glass of red. Patrick seemed not to notice and launched into a discourse about his scope article for tomorrow's Economist to do with scandals in the Sierra Leone diamond mining industry. He was hoping to get some sort of journalism prize for that.

Later that day Michael arranged a meeting with him, Angie, Emmanuel and Dr Emmanuel Adebayo. He knew that the situation might need the input of a Nigerian who had been born and lived in Nigeria till he was twenty-six years old.

'Michael, do you think we have got the right guy?' Dr Emmanuel wanted to check the facts first.

'I cannot see it is anyone else. We have only one video which fits all the criteria and information from Emily and Esther. Of the four people in the video, other than the foreign minister, one is a woman and the other two are older men in at least their forties, who Esther describes as 'old and ugly'. The last man, the one who Esther identifies as probably the right one, is called Goodluck. He undoubtedly is quite a handsome man in the video and Esther is very definite she went with a very handsome man. Patrick identifies him as Ambassador Goodluck Adeyemi and the photos on line of the guy of about similar date, are identical to the man in the video.'

Emmanuel said, 'How do we get in touch with the guy? You cannot just go up to someone important like him and say, 'Hi I'm your long lost son."
Dr Emmanuel agreed. 'We cannot just send him a letter or email to the High Commission or ask for an appointment. We will not get past the secretary or some junior Diplomat or other.'
'What if we went public?' queried Angie.
'We will get nowhere – just some official statement saying that we have got the wrong end of the stick etc. unsubstantiated allegations etc. If he is a senior Diplomat, there might be a complaint to the Foreign Office. Also Emmanuel would never get in contact with his birth Dad which is what he wants – isn't that right Emmanuel? Goodluck would then certainly want nothing to do with him.' His father had always insisted on calling him by his full name.
'Yes Dad that is right. So it seems we are stuck.'
Michael agreed reluctantly not to take things further at present from his end. In all the conversation there had not been a single mention of telling Esther that they had found Emmanuel's birth father.

A day later Patrick called Michael saying, 'I have just watched the social media video of your film of your latest protege Emmanuel and his story. I did note that he bears a remarkable resemblance to the younger Goodluck Adeyemi. Is it possible that Goodluck is

Emmanuel's father? Would you care to comment on that?'
'Michael let me level with you. We don't know and anything else is pure speculation.'
'So I presume that you have managed to locate Esther his mother?'
Michael was silent at that. Patrick was clearly starting to delve and Michael was worried where it might all end. He knew that Patrick would not have a story to tell, unless he managed to locate Esther and persuade her to agree to talk.
'I think it is time to end this call, Patrick.'
'If that is the way you want to play it, after the help I have given you,' Patrick stopped the call angrily.
Michael's reply had made him even more determined to investigate what had the potential makings of an excellent story.

Meanwhile, Dr Emmanuel had been thinking away and was pondering if he could somehow wangle a chat with Goodluck privately. He started to quietly research Goodluck online. He also rang up some friends and his brother, Jack in Nigeria.
'You know who he is, brother,' came the answer back from Jack.
'Yes I have done my research.'
'Did you know that what the Nigerian newspapers began yesterday to label Goodluck as?'
'No I had not quite picked up on that.'
Jack told him. Dr Emmanuel was surprised. It was not a normal nickname given to most politicians in any African countries. He thought that with a label like that, he would not be too keen to hear about a long lost love child. He seemed to have reached an impasse.

Then the idea came to him, in the middle of one night as he lay awake, thinking away. It was perfect. Next morning he explained it to his wife and then to Emmanuel.
'It could work. You have nothing to lose and the London Nigeria association seems the ideal vehicle,' Joy said thoughtfully.
Dr Emmanuel made the phone call.

'Hello, Mr. President, what can we do for you?' came the very formal greeting back.

'I was thinking about the new Community Cultural Centre for Nigerian expatriates, we are due to be opening in Canary Wharf in the next month. I know that, in your role as chief executive, you had asked me to do the official opening as the President of the Association. I was wondering though what you felt if we got the new Nigerian Ambassador to open the Centre together with me? It would be a good gesture to reinforce links with our home country.'

The Chief Executive pondered for a minute and said, 'Why not? Let me sort it'.

Two weeks later a very happy Ambassador turned up to the new centre. The Nigerian Constitution was just about to be amended so that Nigerian expatriates abroad could vote in Nigerian elections. The opening of a Cultural Centre was an ideal opportunity to meet and greet the potential voters and to make a speech on a happy occasion. He was clearly pleased about the plaque which was unveiled at the opening. Not only was Dr Emmanuel's name on it but his name had been added on there, also in a prominent position. That sort of thing was always good, positive publicity.

After the opening ceremony, Dr Emmanuel turned to his Chief Executive, 'Look Charles, I know you have got one or two important guests to speak to. Why don't I take the Ambassador off for a private tour round the centre and its facilities.'

So off the two of them went. At the end they were just about to join the main group for drinks and eats with the great and good of the Nigerian community in London.

Dr Emmanuel took the opportunity to quietly say to Goodluck, 'Mr. Ambassador, I wondered if I could have a chat with you soon, about a larger issue involving...Nigeria, the future of our country.'

The Ambassador looked quite puzzled. He had not been expecting that but said, 'Yes sure. What is it about?'

'It is a more private and how can I put it, a more delicate matter. This is not really the time or place to discuss it.'

The Ambassador hummed for a moment. Now he understood why Dr Emmanuel had taken him off alone for the tour. He wondered if that was why he had got the invite in the first place. His face clouded over as he did not like the words, 'Nigeria... the future of Nigeria.' They had an ominous sound to them.
'Why don't you come and see me in my office in the High Commission.'
'Sure. Very happy to do that.'
The Ambassador dipped into his pocket and fished out his card, 'Just ring my secretary and he will fit you in for an appointment. Here's my card with the number you need.'
'Thanks I will do that.'

CHAPTER 33 - DIPLOMATIC MEETING

The Ambassador was in a thoughtful mood as he was whisked away in the diplomatic Bentley, from the reception back to the Embassy. He was wearing traditional Nigerian garb, because it had been a cultural event. He struggled to fish his mobile out of a hidden pocket. Who was this Dr Emmanuel Adebayo and what the dickens was he meaning by the phrase, 'the future of Nigeria'? He had seemed to be a sensible man, not given to exaggeration. Surely there must be something more behind it.

Ten minutes later, while the car was still stuck in a typical London traffic jam, the Ambassador sat in the back seat, still no wiser. The internet search had given a picture of Dr Emmanuel as a
well-respected London GP, a fellow of the Royal College of GP's, heavily involved in various health boards, President of the London association of Christian Doctors, church elder. He had qualified from Ibadan University in Nigeria but had shortly after, moved to the UK. There was nothing to suggest that Dr Emmanuel was implicated in the politics of his native country or why he should know something relevant to the future of Nigeria. The mystery deepened.

When the Ambassador arrived back in his office, his secretary cum PA said that a Dr Emmanuel Adebayo had rung up to book an appointment for next week. It was definitely time, the Ambassador thought, to get his PA to make some discrete enquiries about Dr Adebayo, in advance of the meeting.

Ten days later Dr Emmanuel arrived in the ornate room which housed the office of the Ambassador. This time they were both wearing suits -the Ambassador a posh bespoke Saville Row one, Dr Emmanuel an off the peg one from a retailer. After the preliminary greetings, the Ambassador got down to business.
'So I gather you want to see me about an important matter.'
'Yes that's right. It's a long story so thanks for hearing me out. I have an adopted son aged twenty seven called Emmanuel too. He was abandoned at birth in London by his mother Esther Afolayan, who then fled from England. Like me, he is of Nigerian origin. He is now due to get married and would love to have his birth parents present at the wedding.'
He went on to explain about the dating organisation and the filming and Michael Cohen. The Ambassador listened carefully but with slight puzzlement. The question on his face was, 'Why am I being told all this?'

'So, we have found his mother, Esther and she has given us what information she knows about the father. In summary, she only met the father once at a party, when she was drunk. His name was Goodluck.'
When Dr Emmanuel mentioned the word 'Goodluck' the Ambassador's face frowned, then his face became totally neutral.
'The only other time she saw the father was on the TV news just in the last month of her pregnancy. He was in a group of officials round the then Nigerian Foreign Minister, who had been making a speech at the UN. Michael Cohen has managed to locate that video and Esther has identified the person she says is the father from that video. We have then identified that person as yourself, Goodluck Adeyemi.'

Dr Emmanuel now was expecting an indignant denial, but the Ambassador said nothing immediately. He was clearly a cool customer.
'Could I see a picture of your adopted son?' Dr Emmanuel passed his phone over.

The Ambassador had a startled look, when he saw the uncanny resemblance between a younger him and Emmanuel. He peered closely through his spectacles and kept the phone in his hand for at least a couple of minutes. He had a look of longing on his face. 'What is that about, that look of longing?' wondered Dr Emmanuel in surprise.
Finally, the Ambassador handed the phone back. 'Nice looking lad,' was his one comment.

Dr Emmanuel decided it was time to press things further.
'Here's a picture of Esther as she was, about the time she fell pregnant.' He offered his phone back over to the Ambassador without asking him whether he wanted to see it or not. The Ambassador took it after some hesitation and looked closely. Dr Emmanuel could see a quick look of recognition cross his face. He knew that he had got the right person and that he had the Ambassador hooked. The Ambassador sensed too that Dr Emmanuel knew he had got caught in his fishing line.
'So Ambassador, what do you think?'
The Ambassador sat back in his chair and put his hands together. He began speaking slowly, carefully, as if well aware that a lot depended on how he handled the next part of the conversation.

'Dr Adebayo, can I call you Emmanuel?' he paused.
'Yes sure,' Dr Emmanuel replied a little uncertainly. He always got a little wary when his patients got a bit over-personal and started using his first name in consultations at his surgery. He had a sense now that yet another person was going to try to get him to believe something that he might not want necessarily to be convinced of.
'Before I got married I did, like many young men, have, how shall I put it.... female friends and I do remember......meeting Esther.' The words 'meeting' and 'female friends' were carefully chosen to cover a multitude of possible events and encounters.
'But since I met and got married to my wife, I have been loyal to

her, totally loyal and she does know that I did have, how shall I put it delicately, one or two flings on the side before my marriage. Did you know that I am a potential future candidate for the Presidency of Nigeria in fifteen months time?'

'Yes I did. I have done a little research on the side before this meeting,' Dr Emmanuel said in a modest tone of voice.

The Ambassador continued, 'The present President could technically stand again for a second term but he won't. His wife has personally assured me of that. He's old, sick and just about to go to Paris for another round of ineffective, expensive, chemotherapy that probably will make him worse – all paid for of course by the Nigerian tax-payer. You probably also may know that the Nigerian newspapers have started to label me as 'Mr. Clean' for want of a better phrase. I quite like the nickname because it expresses what I am about. I am desperately keen to try to rid our country, Nigeria, of the corruption and graft that plague our government, business and natural life. Tell me, do you want to clean up our country? I know you do.'

Dr Emmanuel knew that the Ambassador had managed to turn the conversation round. He was now being played like a piano, by a skilful politician, determined to get the mood music right.

'Of course, I do want our country to be clean too.'

'I know you do, because you could not advance your medical career in Nigeria. You were just not prepared to bribe people to get a job for which you were well qualified. This is why you moved to England. I too, like you, have done my research.'

Dr Emmanuel was silent at that. He should have thought it through beforehand. The Ambassador had investigated him before the appointment because he suspected that it would be a more tricky meeting for him.

The Ambassador carried on, 'The race to be President is at present close run. I will have the support of the current President and his wife which will certainly go a long way. It won't be enough on its own. If negative information about me were to come out, it could definitely affect my chances of winning and with it a real chance to make the lives of my fellow Nigerians better. The other potential contenders are saying lots of nice things but in fact they will just maintain the status quo when in reality we desperately need change as a country.'

Dr Emmanuel nodded slowly in agreement. He too had been doing his research about the various potential candidates. Goodluck's assessment was certainly true to the mark. Then came the sixty-four thousand dollar question directed to him.
'Is there any way you might be willing to keep the information, you have just given me out of the public domain?'

Dr Emmanuel had seen enough of Nigerian politicians to be a bit cynical. He wondered how he could find out whether he was just being cleverly played or whether the guy sitting behind the desk facing him, was genuine. Then an idea occurred to him on the spot. It was perfect but risky. He decided he would test the Ambassador. He would take that chance that if it went wrong, Emmanuel would lose any possibility of getting in touch with his bio-dad.

He wanted to keep a contact line with Goodluck for the sake of the adopted son he was so proud of. He did not however want to be fobbed with a promise from a liar who would certainly break it. If he was genuine in wanting to be 'Mr. Clean' then he would be more likely to keep his word.

Out it came from Dr Emmanuel's mouth in a deadpan voice, 'How many naira (the Nigerian currency) would you give me to keep this information out of the public domain?'
He was looking the Ambassador straight in the face as he posed the question. Dr Emmanuel was now expecting to get an answer like, 'What had you got in mind' or something similar as a prelude to a negotiation about a precise sum as a bribe.

The Ambassador immediately stood up from his desk, plonked his hands on it and leaned forward, slightly menacingly. His face

flared up red and angry and he shouted out, 'How dare you come into my office and try to blackmail me. How dare you? I'm not that sort of politician.'
He bitterly reproached Emmanuel with contempt in his voice, 'I had thought you were a man of faith and integrity as that is your reputation. It's time to end this conversation and for you to leave this office. And I don't care what stuff you spread around about me. I am a man of my word. I am a man of integrity.' The Ambassador was very angry and clearly did not care if he lost votes in the upcoming elections as a result of this turn in the conversation.

Dr Emmanuel smiled and looked him in the eye, 'Please calm down. I was only seeing if you were genuine. I was testing you and was certainly not offering you a bribe. If you had offered me money, I would have refused it. You have passed the test. I do want to carry on our conversation.'
The Ambassador relaxed a little and sat down slowly but was still angry.
'Why did you test me in this way? I don't care for your way of doing things,' he said indignantly.
'Look. I want to make certain that if you were to make any promises as regards my son, you will keep them.'

'Why have you actually come here?' the Ambassador asked still in a bit of a hostile voice. Both knew that they had got to the very heart of their encounter.
'I am hoping you might feel able to have some sort of contact with Emmanuel. Now that he has found his biological mother, he is desperate to have a relationship with you as his biological father.'
'Please,' said the Ambassador pleading, 'I have nothing to offer you in return for you keeping this information private – nothing except a chance for you to help your country.'
Dr Emmanuel said, 'Is there no way you could attend Emmanuel's wedding? I have a personal invite here for you.' He handed

over without asking, a beautifully written card with elegant ornate calligraphy titled at the top, 'His Excellency Ambassador Goodluck Adeyemi'. Angie's sister Josephine was a writing whizz and had pulled out all the stops in designing the invites. The Ambassador took it with his hand, looked closely at it and carefully put it away in one of his desk drawers.

He deflected the question about attending the wedding with a request of his own.
'Could you show me your son's picture on your phone again?'
'Sure, I will show you a slightly different one this time.'
The Ambassador gave a smile of pleasure at seeing Emmanuel in his football gear.
'He is centre forward in a London amateur team,' Dr Emmanuel added.
'You know, don't you, that I was a professional footballer for two years before I went to university and joined the diplomatic service.'
'Yes, you were Emmanuel's position, centre forward in the Warri warriors, weren't you?'
'My, you have done your research on me well.'

The Ambassador held onto the phone and stayed looking at it for ages. He was entranced by the screen, with its picture strongly reminding him of a younger version of himself.
'You know,' he started speaking again, still gazing intently at the screen. 'My wife and I were only able to have one child and that was our daughter. To make it worse, it was by fertility treatment, which we both found horrible, degrading. We both vowed we would never go through *that* again. She, that is our daughter, is now undertaking medical training in the States. But now she is mulling over not having children at all so as to put her hospital career first. That deeply, deeply upsets my wife. She has reached that age where she would love to be bouncing grand kids on her lap. We would have been so thrilled to have had a son.' He had a dreamy look of longing on his face and stopped for a few

seconds,

'Tell me more about Emmanuel, please,' the Ambassador resumed, in a pleading voice, still staring at the screen at the picture of Emmanuel.

'He is something special. He was born on Christmas day and is aged twenty-seven. He has his disability but he has worked so hard to overcome it. He has a first-class degree from Cambridge University in computer studies. I don't understand all he does but he writes a lot of computer code for work, as second in command, at a growing data science firm. He has an excellent voice and sings at Church and he does play his football with skill and determination. He has finally landed this lovely girl Angie and I think they will do very well together. Above all, he has a strong faith.'

Goodluck looked up from the screen, 'Look if you could keep all this out of the public eye, that would be great, but I cannot force you. I would like to keep in touch with you and Emmanuel by private email. I will give you my address and I promise to keep in touch and answer your emails.' He wrote the email address down on a slip of paper.

Dr Emmanuel spoke back, 'I cannot for my part promise to keep it out of the public eye. Other people know what is going on, including this film producer and journalist Michael Cohen, but I will try as best I can. As yet Esther, his mother, does not know that we have located you. I thought it best to find out more before I spoke to her. I still don't know how I will handle Esther. I think I have a clear obligation to tell her about you. What do you think would happen if the news did get out?'

'I don't think it would help my cause. It might just blow over but there is absolutely no guarantee. It could very well lose me the Presidency.'

'Would you deny the information if it were to come out?'

'No, because that would a lie and I will not under any circumstance lie to get to be President. I would either refuse to say

anything at all or I would say that I don't get involved in 'unsubstantiated allegations'.'
'But the 'unsubstantiated allegations' bit is not really true is it?'

'But it is. Look Emmanuel, I believe you and I believe you are honest and sincere in what you told me. At the end of the day though, you are relying on the testimony of a woman who you really don't know well. You have never actually met her face to face – just video calls which is not the same and only one personal video call between you and her. What if the woman had another boy friend at the same time she met me? She was clearly an attractive young lady who was bound to get male attention. She might genuinely believe I am the father of the baby, when in fact the other man is the father of Emmanuel. So, they are unsubstantiated allegations, unless I undergo a paternity test, which I would never agree to. If I was to open myself to have one test, I would certainly open myself up to a whole host of women, who I don't know from Adam, clamouring for a paternity test for their children. The press would make a mockery of me and my political opponents would howl with laughter. They would equally refuse to submit themselves to paternity tests if they were to be asked to do one.'

Dr Emmanuel was silent at that. He did not know what more he could achieve. The Ambassador had not rejected the wedding invite but he had not accepted either. However he had promised to keep in contact. Dr Emmanuel believed he would do so, especially if he sent carefully crafted emails, and guided his son about what messages he sent to his bio-dad.

Dr Emmanuel got up to leave.
The Ambassador stood up too, shook his hand and said, 'Do keep in touch. I mean that.'
He then put on a poker face saying, 'By the way a word of advice. If ever you do want to bribe a Nigerian politician, don't offer him naira. Offer him US dollars instead.'
Dr Emmanuel did not quite know how to take the comment.

Was the Ambassador being serious and was all the long conversation he had just had with him in vain, just empty words? Then he saw Goodluck laughing and wagging his index finger at him. Dr Emmanuel laughed too, pointing his finger as well and stepped out of the office in a good mood, determined to vote for Goodluck in the upcoming election.

Then the Ambassador called him back in, 'Would you very much mind sending me a picture of Emmanuel and Angie?'
Dr Emmanuel smiled, 'Sure. I will send one later today.' He walked away. His good mood only lasted for a minute or two. His phone pinged and he saw the message from his wife.
'Esther has just been in touch with me, saying she has found out today who Emmy's bio-dad. is. She has decided to contact him directly.'
Dr Emmanuel sighed and said inside himself with a sense of horror and disappointment, 'Oh no.' He suddenly knew that life was about to get a lot more complicated.

CHAPTER 34 - THE FALLOUT

'He said what?' the incredulous Esther shouted out down the phone at Dr Emmanuel.

It had been a difficult few hours with much unbridled emotion by more than one person. Dr Emmanuel had tried to calm people down but that had been difficult. He had emerged out of the Nigerian High Commission into a clouded, overcast sky. He walked along the crowded, bustling London streets and texted Esther, Emmanuel's mum. He had developed the ability to text with his thumbs as fast as the youngsters.

'I have got some news for you. I will like to ring you later for a long chat. Could you hold off contacting Goodluck until I have spoken to you please? Thanks Dr Emmanuel.'

His ability to text was really useful in his job as GP and member of the Hackney and East London Clinical Commissioning group, inundated as he was with texts, email and letters from all sides.

He went down the steps and entered the underground. Because the train was quiet, out of rush hour time, he was able to sit down. He then turned his attention to the enjoyable task of choosing a nice couple of photos the happy couple to email to Goodluck. He got out of the train and went up the escalator to do the final quarter of mile walk home. As he emerged onto the street, he pressed the 'send' button on his email. He thought that Goodluck was genuine, but he was not entirely certain. He wondered if he would get a message back, saying that the email address was not recognised or that he would get no reply at all. Just as he got home and was walking through the door, his phone pinged. To his pleasant surprise it was an email reply from Goodluck. 'Thank you so much for the photos. They are a lovely couple. Keep in touch, Goodluck.'

That was prompt and it would make his job easier, trying to convince others that Goodluck was genuine. It was time for a meeting. Unfortunately, it would have to be a video call, again not the best way for sensitive subjects. He knew he had to include Michael Cohen, who he suspected would be the most difficult person to convince. He and his wife sat by the laptop in London. Emmanuel was visiting Angie in Nottingham, so they sat by his mobile phone, while Michael was sitting in his office by his massive Apple Mac desktop computer in West Nottingham.

Dr Emmanuel updated everyone on his visit to Goodluck. 'So, I think Goodluck is genuine, and he has practically admitted that Emmanuel is his biological son but he wants things kept quiet. I also think that if things are not kept quiet, he would break off contact.'
Emmanuel's face revealed his joy. Even though it was only a tentative contact, his bio-dad. had acknowledged him as his son and there was ongoing possibility of keeping in touch. This was exactly what he wanted.
Then Michael came out with, 'That is a pity. It is such a good story. I would love to include it in my second film about you, Emmanuel and Angie.'

Angie frowned. She could say nothing as Michael was her boss. But she felt he was putting making a good film that would sell, above any other consideration.
Emmanuel reacted clearly. He could see what was at stake for him personally. He said firmly with a touch of anger in his voice. 'I know we signed a contract, Angie and I, with you to make a programme. If I find out, Mike, that you have let the information slip out about my bio-dad., I will refuse to cooperate. If I have to fund and organise my wedding myself, I will do that.'

Michael was taken aback. He had not expected such a direct statement from Emmanuel.

Dr Emmanuel weighed in more calmly, 'Michael, I know you will be disappointed, but Emmanuel is right. Also, if you court controversy by exposing one of the prominent candidates for the Presidential election, you might well find this. The Nigerian television which has, I believe, agreed to show the first programme, may get cold feet about screening the second programme.'
Angie put her oar in, 'Look Boss, I know you love a scoop but if Dr Emmanuel is right, then not selling to Nigerian television will dramatically reduce our chances of getting it viewed on other English speaking African countries.'
Dr Emmanuel continued smoothly on, 'With the permission of Emmanuel and Angie of course, I would be happy to liaise with you, Michael, to discuss what you put in your films about Emmanuel's biological parents.'
Emmanuel and Angie nodded vigorously in agreement.

Michael saw he was beaten. He knew that Dr Emmanuel would be a much tougher customer than his son about what he could put in the film. He reluctantly said, 'Okay then. But one condition: I promise that I will absolutely do nothing to let the information come out. But if it does come out publicly another way, then I will want to mention about your father's identity in my second film. I would definitely expect your full cooperation, Emmanuel, in accordance with your signed contract.'
A grudging 'Okay' came out of Emmanuel's mouth in response. The meeting ended.

Dr Emmanuel sent a message to Emmanuel and they logged in again.
'I did not want to tell Michael about Esther's text to your Mum. He might use it as an excuse to contact her, in the hope she might decide to go public. The only thing I can do is to chat with her and try to dissuade her. If she does try to contact Goodluck, I don't know what will happen.'

'What do we do about telling Emily, Dad?'
'I don't see we need to say anything. Let Esther tell her if she wants to.'

Next, Dr Emmanuel now had the tricky job of speaking to Esther. He had only video called her once with Emmanuel and they had spoken for ten minutes. Apart from that and what Emmanuel and Angie had told him about her, he did not really know her well.

Dr Emmanuel kicked off the conversation after the initial greetings.
'I have just had a long chat with Goodluck Adeyemi.'
'Oh yes,' Esther replied in a neutral tone that belied her underlying emotions.
'So did you come to find out about him?' asked Dr Emmanuel.
Esther said nothing at all. There was an extremely awkward silence.
'Shall I tell you about my meeting with him?'
'I somehow think you are not going to let me not hear about it,' said Esther grumpily.
He recounted his meeting with Goodluck and that he had all but acknowledged that he was the biological father of Emmanuel.
'So he probably won't come to the wedding?' Esther muttered sarcastically. 'That is such a pity since I would really like to see him and ask why he never got in contact with me again.'
'I am not hopeful he will come, as he wants to try to keep it all a secret with his upcoming election campaign. He is trying to run on a Mr. Clean bandwagon.'

When Dr Emmanuel heard Esther's reaction, he wished he had not mentioned about the Mr Clean slogan.
Esther burst out angrily, 'That is just hypocrisy. That makes me mad. If he was honest and open, I could understand it more, but this is just pure hypocrisy.'
'I'm sorry but that is his response. The point for me is at least we have the start of a relationship.'

'Have you? Have you really?' Esther replied with a strongly questioning tone. 'How do you know he won't fool you until he becomes President. You can say then what you like about him, but he won't care.'

'Yes I know that there is a risk of that but Emmanuel and I have discussed this already and we are prepared to take that chance. Please Esther, meeting you has been the second best thing that has happened to him for years. I say second best, because first best was coming across Angie.'

'No I am not happy. I feel like contacting Patrick Peyton and giving him my story. I think he would be very interested. A 'Mr. Clean', running for President and refusing to acknowledge his love child.'

'Patrick Peyton? You've been in contact with him? Dr Emmanuel's tone of voice showed his shock. 'Did Michael Cohen put him in touch with you?'

Esther said nothing in response to that. Her mind was whirring away, 'Michael has told Emmanuel and family about Patrick Peyton but has not bothered telling me. And his family has not bothered to inform me either. I am not impressed …..definitely not impressed.'

Dr Emmanuel tentatively said, 'If you do decide to tell Patrick Peyton everything, which I sincerely hope you don't…. would you feel able to send me a message first?'

'Why should I? You went behind my back, doing things without telling me. You knew three weeks ago and did not deign to tell me about Goodluck. Why should I?' Esther shouted angrily down the phone.

She then just put the phone down in disgust.

Dr Emmanuel felt betrayed, after his recent chat with Michael Cohen. No wonder Michael had extracted a promise, that Emmanuel would go through a filmed wedding, if all the information came out in public. That was because he knew that Patrick Peyton would be revealing it all. And that was because he had

put Patrick Peyton in touch with Esther.
He started to worry if Esther did reveal things, what the effect would be on his son, Emmanuel and Goodluck. Goodluck would drop contact with him and Emmanuel would be devastated.

CHAPTER 35 - PATRICK DELVES

Retracing our steps in the story, to after his lunch with Michael Cohen, Patrick had managed to see the video of Mike's first film and had got such information as was given in it about Esther and Emily. He had searched and searched and come up with nothing for either name Esther Afolayan or Emily Sutton. Then he decided to do a different approach – to search for registered midwives, that is assuming that Emily had completed her training. No joy but then he noted that you could search for previously registered midwives by name and found three Emily Suttons.

One Emily Sutton had qualified and worked in Manchester all her professional life, another had retired after thirty years service ten years ago which meant she was probably too old. That would mean she was probably now in her late sixties. The last Emily Sutton had worked in the North London hospital and had qualified about two years after Emmanuel's birth. Things were looking up there with this one. Then he noticed that you could click on a link to see all the registration information for that midwife for each year. Three years after registration, the name had changed from Sutton to Tomenko and had stayed Tomenko until her registration ceased four years ago. Patrick surmised that Tomenko was probably a married name. Emily would have been about the age, at which many young people got wed.

Emily Tomenko, now that was not a common name. Where did that name come from? It turned out it was Ukrainian and a search for Emily Tomenko only revealed one entry in the UK.

It was a posh estate agent firm in some spot in Devon. Patrick clicked on the link 'Dreams to reality with Tomenko estate agents'. It showed a picture of Emily and Ralph Tomenko – a smiling, balding chap in his early fifties with a pleasant looking lady of similar age. The blurb read, 'At Tomenko's, retired midwife Emily, together with her Devon born and bred property developer husband Ralph, help people give birth to their dreams of owning a lovely home ....'

Yes that was definitely her. It looked like she had probably married a Brit with Ukrainian ancestors. Ralph did not exactly sound like a Ukrainian name. There was the normal web site enquiry form but also a landline number for the business. It was 1.45 pm on a Tuesday afternoon and it was very definitely time for a phone call to the estate agent office. Patrick picked up his mobile and dialled.

'Hello, Tomenko estate agents. Emily speaking.' She was in sunny mood and her voice was smooth, friendly and professional. The river Dart was gleaming in the sun. The view from their river front office was amazing and to top it all, she had just sold two large houses developed by her builder husband. The day however, was just about to get a lot less sunny for her.
Patrick thought to himself, 'Great it sounds as I have got through to Emily Tomenko'.
'Is that Emily Tomenko?'
'Yes speaking,' came the pleasant, neutral voice back.
'The Emily Tomenko nee Sutton who is a friend of Esther Afolayan and involved with baby Emmanuel as he then was?' Patrick had already decided that a direct approach was most likely to yield results. He was half expecting a smooth reply back in professional tones like, 'I think you have got the wrong person' or something similar.
'Who's this?' came the reply straight back in much less pleasant tones. She sounded rattled too.
Patrick smiled. This was sounding hopeful. He continued

smoothly on, 'My name is Patrick Peyton P E Y T O N a freelance journalist working with the Economist and Financial Times. You can google me if you like.'

'Who gave you my contact details? Michael?' came the even more agitated reply back.

'Michael Cohen?'

'Yes, Michael Cohen?'

Emily felt badly let down. Angie had promised her that her personal details would not be revealed but that her role in the second programme would be as Emily Sutton, without giving details of her present name or job. Why had Michael given this information to an investigative journalist of all people?

Patrick put his fist in the air with elation. He had hit the jackpot. He sidestepped the question.

'I'm a friend of Michael Cohen. We have worked together before and he asked for my help to find Emmanuel's father. I believe we have found him.'

'What? You have found Emmanuel's father!' Patrick could hear the astonishment in her voice. So Michael had not bothered to share that bit of information with Emily. Did that mean that Michael or the family had told Esther yet?

'Yes I think so. Didn't Mike tell you?'

'No but who is the father?'

'I think in fairness to Esther I had better tell her first unless she knows anyway.'

'No she certainly does not know.' Patrick knew again he had hit the jackpot. If he could be the one to give her the news then it would be fascinating to hear Esther's reaction.

 Why have you contacted me?' asked Emily.

'I want to be able to speak to Esther directly and Michael won't let me do that. I believe she has a right to know about Emmanuel's father.'

'Look I cannot give you her contact details directly. I would need to first ask to get her permission.'

'How would you do that?'
Emily thought it through. 'I will send her an email today.' came the confident reply.
'Look, I can see your office email address on your web page. I will send you an email now so you can forward my email to Esther.'
'Why do you want to contact Esther directly?'
'I am a journalist. I make my living by publishing stories. I believe that there is a story to tell, because in my opinion, the guy, who is the father of Emmanuel, is one of the biggest frauds out in the history of Nigeria. How do you think Esther will react? How is she doing these days?'
Patrick asked the last question in the hope that Emily might start spontaneously giving him information.
Emily took this news with a sense of shock. What was all this about?
'She is doing well, happy in her new life. I think she will be shocked by the news,' was her slightly guarded reply.
'Are you able to tell me more about her new life?'
'Not without her permission.'
'So look, do me a favour. If I send you my email, can you at least reply to me if she is willing to talk to me or not.
'Okay, I will do that.'

The call ended and a couple of minutes later her Apple Mac laptop pinged. She was a fan of Apple Mac because it was better than a Windows one for the media stuff, pictures and videos, that she handled regularly as an estate agent. She had a new email from Patrick Peyton. She googled him and found he was exactly who he said he was. She wondered what to do, and decided it would be best to do a video call to Esther, later that day after work. Doing it from home would be better. At least she could be guaranteed some privacy. An email would not do for this.

At 7.30 pm she sat down in her new house in the above town area of Dartmouth. Her living room looked down upon the river. It was getting dark and some of the boats were lit up with fairy

lights. She fired up her laptop and clicked on the link to start the video call.
'He what?' exclaimed Esther in shock.
'Yes he told me that Mike Cohen was stopping him from contacting you and that he knew the name of Emmanuel's father.'
'If that is right, then Emmanuel, Mike Cohen, Dr Emmanuel and Angie have been keeping information from me. How dare they? How dare they think that I don't have the right to know. I am angry. I could contact Emmanuel's parents directly but I need to hear what this Patrick Peyton has got to say.' Esther just let it rip out, all her anger and emotions, with a woman who was one of her best friends. She told her decisively, 'Send me his email.'
They chatted on for a few minutes then said goodbye.

Esther sent an email from her email address mariammaceesay109@gambiamailone.gm to Patrick.
'Dear Mr. Peyton,
I gather from your email that you want to share some important information with me. Can you give me more details?'
Esther.'
Patrick received the email and decided to put the email address in a search engine. He immediately hit on the page of 'Senegambia Trading' and on the top of the page was a picture of Mariamma Ceesay, the owner and Managing Director. At the bottom was the email contact address. The picture bore a clear resemblance to the photo of Esther shown in the first film, merely an older and a bit fuller in the face version.
'Got you,' said Patrick to himself, 'You have changed your name. Now was that done legitimately or not?'

He took the decision not to reply immediately but find out what he could about her. Keeping Esther dangling for a while, was not such a bad idea. She might be more willing to cooperate. If she had abandoned the name Esther Afolayan unofficially, then she might not be willing to expose herself publicly. However if she had changed her name legitimately, she might be willing to talk.

It was vital for his purpose that she be up for making a public statement. Time to ring up his contact in the Gambia, a lady called Fatou Drammeh.

After the preliminary greetings Patrick and Fatou got down to business.
Look Fatou, I want you to find out for me if a Nigerian woman who called herself Esther Afolayan has legitimately changed her name to Mariamma Ceesay. She runs Senegambia Trading. She may have possibly used a pseudonym to enter the Gambia. Also I would like to know if she is a Gambian citizen or not and any other information you can find out about her.'
'It will take a little time and money, delving into court records and court fees and all that.'
Patrick wondered if 'and all that' was a polite term for bribery but decided not to enquire too deeply. After some haggling they agreed on a price of £500.

Three days later Fatou came back to him with the information sent to him by email as well as a long phone call.
'Esther Afolayan changed her name legitimately in December 2007 to Mariamma Ceesay and became a Gambian citizen at the same time. Funnily enough, she also legally renounced another name too at the same time, Blessing Okafor. That was a name which she had also apparently used too.'
Patrick wondered if that last name she has used to enter the Gambia with. That might be useful information. Time now to send an email
'Dear Esther,
Thanks for your email. I am very happy to divulge the information about Emmanuel's father. I would, however, only be prepared to do it via a video call. Please send me a link and a time for the call.
Thanks Patrick.'

Esther read the email and knew that she was cornered. She desperately wanted the information. She was even more so,

when the video call started and Patrick said,
'I need to record this before I give out my information. Are you in agreement?'
'I suppose so.'
The recording started.
'Are you Esther Afolayan currently now Mariamma Ceesay?'
'That is correct.'
'Do you give your consent to being recorded.'
'I do.'
'Right. Do you admit to recognising the father of Emmanuel your baby in a TV programme at the time when you were just about to give birth to Emmanuel?'
Patrick silently said, 'Come on Esther just say 'yes' then I have got my story.' He absolutely knew that he would need a clear statement from Esther in order to be able to sell his story to a newspaper editor. They, that is the editor, would either want a signed statement, or better, a video call recording especially for something as sensitive as this. He needed more than some wild assertions or conjectures on his part.

Esther sensed that she was being reeled in like a fish but refused to take the bait.
She said nothing.
Patrick then said, 'Can I share the video on my screen with you?'
'Yes you can share whatever you like,' Esther said with a slightly contemptuous voice.
They watched the video together. Patrick then said, 'That was the video I think you saw so many years ago, in which you identified one of the people as the father of Emmanuel,' said Patrick making an intelligent guess. 'I first saw that video three weeks ago together with Michael Cohen.'
He repeated the question, 'Do you identify the man, on the far left of the screen, as the man who fathered your baby Emmanuel.'
Esther again said nothing. Patrick had hoped that seeing the video might jog her memory and her voice into action.

He then said, 'This man, the father of Emmanuel, is Ambassador Goodluck Adeyemi, who is head of the Nigerian High Commission in the UK.'
Esther merely nodded in reaction to that.

Then Patrick tried his last desperate fling to get something out of her. He practically shouted in his frustration and desperation. 'This man went with you and then betrayed your trust, never calling you even you had given him not one but two business cards. Do you know what he is now proposing to do? He wants to stand for election as President of your native country, Nigeria and can you guess what he is going to stand as? It is as 'Mr. Clean' - the one who will stop corruption in your country. What a hypocrite! What a disgusting hypocrite!'

Esther felt sudden rage inside herself that this man, this man who had betrayed her trust, was now going to ask the Nigerian people to put their confidence in him. However she was not going to give this slimy Patrick chap the story he craved for, without some thought. She would not let him use her for his own purposes, like she had let Goodluck use her. If she did give him the story it would be on her own terms and in her own time.

So in response to his statement, with a supreme act of self control, she refused to let her anger show, merely flickering her eyelashes. She quietly decided to take control of the situation.
'Mr. Peyton, have you anything else to say to me?'
'Don't you think I have said enough?'
'In that case, I will end this video call. If you wish to say anything more to me, you have my email address and likewise, if I wish to communicate anything to you, I have your address. Goodbye.'
Esther ended the call fuming inside. She felt that Michael Cohen had betrayed her bringing in this arrogant outsider Patrick Peyton, without her knowledge. She was mad too with Emmanuel and his family also, because they had kept her in the dark.

She wondered what to do next. It would be easy to fly off the handle, but she decided she needed to hear what Emmanuel's family had to say. Emmanuel was a little bit too young. He was very reliant on his parents, for advice on the tricky issues he had had to deal with in his search for information about his birth parents. She did not know Dr Emmanuel very well and she wanted to talk to a woman, a fellow Nigerian. She did however know Joy, Dr Emmanuel's wife better, and had had a few video calls with her before. So she rang her.

CHAPTER 36- ESTHER DECIDES

Esther had had the conversation with Patrick Peyton and had just then had the call with Dr Emmanuel, who had been trying to calm her down. She was angry with everyone and was crying, tears running down her face. Emmanuel and his family and Michael Cohen had not told her they had located his father. He was a man who not only had fathered her child but a guy she had unfinished business with. They had no right to keep that information from her, absolutely no right.

That Michael Cohen had gone around getting others involved – that Patrick character, without asking her permission. She just felt like contacting some Nigerian journalist instead, and giving her story. Let one of her own countrymen have the scoop of exposing a fraud, pretending to be a Mr. Clean, as a Presidential candidate. She would not tell that slimy South African chap. She wanted to tell the world of her pain, of her betrayal. She sat in her bedroom in her house in the Gambia, the house that had been Uncle Samuel's when he had been alive. She was thinking. Who could she talk to? Who could she confide in about her situation?

Her oldest daughter, Hawa came into the room. She had heard Mum crying. She was only twenty-one but had a steady head on her.
'What's the matter, Mum?'
Mum decided to unload all. At the end she said.
'I just feel betrayed. That man Goodluck betrayed me twenty-

eight years ago and he has betrayed me again – not being prepared to admit publicly what he has done. If he was a real man, he would come to Emmanuel's wedding and publicly say, 'I am Emmanuel's father'. It is going to go public anyway what happened about Emmanuel and me so I might as well say the other part of the story.'

Hawa sat listening. Then when Mum had said all she had wanted to pour out to her, and had started to calm down a bit, she began to ask a quiet question of two.

'Mum, why did you give your interviews with Michael Cohen, which he is going to show in programmes about the wedding?'

'A variety of reasons I suppose. I was initially grateful to Michael Cohen for bringing me and Emmanuel together when I had been starting to so long to see him again. I wanted to repay him. I have grown to really love Emmanuel, my long-lost son and he has very much wanted me to tell me my story.'

'Why has Emmanuel very much wanted you to say your side of things?'

'Because he knows that if I tell my side, then the second and subsequent programmes made will be much more powerful and sellable. That will enhance his fiancee Angie's career as she has the job of trying to sell them in the African television market. Obviously he wants to help the woman he loves and I do understand that.'

'I know that and that is why Angie was so keen to get Emily giving her story.'

There was a pause and Hawa continued, 'Is there any reason you are telling the story for yourself, as opposed to helping others?'

'Well, I suppose I wanted to get the other half of the story out about why exactly I abandoned Emmanuel at birth and also to show how I rebuilt my life. Also that I am being open and honest, recognising Emmanuel as my son and acknowledging my mistakes.'

'And ..... ' Hawa left the question hanging.

'I wanted to show what we African women are about – that I

could build a successful life after a mistake – to give an example to others.'

'What do you think might happen if you decided to contact a Nigerian journalist?'

'I don't know. I have not thought it through yet.'

'Well, I will tell you, Mum, what I think will happen. Firstly, Goodluck is likely to clam up and break off contact with Emmanuel. That would upset him badly and would cause a massive rift between you and him and Angie. Secondly, is it a particularly good thing, upsetting a prominent Nigerian politician who might be President of the country? Senegambia trading is starting to develop significant business with Nigeria and angering Goodluck could harm the business. Lastly, telling all to the world will make you seem like a woman, just out to get revenge. Is that the image you want to give the world, of another bitter twisted person in this world? Remember that these days, once you let the information out publicly, you cannot then take it back.'

Esther was silent at that. Hawa was hitting home with what she said.

'Mum why did you and Dad call me Hawa?'

'Because you were our first daughter and Hawa is the Gambian and Arabic name for Eve in the Bible who was the first woman.'

'But there is another reason why you called me Hawa and why my brothers and sisters are called Mariamma (Mary), Adama (Adam), Ensa(Jesus), Yaya(John the Baptist) and lastly Ibrahima(Abraham). What is that other reason Mum?'

'Because your Dad was a Muslim and I am a Christian and we wanted Gambian names that were common to both the Bible and Islam.'

Hawa continued, 'Look Mum, I know that you have turned more religious recently. You have started to go to that Nigerian gospel church in Serekunda. What have they been telling you about, the stuff you have been relating to us back at home?'

Hawa arched her eyebrows and looked at Mum, knowing exactly what she would say in response.

'They have been talking about forgiving others as Jesus has forgiven us.' Esther mumbled it out, feeling rather embarrassed at her nominally Muslim daughter picking her up.
'Look Mum, I know you never converted to Islam when you married Dad and I know you do the Christian thing. You know as well that I am not particularly religious for anything. Maybe, just maybe, your church is saying some sense. Why not just let Goodluck go mentally? You will feel better for that.'
'So you are saying I should not do anything.'
'Exactly. Also if you decide to tell all to some journalist, the rest of us, your family will find ourselves in the firing line – possibly the centre of attention. Do you really want that? Please just leave things be.'
'I will think about it.'
'Just one last thing. You made a promise to Emmanuel in that note you left in the basket at birth saying 'I will love you always'. I think that saying nothing is the best way of showing your love to him.'
Esther frowned at that and said irritably, 'You really did not need to say that, Hawa.'
'Okay, I will say nothing more.'

Dr Emmanuel and Emmanuel and Angie had a worrying week wondering if Esther would speak out publicly. They kept checking the media to see if there was anything. Emmanuel said to his Dad, 'Do you think I ought to ring her and ask her what she is doing directly?'
'No. From the tone of her last conversation, I don't think she has made a definite decision to go public. I do think if you ring her now, you might push her into doing just that. Let's just leave her be.'
Ten days later they had a call from Esther and she was nice and happy with no mention of contacting journalists.

CHAPTER 37- CHURCH

Emmanuel and Angie were keen to get married and decided not to wait but go for a winter wedding. Michael was entranced. Filming a winter wedding would be different. He started praying for snow on the day. That would be even better!

The invitations went out and one made its way to Dartmouth. When Emily read it, she exclaimed with some sense of disappointment, 'I do so want to go but we won't be able to have the family round as normal if we do go to the wedding.'
Ralph read it and groaned, 'I won't be able to get my turkey and brussels and plum pudding. They never serve that sort of fare at wedding receptions but we should go even so.'

One invite wended its way in the post to the Gambia. Esther sat on it for days before finally deciding she would go. She had reservations about attending, in spite of having got to know Emmanuel and his family quite well through video calls. She had heard the long and short about how they discovered about Goodluck. Patrick Peyton had been upfront with Michael, about how he had managed to come across Emily and Esther. Fences in relationships had been mended. She still felt she would be in the way, an awkward and embarrassing spare part from the past. She did need emotional support though to do it. Hawa, her daughter, could not come to England. She was the one Gambian, Esther needed and trusted to run the business back home. So she asked her sister Joy, who lived in Abuja back home in Nigeria, to come with her to England.

Esther flew to Abuja from the Gambia to meet her sister and stay a few days with her. They were planning to fly to England on 23rd December well in time for the wedding. It was the first time Esther had been to England for twenty-eight years and they had arranged to stay at the wedding hotel in Derbyshire.

They turned up to the airport on the morning of the 23rd, ready for a flight of nearly six hours. The air was dusty and blowy – a reminder that Nigeria was just south of the Sahara. There was a dry, dusty, north easterly wind called the Harmattan, obscuring visibility.
Joy said to Esther, 'Hopefully it won't stop the plane flying'.
'Does that happen often?' said Esther. It was her first time in Abuja and sandstorms sufficiently strong to stop planes flying did not happen in Banjul.
'Sometimes,' came the not reassuring reply.

But they were not in luck. The flight was cancelled due to a real sandstorm on the runway and they were told to come back next day. Esther sent a message to Angie saying that there were problems with the flight but they, 'hoped to be there.'
Emmanuel's reaction when Angie passed on the news was, 'Oh no. I'm being rejected yet once more. They won't come. It's just excuses.'
'Don't be so negative,' said Angie looking on line at her phone. 'There is a real problem at Abuja airport with the visibility down on the runway, due to dust from the Sahara. Let's see what happens.'

The next day was December 24th and they turned up to the airport at 6pm for a 9pm flight to London Heathrow, arriving at 3.30 am Christmas day morning. The flight was delayed but they finally boarded the plane at 11pm and were sitting aboard for seemingly hours before setting off at 12.30 am Christmas day morning. They were due to arrive at 7 am but Esther began worrying whether they would arrive in time for the wedding at Midday.
'It will be maybe an hour from landing to being out to the taxi

rank. We will be ages in passport control because they will want to check all our paperwork carefully. It is nearly three hours from the airport to the church in Derbyshire. We have also got to change into our wedding outfits. We are starting to cut it a bit fine for time.'

The plane flew to Heathrow but was then stuck in a holding pattern with endless circles for another hour. They finally landed at 8.30 am. Thankfully the airport was quiet on Christmas day. They raced through passport control and emerged to the light of day at 9.00 am. The taxi rank was quiet too but they had difficulty finding a driver who was willing to spend over half of Christmas day going to Derbyshire and back. At last they found a Muslim guy who was very happy to work Christmas for a big amount of extra cash.

'I don't worry about having Christmas dinner,' he informed them with a grin.

They set off at 9.30 am.

Joy said, 'What about sending Angie a text saying we are going to be late?'

Esther had been texting Angie about the practical aspects of the wedding. So she sent the text at 10.30am, 'We are running late due to plane landing late. Not certain when we will arrive. xx Esther'.

Angie did not receive the text before the church service. At 10.00 am she had handed her phone to her chief bridesmaid Poppy saying, 'It's time for me to get my hair done and then put on the dress. You take charge of my mobile. Just tell me if there are any important messages or calls.' Poppy saw the text from Esther. Not knowing exactly who Esther was, she did not think it important enough to mention to Angie while she was immersed in having her prenuptial wash and blow dry.

Joy remarked to Esther in the taxi, as they went up the M1 motorway, 'We were planning to get changed in the hotel but we won't have time. Where are we going to get into our wedding outfits?'

The taxi driver heard the remark and interrupted, 'Excuse me butting in, ladies, but last month I took a girl going to a wedding in Leeds. We stopped at the Watford Gap services which are coming up now. She went to the disabled toilet, as it has got plenty of room to change. You could do that.'

So plan made. The ladies went to the disabled toilet going in with Western clothes and coming out with gorgeous Nigerian outfits, past the shops and food outlet. The shop staff gawped as they gazed on the outfits. Back to the taxi. The driver decided it was time to try to speed up to get them to the church on time. It was finally 12.25 pm when they arrived and the church doors were shut. They debated what to do and gingerly opened the heavy creaking wooden door of the old church. They tiptoed in. The congregation was quiet and the priest at the front was talking. They were too late. Emmanuel and Angie must now be married. Esther felt a deep sense of disappointment.

They needed to sit down at the back of the church but which side of the aisle should they choose? They wanted to be on the groom's side of course. There were black faces on both sides of the aisle, so that was no use helping them decide. Then Esther noted at the front of the church, several folk in obviously Nigerian outfits with their backs to them but they could not see the faces. Presumably that was Emmanuel's close family and therefore the groom's side. So there they sat in a centuries old wooden pew, watching proceedings.

At the end of the service Emmanuel and Angie started to process down the main aisle out of the church. Emmanuel was feeling elated and happy – married to the right girl at last. He looked very cool in his white suit and Angie was absolutely stunning. Then he saw Esther and he stopped. His heart gave a leap and he turned to Angie who was looking the other way, quickly greeting a friend. He whispered, 'Angie my bio-mum has come after all.' Angie turned and saw Esther. Emmanuel gave Esther a huge smile and she waved shyly back with a smile. Angie mouthed at her the words, 'thank you.'

Emmanuel felt that this was like the cherry on the top of the Belgian bun. His biological mother had come thousands of miles especially to see his wedding. He did not quite understand why she was late but she had come. He would have time at the reception to catch up with her. It was a pity his biological father could not be there but he knew that was not possible.

Outside it was snowing lightly. Michael's prayers had been answered. Esther saw her son Emmanuel help his new wife into the open, horse drawn, old fashioned carriage. She had a white long cloak and hood to cover her wedding dress. He had a Victorian style long overcoat, what used to be called a greatcoat, and a large top hat. The plan was to take the formal wedding photos at the hotel. Joe, Michael's trusty cameraman had already launched the filming drones and he was looking at his mobile laptop screen with satisfaction at the video feed from the drones.

There would be some great TV pictures. It was a surreal scene. The horse drawn carriage was being slowly pulled by four old squire horses and a driver perched on the front platform. In the seats sat Emmanuel and Angie, well wrapped up but still shivering in the cold. The snow was now falling more heavily and the wind was now beginning to blow noisily. There were four drones which buzzed round like flying insects at varying distances from the carriage, sometimes coming on and sometimes coming away, taking pictures all the time.

Emmanuel said to the driver, 'How long will it take to get to the hotel?'
'About another half an hour.'
'What?! My wife and I are shivering away. Can't you hurry it up?' Emmanuel felt a certain pride, saying for the first time the phrase, 'my wife and I'.
The driver, who was wrapped up with a ski vest and long johns,

took pity on them and said, 'Yes sure. The road will get a bit bumpier and I cannot go too fast in case the horses slip in the snow. If you lift up the seat lid underneath you, you should find some blankets you can wrap yourselves in them.'

The blankets helped a bit but they were still cold. It was now a definite blizzard.
Angie with teeth chattering with the cold remarked, 'You know what I could do with, Emmy, a hot alcoholic punch. That would warm me up nicely.'
'Agreed Angie. This was a silly ideas of your boss to get us to do an open carriage ride on a really cold winter's day from church to hotel.'
'I'm beginning to think so too and you know he has planned the wedding photos outside too – with the drones taking them and the cameramen inside nice and cosy, operating the drones remotely.'
'You never told me that bit. I'm not impressed.'

The road started to go through a large dark wooded area without fencing but with large bushy undergrowth on either side of the road. There was no other traffic on the road and there was total quiet. Not a noise could be heard. Even the sound of the horses' feet was muffled by the thin layer of snow on the ground. Tall pine trees towered up high above them, mostly keeping out the snow, which was now getting heavier and heavier. It reminded Angie of the childhood stories of fairy tales and enchanted woods. In the stories any moment you might expect to see a wolf or peasant wood chopper or a fairy emerge.

There was a standard red roadside sign, warning cars that there might be wild deer crossing. Everyone though knew that it was practically unheard of, to actually see a wild deer in this day and age. The sound of the cars probably scared them away. Then suddenly there it was. Two beautiful deer slowly emerged from the undergrowth and stood still on the road. The driver stopped the carriage and Emmanuel and Angie stared at them in amazement. They were young, sleek, beautiful, brown creatures with delicate heads and faces. They stared back at the humans and the horses. Then after a minute they seemed to lose interest, trotted across to the other side and dived into the bushes on the other side. Emmanuel and Angie looked at each other and smiled and silently mouthed, 'Wow' to each other. They forgot the cold for a moment. Without another word they knew that what was a wonderful day for them would be forever magical.

CHAPTER 38- RECEPTION

When they finally got into the hotel and walked into the reception, they were greeted by a cheer from everyone. The others had come by car, by a different and faster route to the scenic one taken by Emmanuel and Angie. The hotel had decided at the last minute in view of the inclement weather, to offer the wedding guests a hot toddy if they wanted it in place of the traditional champagne or orange juice.

The Maitre de of the Reception greeted them both with a bow, 'Congratulations Mr. and Mrs. Adebayo. Would you care for a glass of champagne or a juice or even maybe a warming hot toddy?'

'Hot toddy,' Emmanuel and Angie said together and then laughed.

Michael greeted them too and said, 'We had hoped to have the wedding photos outside but unfortunately everyone else has flatly refused to venture outside. I am sure though that we can get a few shots of you two outside the building. Again it is good publicity for the hotel and that is important for costs.'

Emmanuel looked Michael in the face and said firmly, 'Mike, we are NOT doing that. My wife and I are frozen to the bone.' Did Michael really have to mention money on their wedding day?

Angie more tactfully interrupted saying, 'Boss I *am* a bit cold and I'm sure that there must be somewhere nice inside this beautiful place to take some decent photos.'

Michael could see he was defeated and reluctantly mumbled, 'Okay, just give me a few minutes to sort something.'

He walked away sulking. He was more than consoled, when he saw the footage later of the carriage ride through the woods and the deer. He could give the hotel, some fantastic photos of Emmanuel and Angie arriving in their carriage, outside the hotel entrance. After all, the hotel owner had said that he hoped that this wedding reception would be the first of many such Christmas do's.

The wedding photos seemed to take an age and everyone's tummies were rumbling. Two hours later they were in the large hotel dining room, all ready for the first course of the wedding breakfast. The cameras were everywhere. The hotel's Maitre de approached discretely, the top table where Emmanuel and his family were sitting.

He quietly spoke, 'There is a delivery driver outside with a package. It's for Emmanuel Adebayo. He says he has strict instructions, only to give it personally to him.'

Emmanuel got up to go outside. The Maitre de coughed discretely and said, 'It's for Doctor Emmanuel Adebayo.'

His father got up, put his white napkin down and went outside to the young delivery driver.

'Dr Emmanuel Adebayo?'

'Yes that is right.'

'I have got this for you,' He handed over a letter and a huge bouquet of flowers enveloped in clear plastic.

'Sign here please, with your name in block capitals.'

Dr Emmanuel was really surprised to see a delivery on Christmas day.

'Do you normally do many deliveries on Christmas day?' he asked the delivery man.

'No this is my only one today. Its a special one. I picked it up at ten o'clock from a small florist in Finchley in North London. The girl who gave it to me said it was an unusual one and we got chatting. Apparently a very tall, slightly older African gentleman came to the florist a few days ago and ordered the flowers and paid in cash.'

'Do you have a name and address if you had been unable to deliver them?'

'No. The guy did not give an address merely a name – Mr Goodluck.'

When Dr Emmanuel heard the name he realised who they must be from. Goodluck had clearly covered his tracks well. Finchley was way away from the Nigerian High Commission building and he had only given his first name. Finally he saw on the delivery note that the bill had been paid in cash, so no credit card trail.

Dr Emmanuel looked at the huge bouquet. He was an enthusiastic gardener in his petite garden and recognised the gorgeous white flowers that it was 'Star of Bethlehem'. At least someone had chosen the right flower for Christmas time. He said to himself, 'But these flowers don't grow in the UK at this season. They must have been imported from abroad. Delivering them today must have cost a bomb.'

He read the letter.

'Dear Dr Emmanuel,

Thank you again for coming to see me three months ago. Please could you give this bouquet to Emmanuel and Angie privately and discretely. Please do contact me from time to time with news of them both and I would love (underlined) to see some wedding photos, Goodluck.' Smiley face.

Dr Emmanuel said to the Maitre de who was standing nearby, 'Would you be able to get Emmanuel and Angie, here for me quietly without any fuss. I don't want the cameraman out here.'

The Maitre de disappeared quietly and came back with bride and groom. The rest of the guests were munching their way through turkey and trimmings and nattering and there was an excited buzz of contentment in the room of celebration. Ralph Tomenko was particularly happy. He had got his beloved Christmas turkey and Brussels sprouts and roast potatoes after all and a goodly portion at that. To top it all the printed menu promised plum pudding with crème anglaise, the fancy name for custard, and clotted cream for dessert.

Emmanuel said, 'What's this about Dad?'
Dr Emmanuel glanced at the Maitre de, who left as discretely as he had called Emmanuel and Angie outside.
'I have had this letter and this bouquet. The flowers are the Star of Bethlehem, very appropriate to give at Christmas time.'
Emmanuel and Angie took the bouquet and saw there was a little card in an envelope attached to it.
Angie carefully opened up the envelope and read the card out loud.
'To Angie and Emmanuel on their wedding day. I have seen the internet videos. Angie, you are the luckiest girl in the world, having such a fantastic guy as your husband. Emmanuel – you have married a very beautiful and clever young lady. All the best for the future together. Dad/ Goodluck.'

Emmanuel was overwhelmed. This was more than he had ever expected. His Mum and Dad were present at his wedding as he had always known they would be, fully supporting and encouraging him. But his bio-mum had turned up too. She was busy chatting with his Mum, swapping stories happily about university life in Nigeria from yesteryear as they were both Lagos graduates. Emmanuel was crying tears of joy. He had never imagined that he would find his bio-dad. and that he would acknowledge him as his son. He looked up at Dr Emmanuel in astonishment with eyes wide open, and said,
'He has called himself Dad to me. He has acknowledged me as his son.'

Suddenly Dr Emmanuel started crying, slowly quietly crying. Emmanuel suddenly became aware that his adopted Dad was now an old man. He was stooping over, weeping. Emmanuel towered over him normally but now he was a positive giant compared to him.
'What's the matter?' he asked him concerned.

Dr Emmanuel had so many thoughts running through his head. He had always to be the strong one in the family, the head of the family, supporting everyone else, listening to their worries, their concerns their fears. It was the same at work where he was the senior doctor in his GP practice. When the staff had a meltdown, he had to sit down and listen and pick up the pieces. But no one was there to support him when he had his weak moments, except of course his wife. But he could not even share everything with her. This lad Emmanuel, he had nurtured and shaped and helped and wiped away his tears when he had been bullied for his disability. He had paid thousands to put him through university, not that he minded spending a penny of it. He had done that because he was committed to Emmanuel and deeply loved him. And now this lad, who he thought of as his son, had found his biological father and would be calling him Dad instead.

Dr Emmanuel spoke out the words slowly, reproachfully with sobs, 'So now you will be calling Goodluck, Dad.'
Emmanuel now realised the issue.
'Dad, I could never call Goodluck Dad. Yes, he is my biological father and I am pleased to have closed the circle and found him but he will never never never be my Dad. I refer to him as my bio-dad. only for convenience. I love you, Dad and I love Mum too, and I will always love you and I am so, so grateful you took me in.'
He gave Dr Emmanuel a massive hug and got out a handkerchief and wiped his Dad's tears away for him. Dr Emmanuel gave him a hug back and started to smile while still crying.

Angie had turned away a little bit embarrassed, wanting to give them both a moment of privacy. She was busy looking at the flowers and then she had a sudden thought. She started counting them out loud. 'one, two, three ……. twenty-six, twenty-seven, twenty-eight. There are twenty-eight flowers, Emmy,' she exclaimed in a surprised tone.

'Yes so what?' Emmanuel said in a questioning tone.
'What day is it today?'
'It's Christmas day.'
'Yes what else?'
He looked puzzled, 'It's our wedding day.'
'Yes but what else?'
'I don't know.'
'It's your birthday.'
'Oh yes of course I had forgotten about that.'
'How old are you today, silly?'
'I'm twenty-eight today.'
Then he got it, 'He has sent me twenty-eight star of Bethlehem flowers in honour of my birthday.'
He said with a look of dawning amazement.
'That was really thoughtful of him, really really thoughtful of him.' He was just amazed by his bio-dad's careful choosing of the number of flowers.

Angie said, 'What shall we do with them?'
Dr Emmanuel, ever the practical one, said, 'Leave it to me. You go back and enjoy the wedding breakfast before the food gets cold. You need to eat, to keep your strength up for what will be more of a long and tiring day ahead, with the evening reception.'
Off they trooped back in. Dr Emmanuel left the flowers outside. He found the Maitre de and asked him, 'What is the best thing to do with the flowers?'
'We could put them up in the Bridal Suite. We have employed our part time florist to come in advance and arrange the flowers in the room for special guests like your son and his wife. But it's Christmas day and we cannot get him in, to add in more flowers.'
'Oh,' said Dr Emmanuel, disappointment in his voice.
'But what I can do is ask my wife Marie, who is working reception today. She is a talented, amateur flower arranger and could place them tastefully round the Honeymoon Suite.'
'Yes please, if you could do that.'

Many hours later, when Emmanuel and Angie retired into the honeymoon suite, they were met with blooms everywhere – a beautiful mixture of red roses from the hotel and the white star of Bethlehem flowers. Angie took one look and exclaimed, with mouth open with wonder, two words only, 'Floral heaven!'

CHAPTER 39 - EPILOGUE

'Oh I cannot cope with the pain any more. Do something. This gas and air stuff is doing nothing,' cried out Angie in her distress. She was writhing round, holding onto the mask and panting away. She shouted away, even more loudly, 'Do something! Do something!'
The midwife calmly said, 'Do you want an epidural now?' She had seen this all coming and wished Angie had accepted her offer of an epidural two hours before. She had more than enough experience of modern British women in labour, with their elaborate birth plans, to know that they had their own distinctive ideas of what they wanted to happen at this big moment.
'Yes Yes.'
'I need just to check first that you are not about to give birth.'

A few moments later the midwife looked up from peering through her spectacles and said, 'I can see the baby's head. It's time to push, my love.'

It was thirteen months after the wedding. Angie had been in labour with her first baby for twenty five hours and was clearly exhausted. She had a drip attached to her right hand, to stop her getting dehydrated. Emmanuel was at her side, holding her left hand and not knowing quite what to say or do, with his wife in labour for the first time. He too was tired and hungry and thirsty. He had a sudden longing for one of his Mum's goat curries, washed down with a beer. He clearly was not going to get that for a while. He looked round. The room was quite clinical and bare, with tiles and lino floor – easier to wash the blood and gubbins off, he grimly thought. With them were two midwifes and a little collection of monitors.

Emmanuel's phone pinged and he automatically let go of her hand to reach for his mobile.
Angie glared at him and growled out, 'Leave it. Hold my hand.'
She could have said more, like: 'No one important is going to be sending you an urgent message now,' but barely had the energy to say more. Emmanuel did just that. Ten minutes later Emmanuel's phone pinged again. He totally ignored it this time. Half an hour later, the baby was born without complications. Twenty minutes later Angie was being washed and cleaned up. Emmanuel took the opportunity to pop out of the room and make the phone calls to family.

'Dad it's a boy, seven pounds and five ounces, lovely and normal, born at five minutes past ten. A normal delivery too. Angie is fine, just exhausted. We've got a name too,' Emmanuel just could not keep the excitement out of his voice.
'Congratulations son. Your mother and I are so pleased, so happy. So what are you going to call him?'
When Emmanuel said the name, he immediately added, 'It's in honour of you, Dad, not me. Angie and I unanimously agreed on it. If the baby had been a girl, we would have honoured Mum in the same way.'
Dr Emmanuel did not know what to say except, 'Thank you son, thank you so so much. What made you choose the middle name, son?'
'It just seemed to make sense, Dad.'
'Okay, I will get an email off.'
'I'd better stop, as I have got to ring Angie's parents next and then the rest of the family.'

Finally twenty minutes later, Emmanuel popped back into his wife and baby and chatted excitedly away, holding his new born son. It was not for a further hour before he got round to looking at his phone. There were two notifications. The first one he looked at was from the family social media group. It was from his Dad and the first one he had received when Angie was in labour.

'Hi family, I have just been appointed Chief executive of Hackney and East London Clinical Commissioning Group. It is the greatest honour I could ever receive, to be responsible for the primary care health of millions of my fellow Londoners.'

Emmanuel was pleased for his Dad. He was a really good chap and thoroughly deserved the honour. So typical of modest Dad that he did not mention it, when Emmanuel rang to tell him of the birth.

'It was the icing on the cake of the day or was it the cherry on the cake or something like that,' he thought.

Then he saw the other notification, which was from the BBC news. 'Goodluck Adeyemi elected the new and 18th President of Nigeria in a close fought contest. His slogan, 'For a better Nigeria' resounded in the hearts of many voters, tired of the corruption that has plagued the country for many years. Incidentally and appropriately, the surname Adeyemi means, 'The crown befits me' in Yoruba.'

Emmanuel burst out laughing at that. Not only had his Dad got responsibility for the health of millions but his bio-dad now had the responsibility for the lives of over a hundred million people. What a day it was turning out to be!

Two days later, a very tired President elect sat in his new office in the Presidential Palace in Abuja Nigeria. It was the end of another exhausting day with rounds of meetings and phone calls. It was 10.30 at night and he finally got round to opening his private emails. There it was. It was a message from Dr Emmanuel Adebayo and was two days old.

'Dear Mr. President,

Many congratulations on your election. Angie delivered a little boy today weight seven pounds five ounces. Mother and baby are doing well......'

He thought what a day election day had been – becoming President and grandfather in the same day. The President elect Goodluck Adeyemi smiled with satisfaction, when he saw the last sentence of the email, 'The baby has been named 'Emmanuel Goodluck Adebayo.'